Hook, Line, Professor
PART II

SHAYLA HART

Quote

Love doesn't need to be perfect, it just needs to be true.

 Copyright

"Copyright © 2022 by Shayla Hart
All rights reserved.

No part of this book may be reproduced in any form or by any electronic or mechanical means, including information storage and retrieval systems, without written permission from the author, except for the use of brief quotations in a book review."

Acknowledgements & Dedications

Behind every author is a fleet of talented individuals. I know I would be lost without them.
A special thanks to -
Liji Editing for being so very patient with me while working on this book.
LJ_Bookreviews for her awesome proofreading (last minute again!)
Naqmeh-Art - For illustrating the kick ass drawing of Rein for the paperback cover.
Irishink publishing services -
For the paperback cover design.

I would like to dedicate this book for those who are still searching for their soulmate. Don't give up, they're out there.

About Shay

Shayla Hart is an emerging author of contemporary adult romance. This is Shayla's sixth book with seven more in line for 2022!

"When Shayla isn't locked away in her writing cave she's busy planning weddings and social events as an Events Co-ordinator. In addition to having a full time job and chasing her dreams of becoming a full time author, Shayla is also a social media influencer.

Follow her socials below for more updates on upcoming works and entertaining videos on her TikTok's where she acts out scenes from her books. Click here

Shayla also has Merchandise for her books which you can find here. Shayla Hart Merchandise

To find out more about Shayla visit her website - Official Shayla Hart

More by Shay

Hook, Line, Professor - Part 1
The Accidental Wife
Love Me Again
Cuffed By Love
An Assassins Oath

Coming soon…
When Love and Hate Collide
When Love and Fate Collide.

Chapter 1
Talon

NEVER GONNA BE ALONE - NICKELBACK

"It took me a good while to figure out what I wanted to major in, but my parents always told me I was filled with creativity growing up..."

I narrow my eyes and nod slowly, feigning interest in Polly's mind-numbing drivel over her struggle choosing what to major in. Involuntarily, my eyes drift over her shoulder to the table a couple of feet next to ours, staring at the object of my fixation who is sitting next to her date and looking like she'd rather be anywhere else than on that date with that pompous twit. He keeps touching her, and I don't like it. I'm not a possessive man, but she's making me want to be. Every time he takes hold of her hand or leans in to whisper something in her ear, I swear to God it feels like someone is tightening a vise around my gut and I need to remind myself I've got no business getting worked up.

As if sensing me watching her, Rein's eyes veer and catch mine when she takes a sip of her water. I don't look away and neither does she. I assumed coming on this date would help distract me from missing Rein, but it's had the opposite effect. If anything, I want her even more now. I crave her company desperately. I want to gaze forthrightly into those dazzling eyes and forget everything–including myself.

I knew going in I was going to struggle walking away from her once I got a taste, but I never imagined I would be this transfixed with her–and so abruptly.

My mouth waters when she enticingly uncrosses and crosses those sexy legs under the table, gallantly evoking images of her very bare pussy. My cock aches, reminding me of my very apparent need for her.

She's making me fucking crazy. Crazy enough to seriously consider striding over there, taking her by the hand and walking right out this restaurant, leaving behind a pile of fucks I honestly couldn't give.

"Talon?"

I drag my eyes away from Rein's and look at Polly, who's watching me probingly. "I'm sorry, my thoughts just got away from me for a second. What did you say?"

Polly reaches over and places her hand over mine on the table. My gaze drops to her hand resting on mine and I resist the urge to recoil against the foreign sensation of her skin touching mine.

Shit.

How do I move my hand without affronting her? From the corner of my eye, I can see Rein watching me. I don't even have to look in her direction; I can feel her gaze penetrating right through me. I peek anyway and curse inwardly when I'm greeted by her scalding gaze. Would you look at that... it seems I'm not the only one that's feeling peeved after all. The covetous look that simmers deep in her eyes gratifies me. Never have I ever witnessed jealousy look so damn good on a woman before.

Goddamn.

I feign a cough and pull my hand away from Polly's to cover my mouth. "I was saying that you seem distracted. Are you okay?" she questions, concerned.

I nod and take a slow sip of my glass of water. "Yes. I'm fine." I set the glass back down. "I just remembered I've got a stack of assignments on my desk that are waiting to be graded."

"I'm sure it can wait *one* more night," she purrs suggestively, nibbling on the straw to her passionfruit mojito, her brown eyes gazing at me longingly. Good heavens, she's gone and assumed the night is going to end with us leaving the restaurant together and having sex.

I need to shut this down once and for all. I'm growing incredibly tired of her advances. "Look, Polly, I think you're an incredibly intelligent woman and a terrific Professor in your field. However, I don't want you to presume I agreed to go out on this date with you because I'm interested in pursuing a relationship with you. I don't date," I state frankly. Polly's face falls, the dissatisfaction that supersedes the flirty glances she was donning less than a second ago is blatantly apparent. "I have—and I cannot stress this enough—no interest in dating anyone, especially someone I work with."

What I wanted to say was, 'Absolutely not you, because you're the furthest from my type and don't appeal to me in anyway, physically, or emotionally.' Yes, she is very beautiful, and any man would give up their left nut for a chance with a girl like Polly, but not me. We don't mesh–there is nothing about her that excites me.

"Oh, then why did you agree to go on this dinner with me?" she questions.

I feel my brows crease. "You've been *persistent* to say the least with your pursuit of me, and honestly, I was starting to run out of excuses, so I thought that instead of outright declining, I would accept and communicate face to face so that we don't waste any more of each other's time. I truly hope I didn't affront you, because I would hate for there to be any animosity between us."

Polly leans back in her chair, exhaling audibly. "I appreciate your honesty, Professor Saxton. In my experience, most men I've dated previously would take what they wanted and never be heard from again, but I was right to assume that you're not like most men, and that's what I liked about you. Your integrity and work ethic is truly admirable."

Oh bloody hell. My integrity and work ethic are degenerating quicker than I'd like to admit.

If only she knew what absolute scum I truly was, she would run a mile and never look back. "That's very kind of you to say, Polly," I say and look over when I see Rein, her friend and their dates are getting ready to leave the restaurant.

"Isn't that one of your students?" Polly questions, following my gaze.

"Yes, it is." I nod in greeting when Paris and Rein both wave as they walk by our table.

Polly looks over Rein and her date as they pass by. "Rein Valdez, right? It didn't take her very long to move on after her breakup with Hunter Harris. Their breakup was quite the topic in the teacher's lounge the other day. Though, by the looks of it, she's levelled up and nabbed herself a rather attractive sugar daddy. Clever girl."

I grind my molars together and resist the scathing remark just itching to come out and put her back in her place. I catch the waiter's attention as he walks by and gesture for the bill. He nods, scurrying off to fetch it.

I'm not going to bite.

"Your bill, sir."

"Oh, we're skipping dessert?" I almost roll my eyes but catch myself at the suggestive tone of her voice. Did I not just make it perfectly clear I was not interested in pursuing anything with her? Personally, I would rather hump a cheese grater than shag her any day of the week. I hand over my credit card and they process the payment. I don't even wait for a receipt before I'm up on my feet and pulling my jacket on. Thank fuck we drove here in separate cars, because I cannot bear to stand another second with this obnoxious woman.

"We are. I'm not really a dessert kind of guy."

Polly turns to look up at me, her dark brown eyes bawdy like she's ready to pounce on me at any given moment. "Well, Professor, I happen to have something even better in mind than dessert. Something that will satisfy both our appetites."

Oh, *fuck no*. What appetite is she speaking of? Was that supposed to make me change my mind and suddenly be like, yes, I am swayed, I must have you now? Jesus, for a highly cultivated woman, she is quite dense. Or she's just deliberately ignoring all the signs and the very clear fact I already told her *openly* that I am in no way interested. I made a terrible mistake by ever accepting to go on this fucking date and now I'm paying for my idiocy.

"Polly, please stop. I hate to be blunt, but either I'm not making myself very clear or you're just refusing to acknowledge it. I am not sleeping with you, not tonight, not ever. Do you understand? This whole date was nothing but a mistake. I'm truly sorry if I've misled you in anyway. It's not your fault, its mine. I should have made my intentions–or lack of interest–clear from the get-go."

The fire in her eyes from moments ago dies out and is quickly replaced by disappointment once again. Polly forces a smile on her face and nods. "Well, you can't blame a girl for trying," she jests, though her smile doesn't quite reach her eyes and she looks slightly mortified.

Maybe I could have handled it better and been a little less insensitive but sometimes you must be firm to get the message across. I've put up with her advances for as long as I can tolerate and been civil, but enough is enough. I don't have the patience nor the stomach for it any longer.

"Of course not, but I'm not the man for you. Shall we?" I gesture towards the exit and she nods, wrapping her ivory cashmere shawl around herself.

We walk out and hand our cards to the valet who rushes off to get our cars. I see Rein and her date a couple of feet in front of us. My eyes stare agitatedly at the hand placed on the small of Rein's back as he leans in to speak to her intimately. The two black Porsches roll up and they get in. "Thank you for dinner, Professor.

Even if it didn't quite go as I had intended, I appreciate that you took the time to join me."

I nod. "I apologise for my bluntness back there. You deserve a man that will reciprocate your feelings and affections. Unfortunately, I'm not that man," I tell her earnestly. From the corner of my eye, I see the Porsche that Rein got into pull off rather hastily, the tyres screeching against the asphalt.

Fucking arsehole.

"I get it. Thank you for your honesty."

"Have a good evening." I shake her hand and take the key from the valet and jump into my car. I have an uneasy feeling gnawing away in the pit of my stomach. I know Rein is old enough and smart enough to take care of herself but there was something about the guy she's with that didn't sit right with me. And no, it's not just that I'm jealous. I'm genuinely concerned.

So, I do the only logical thing–I follow them. I mean, is it considered following if we are going the same way? I think not.

I manage to stay relatively close until we stop at a set of traffic lights. The Porsche with Paris and her date pulls up beside the one I'm currently tailing, and he revs his engine provokingly.

You're not about to do what I suspect you are... Rein's date revs his engine back, and my suspicions are confirmed when the light turns green and I hear the screeching of the types on the asphalt when they both speed off. "Son of a..."

For an entire second, my brain doesn't react, almost like it's stopped functioning. And then it hits me all at once. I picture Taylor getting hit by that car, then Rein in her accident and how she shook–absolutely terrified–in my arms when she had to relive that moment. And then I envision the crippling fear in her eyes and the possibility of losing her too and my panic grows tenfold. I put my foot down and race after them.

I've not felt this level of rage since I saw the prick that took the life of my Taylor and our baby in court where he was sentenced to twenty years. It's one thing to endanger your own life and those around you by speeding and driving recklessly, but to endanger someone who entrusts you with their life by getting into your car is something else altogether.

My fingers tighten around the steering wheel when the Porsche swerves in and out of traffic at alarming speed. I'm pushing one hundred and he is two cars ahead of me, which means he must be going at least a hundred and fifteen miles per hour. "Oh, when I get my hands on you, I'm going to make you a permanent fixture of that car, you fucking prick!" I growl hotly.

My heart squeezes and I watch in horror when a car swerves in front of the Porsche and he slams his foot on the brakes and the car spins out. "NO!"

The screeching of the tyres hangs in the air for a couple of seconds, the sound echoing in my ears. Traffic halts and I slam my foot on the brake and–in a panic–throw myself out of the car and race toward the Porsche. "Rein!"

I can't see her through the tinted glass. I pull the door open and see her in the passenger seat, her head in her hands, her shoulders rising and falling quickly. "Rein, hey, hey, it's okay. Look at me, look at me!" I pull her hands from her face, and she peels her eyes open. She looks down at herself then turns to face me. The fear she holds in her eyes honestly cripples me.

"Talon," she whispers, her voice breaking.

"Are you okay?" I ask, taking her face in my hands and looking her over. "Are you hurt?"

Rein doesn't say anything, she just stares at me, her eyes swimming in tears. I can feel the tremors passing through her and it sends my rage skyrocketing. Satisfied that she's not physically hurt, I pull back. "Don't move, I'll be right back," I tell her and walk around the car to the driver's side. I rip the door open and glare menacingly at the driver who turns to look up at me, eyes wide and full of fight, undoubtedly still in shock.

Don't you worry, I've got just the thing to snap you back to reality, you impetuous dick. "Get out of the fucking car." I grab him by the lapels of his designer jacket and drag him out of the car before I slam him hard against it. "I'm giving you three seconds to give me one good reason as to why I shouldn't break your fucking legs, you senseless little prick," I growl angrily, glowering into his bleary eyes.

"The hell are you doing? Get your hands off me. Who are you?" he utters faintly and lifts his hands to take hold of my wrists in an attempt to push me off, but I tighten my grip and tug his face closer to mine until we're nose to nose.

"Who am I? I'm the guy that's going to ensure you damn well never get behind a wheel again. You'll be lucky to even ride a fucking bicycle when I'm through with you, you dickless twit. You think speeding is a goddamn joke? Huh? You and your buddy think it's funny to put other people's lives in danger so that you can show off? You could have fucking killed her!" I holler, taking a step back and punching him hard across the face. I watch him hit the floor like a sack of rotting badgers, blood seeping from his mouth.

"Ahh, what the fuck, man?" I lean over and pull him up by the collar when he tries to scoot away from me. "Let go of me, I didn't mean–"

"Shut the fuck up!" I grouse stormily and punch him again. "You're damn lucky she's not hurt because I swear to God I would have beaten you to within an inch of your life!"

"I'm sorr–" I pull my fist back to punch him again and my hand halts in mid-air when I feel a grip on my arm.

"Sorry isn't good enough!"

"Talon! Stop, stop, please stop," Rein whimpers. I turn my gaze and look at her. "Stop," she whispers. One look into her fretful eyes and the rage in me drains away. I let go of my hold on the prick and turn to look at him.

"You're not to set one fucking foot near her, you hear me?" I bark vehemently. "Let me catch you even glancing in her direction, and I'll make you wish you were dead." When he nods, wiping away the blood dripping from his mouth, I allow Rein to pull me away.

I pull her to me and look her over. "Are you okay?"

Rein nods meekly. I notice her hands are trembling still, so I take them in mine and press them to my lips. "Christ, Rein, I thought you were going to crash straight into that car. I thought..." I declare, gazing into her teary eyes and shaking my head. The thought alone of losing her too is soul crushing.

"I was so scared, I begged him to stop but he didn't listen to me and I..." I draw her into my arms and hold her tight against me. Her body shakes with hoarse sobs.

"Shh, it's okay. You're okay, Snowflake, you're safe," I whisper repeatedly till her body calms and every so often a little sniffle escapes her.

Between my panic and rage I hadn't even noticed the crowd of people that have gathered around until I hear the police sirens approaching. I can vaguely hear the muttering of Rein's date behind me, threatening to have me arrested for assault.

I've got the right mind to go over there and finish what I started, but the way Rein is holding onto me so tightly, I can't bear to let her go.

The police came and took our statements. Despite his bitching and threatening to have me arrested, he was the one that got led away in cuffed for dangerous driving and driving under the influence of alcohol and drugs. Not only was he over the limit but the bastard was high on cocaine.

I dread to think how horribly this all could have turned out, but I'm so thankful that Rein is in one piece. Someone up there must really be looking out for her, because had they collided with that car at the speed they were going... neither of them would have survived.

"Maybe we should take you to the hospital and have you checked out?"

Rein shakes her head against my chest whilst we walk back to my car. "There's no need, I'm okay, really." She turns her gaze to me. "Nothing a long hot shower and comfort food can't fix."

"Rein..." I protest, but she shakes her head, having none of it.

"Tal, I'm okay," she assures me once more. I search her eyes and heave a sigh.

"Fine, but if you feel any discomfort or pain *anywhere* then you tell me and we'll go to get you checked, understood?" I assert, and she nods in response, nestling her face into the crook of my neck when I wrap my arm around her tighter and press a kiss atop of her head.

"Take me home, Professor."

Chapter 2
Rein

MIDDLE OF THE NIGHT - ELLIE DUHE

THE DRIVE back to my apartment was a quiet one. My life has been spared yet again, and I can't help but wonder... *why?*

My fingers play with the necklace my mother gave me whilst I stare out of the passenger window, and my other hand is resting on Talon's thigh, covered by his long fingers brushing soothing circles over my knuckles. My phone vibrates in my lap, and I don't need to look at it to know who it is–Paris and I have our vibrates set to heartbeat, so when our phones ring, we'll know who it is. She's probably heard about what happened by now and is calling to check in.

Despite not really wanting to talk, I answer. "P."

"Oh, thank God!" she shrieks down the phone. "I just heard what happened, Rein, are you okay?" she asks in a flurry.

"I'm fine, P."

"Where are you? Miles said Dean's been arrested? He's gone to the station with their lawyer. Apparently some guy beat on him and then took you away. Who are you with?"

I glance over at Talon, and he looks over at me curiously, his blue eyes narrowed. "Just another driver that witnessed the whole thing. He's kindly taking me home."

"Wait... Hold on a damn minute. Some random guy saw you almost crash into a another car then took it upon himself to beat on Dean and you decided it was totally sound to jump into a car with him?" she iterates and then gasps. "Oh my God, have you been kidnapped? Cough twice if you have. I'll have the CPD, the FBI, and the S.W.A.T on your ass quicker than you can blink."

I roll my eyes. "No, I haven't been kidnapped, don't be ridiculous, P."

"I'm not being ridiculous; I think I'm being damn well logical. Since when have you ever gotten into a stranger's car? In fact, you tell me off for doing it, so what the fuck gives, woman?"

I pull the phone away from my ear and wince. "Will you stop shrieking down the phone. Look, I'm fine and perfectly safe. I'm going home; I just want to shower and go to sleep. Can we talk later, please?"

"Nah uh, I'm coming over."

"No, P, there's really no need. I'm okay, I'll come and see you tomorrow."

"You swear you're okay?"

"Yes."

"Swear it!"

"I swear, jeez!"

Paris exhales. "Okay, fine, but if I don't hear from you by midday, I'm coming over all guns blazing." I close my eyes and smile.

"Fine, you have my full approval to come over with the whole of Chicago if you wish."

"I'm sorry, Rei Rei." My heart squeezes at the gloom lacing her tone. "You could have been killed and it would have been all my fault. I'm truly senseless. I didn't even stop to consider how you would have felt in that car after everything that happened to you. I told Miles to stop, but he wouldn't listen to me."

I chew on my bottom lip. "It wouldn't have been your fault. I'm old enough to make my own decisions, P. I'm not holding you accountable for anything, so please don't blame yourself, okay?"

"But I—"

"No buts, I'm fine," I interrupt cogently. From the corner of my eye, I can see Talon looking from the road then to me. "Love you always, bitch tits."

"Love you forever, sugar tits." Paris sighs. "Call me tomorrow, okay?"

"I will, I promise." Satisfied by my response, she finally hangs up and I exhale slowly, resting my head against the headrest.

"You all right?" Talon questions.

"I hate lying to her."

Talon stares ahead and wets his lips. "You know you didn't have to."

I veer my gaze to look at him questioningly. "No? What would you have rather I said? I'm not with a stranger, Professor Saxton showed up, knocked the wits out of Dean, then whisked me off to his apartment complex where I'm currently staying, by the way."

Talon's shoulders rise when he sucks in a deep breath and exhales slowly. "We were at the same restaurant, Rein. I could have coincidentally seen you on my drive home and offered to drive you back to your place."

I cross my arms over my chest. "Sure, that's logical enough, and it might have even worked had you not pummelled your fist into Dean's face."

With a shake of his head, Talon rolls his eyes, his fingers tightening around the steering wheel in agitation. "He's lucky that's all I did. Senseless prick," he grouses irritably.

"You put yourself at risk, Talon," I argue, shifting in my seat so I can face him properly. "What if Paris saw you? Or worse, what if you got arrested for assaulting him? How would you ever justify that?"

Talon stays silent for a couple of seconds. "I don't know, Rein. In that moment, I didn't stop to think about it, I just reacted, okay? Maybe not in the most rational of ways, but that dipshit deserved every punch, if not more," he claims heatedly, glancing at me sideways when we stop at a traffic light. "He could have killed you." I stare at him wordlessly. There's this look he's got deep in his eyes, but I can't seem to place it. "Why are you looking at me like that?"

The guy that was pounding his fist brutally into Dean's face and the Talon I've gotten to know seem to be total opposites. The ireful expression on his face, the pained look he held in his eyes when he dragged Dean out of that car almost seemed like this uninhabited side to him that he's keeping hidden suddenly surfaced and he lost control—which is so unlike him.

I can't help but wonder what it was that triggered him enough to lose his head like that. I must be honest though, while I am a little displeased with him for reacting in such an inane manner, I'm also a little turned on.

"Nothing." He stares at me for the longest moment, his eyes searching mine, clearly not accepting my answer as the truth. "The lights green."

"I know."

"Aren't you going to drive then?"

Talon glances at the lights and then back at me, licking his lips. "I will when you tell me the reason... the *real* reason behind the look you were just giving me."

Cars start to honk behind us. I turn and look back at the line of vehicles honking impatiently. "Talon, we're holding up traffic."

He shrugs, keeping his intense gaze on mine. "Answer me and I'll drive."

I gawk at him and look back at the line of cars honking incessantly.

"God's sake, fine." I huff. "I was thinking that I may have, sort of, found that barbarously protective side to you sexy." My cheeks burn red hot under his fiery stare.

"Right." I scowl at him. Right? *That's it*? What in the name of baby Jesus is this guy on? How can he look at me with such burning desire one second and completely switch off the next? I've got the urge to smack him upside the head, but I begrudgingly settle for shaking my head and turn to look out the window. What was I expecting? That he would rip my clothes off right here in the middle of the street? Maybe not that far but a flirty remark would have been nice. It's so easy to forget when I'm around him that we ended our brief yet very illicit fling.

Twenty minutes later, we pull up outside my apartment complex. "Thank you for driving me back."

Talon turns to look at me sideways. "I'll walk you up."

"You don't have to."

Talon nods and unfastens his seatbelt. "I know." Before I can say anything else, he's already out of the car.

Okay then.

I follow suit and we walk side by side through the underground car park towards the elevators. "What happened to your date?"

Talon pushes the button and leans one shoulder against the wall. "We parted ways at the restaurant."

Oh?

"Second date?"

Talon narrows his eyes while he observes me. "Maybe."

I pay no heed to the pinch in my chest and nod, lowering my gaze to look at my feet. "Oh, okay."

"Jealous?"

My eyes snap up to his. I snort. "No."

Talon smirks. "Good."

We stare at one another for a long time. Sodding hell, the urge to jump into his beefy arms and kiss him till my lungs implode is stronger than ever. The ding and the sound of the woman informing us the elevator has arrived on the basement level forces us to break eye contact. Talon gestures for me to go first. "After you." Without a word, I walk past him and into the elevator. Talon follows me in and presses the button to the tenth floor. The air in the elevator is suffocatingly thick. Talon and I don't speak the entire journey up. We only glance at each other, one catching the other in a stare.

The two minutes we spent in that elevator felt like years. It wasn't awkward, just intense. It feels like there are one too many unspoken words floating between us, just waiting to be addressed, but we keep ignoring it in hopes it will go away.

The elevator slows to a stop and then pings before the doors slide open. I walk out ahead of him and down the dimly lit corridor towards my apartment as Talon follows. My steps are deliberately slow. Usually, I'm whizzing around, but right now, I'm dragging out every second simply because I just want to be close to him.

Regrettably though, we eventually reach my apartment and I turn to face him just after I slide the key in the lock. "Thank you for saving me yet *again*, Professor."

Talon nods. "Do you think you can stay out of trouble till tomorrow morning? You're not going to start a war with anymore appliances, I hope."

I smile widely and shake my head. "I'm not planning on it, but the night is still young, who knows what shenanigans I might get up to all alone in there."

Talon flashes his insanely sexy trademark grin that without fail makes my panties moist—well, if I were wearing any, that is. He rubs the back of his neck and chuckles. "See, usually, I would laugh it off as a joke but with you anything is possible. I'm honestly concerned you'll end up in a headlock with the fridge or something."

I laugh and hit his shoulder with my clutch. "Shut up. My life may be a little chaotic but I'm not *that* bad," I contest. He catches my wrist, his fingers curling around it snugly.

Talon's brows rise to his hairline, and he gives me a dubious look, those gorgeous blue eyes glittering with mirth. "A little chaotic? Shall we rehash the last couple of weeks?"

I groan and shake my head. "I'd really rather not."

Talon licks his lips, his thumb brushing over my pulse point which jumps with every gentle stroke. "I better go."

Stay.

"Okay."

My eyes lower to his mouth when he bites down on his bottom lip. "I'm going to go."

Please don't.

"Good night, Professor," I murmur, lifting my eyes to meet his, and the moment I do this inexplicable heat consumes me–my stomach clenches and unclenches with anticipation. The avaricious need flaming deep in his eyes leaves me feeling defenceless.

An invisible almost magnetic force draws us closer. "G'night, Snowflake," he drawls, the words rolling off his tongue in that erotic Australian accent that makes me stupid with desire for him.

I can't think or see straight. There is only one coherent thought in my mind and it's this unquenchable, unwavering craving I have for him. The smell of his aftershave makes my head go faint and I sway on my feet ever so slightly.

And just when I'm convinced he's about to close the miniscule gap between our lips, he pulls away, taking his heat, taste and smell with him.

I keep my eyes closed for a moment to compose myself until the surge of disappointment ebbs away. When I open my eyes, he's backing away, still watching me ardently.

One, two, five, ten steps. With each step he takes, every inch further away he gets, my disappointment intensifies.

Disheartened, I turn to face the door. My fingers tremble slightly when I turn the key in the lock. Suddenly, my heart leaps up to my throat when two arms appear on either side of me, caging me, palms pressed against the white door.

"One last time." My eyes slide shut, and I bite down on my lip to keep from moaning against the heat of his breath on my ear. "I need to have you one last time. Let me memorise every sound you make, soak up the way you taste, and fill my senses with the intoxicating scent of you, Snowflake."

I moan zealously and push the door open, tilting my head back while he skims his lips down the length of my neck to the dip in my collarbone. My knees wobble when he teasingly licks and sucks the flesh.

"Oh God, yes." I toss my bag and keys inside the house and spin to face him. Our lips draw together with urgency. Talon's lips glide tantalisingly over mine, parting my lips so he can sink his tongue into my mouth. He walks me back into the apartment, the fingers to his left hand curled in my hair and the other gipping my waist and drawing me closer until I'm pressed up against him while his mouth continues to devour mine.

Hand on my heart, I can say I was ready to come apart for him there and then. I've kissed my fair share of guys, but Talon's kiss, it's going to sound so cheesy and cliché, but damn if his kiss isn't mind-blowing, something dangerously addictive, and the more he kisses you, the more profound the craving becomes.

Panting, Talon pulls back a little and his lips ghost over mine as he speaks in a slow, gruff tone. "I honestly can't decide if I want to rip your clothes off and fuck you all over that kitchen counter or go slow and take my time." He almost growls, pressing his forehead to mine. "You're driving me fucking insane."

I moan and sway in his arms when my head swims with utmost need. "Do both." Talon groans, watching me with hooded eyes when I bite and tug on his bottom lip. "If this really is the last time, let's make it count, Professor."

Talon bites his bottom lip and smiles deviously. He tucks his index finger under my chin and tilts my head up a little, so I'm gazing up at him, lips parted slightly. "You read my mind, Miss Valdez." I lament lasciviously, and my eyes close when he lightly drags the pad of his thumb over my bottom lip.

I open my eyes and raise a brow. "Great minds tend to think alike."

Talon smirks, his eyes slowly skimming over my face. "So I've heard. Though, I'm becoming very fond of this exquisitely salacious mind of yours, Miss Valdez. What are we going to do about that?" he burrs hoarsely. The deep husky tone of his voice combined with his accent makes my knees go weak and my lady bits moisten that much more.

"I have a couple of tricks in mind that I'm damn certain will ease off some of that pent up tension, Professor," I whisper as he slowly backs me up against the kitchen island. He cages me in by gripping the countertop on either side of me and lowers his head so he's at eyes level with me.

"Oh yeah?" Biting down on my lower lip, I stare at him and drag my finger up the length of his erection. Talon's eyes close and he hisses, his jaw set tight, his cock pulsing under my touch through the fabric of his jeans. "Fuck."

Damn. That's so hot.

When Talon opens his eyes, they're a darker shade of blue and full of hunger. "Fuck me like I'm yours, Professor."

A dark smirk graces his handsome features. Talon brushes his nose over mine, his gaze fixed to mine. "If I do, Snowflake, there is no force on this earth that will compel me to stay away," he utters lowly, his lips gliding over mine as he speaks.

"Then don't—" The words haven't even left my mouth fully before he swallows them up when his mouth attacks mine. We kiss frenziedly, and my hands push his jacket off his muscular shoulders. I gasp when he finds the zipper of my dress and tears it open in one swift motion. While his tongue teases mine, I clumsily unfasten the buttons to his pale blue shirt–it's mighty difficult to focus on the task at hand when he's sucking on my tongue in that mind blowing way he does. With a frustrated whimper, I tear the rest open and yank it off. Talon grins against my mouth.

"You're fierce, Rein Valdez."

"You make me crazy, Professor." Talon tugs my dress down and over my hips until it slides off and pools around my ankles. With a flick of his fingers, my black lace bra unclasps and joins the dress on the floor.

Talon breaks the kiss and takes a step back. "Hold on, darlin', let me take a look at you." I stand before him in nothing but a pair of red stiletto heels. The fire burning in his eyes as he looks me over makes me feel something I've never felt before. For the first time in my life, I feel sexy and appreciated, and there is something so powerful in that.

"Christ, you're so fucking beautiful. I'm going to thoroughly revel in devouring every inch of you, Snowflake," he affirms, walking towards me. I smile sultrily and hook my finger in-between the gap of his jeans riding low on his sensational hips and tug him to me. My fingers appreciatively glide over his smooth muscular chest and over his taut abs which flex under my touch.

"There is absolutely nothing I don't like about everything you just said, Professor," I purr, craning my neck to gaze up into his ocean blue eyes. "I'm ready and yours to tame."

Talon smirks and brushes the backs of his fingers down the side of my cheek. "I wouldn't dream of taming you, baby. Your wild and fiery temperament isn't something I would ever want to extinguish–if anything, I crave to spend the night burning in it, and that's precisely what I plan to do."

Talon scoops me up into his arms–bridal style–like I weight nothing at all, and his lips sweep over mine sensually while he carries me to the island in the kitchen. I hiss when he lays me down on top of it, the coldness of the marble worktop raising goosebumps all over my body. "I'm sorry, baby, I know it's cold," he apologises, dipping his head and curling his tongue around my hardened nipple, his large hands caressing my body, warming me instantly.

"God, Talon." I moan, arching up to his mouth when he sucks my nipple teasingly, causing my body to shudder with need.

"Better?"

"More." I breathe, curling my fingers in his hair. My eyes find his and he smiles, biting my nipple and tugging gently. My body jerks with the jolt of pleasure that swims through me and I grip the side of the island. I bite my lip to smother the whimper that's about to escape me.

"Ah ah, no holding back, Snowflake. Let me hear you, I want to remember every sound you make," Talon commands, pinching and rolling my other nipple while his mouth sucks the flesh of my breast, leaving a nice red mark behind. "Don't move."

I groan with displeasure when his mouth disappears and he walks over to the fridge. I observe him looking through the fridge, gathering various items, marvelling at the way his muscles flex and stretch across his back.

He's just so effing hot. Most of the time, I have to pinch myself to make sure this is all real and not my imagination playing tricks on me. I find myself wondering why on earth a man like him would waste a second of his time on a girl like *me*.

I don't have much time to dwell on it because Talon comes back with a bowl full of strawberries, a can of whipped cream and chocolate sauce.

Oh boy.

I lift my head and raise an inquisitive brow. "Are you making a snack?"

Talon flashes me a beautiful broad smile, his eyes lit up so bright it steals the breath right out of my lungs. "I sure am," he affirms, shaking the can of whipped cream. "Lay back."

I obey his command and lay back, watching him closely as he moves around the island until he's back where he was. I gasp when he squirts cream over my nipple. The chill of the cream hardens my already erect nipple, and it sends a mass of tingles shooting up and down my spine. I fist my hands by sides. "Oh God..."

Talon's tongue darts out and he licks the cream off my nipple with a moan and sucks hard making me whimper. He repeats the process with the other nipple and slowly works his way up to my lips. "Stick out your tongue."

I smile and push my tongue out. Talon squirts cream on the tip of my tongue and leans down to suck it off. I moan, curling my fingers at the nape of his neck and kiss him ardently. He pulls away from the kiss, leaving me in a stupor, and picks up a strawberry and puts it between his teeth and feeds it to me.

I love strawberries, but this one is by far the best I've ever had. It tastes exceptionally sweeter, more addictive combined with the taste of us both. When he said he was going to thoroughly enjoy every inch of my body, he damn well meant it. The amount of chocolate and cream we consumed off one another's bodies, I was convinced we'd both wind up in a sugar coma.

"Christ, Rein." Talon growls, watching me while he pushes his cock deeper into my mouth while I hang loose on the edge of the island. I'm thankful I don't have a gag reflex, or this position would be mighty uncomfortable. The way he considerately glides his cock in and out of my mouth without trying to force it makes the whole experience even sexier. His large hands grasp handfuls of my tits, his body juddering with every thrust, and his grunts and moans getting louder. "Goddamn, atta girl, just like that. Fuck, I'm losing my mind," he hisses through clenched teeth. "S-Stop, Snowflake, stop." I look up at him, panting when he withdraws, his eyes closed, his bottom lip between his teeth. "As much as I would love to come down your throat and watch you drink up every drop of my seed, I need to feel your tight little cunt clamped around my cock as I come deep inside you."

My pussy aches zealously and my clit pulses with anticipation despite him already making me squirt twice with his mouth. We're both a sticky mess, covered in chocolate and whipped cream. Talon leans down and kisses me affectionately before he helps me sit back up. My head goes woozy when the blood starts to flow back the other way where it had rushed to my head from hanging off the side of the island. My eyes close and I rest my head back against Talon's shoulder when he kisses along the side of my neck. "You okay?"

I bite my lip and nod. "Never better." My lips find his and we kiss passionately for a minute or two. Talon spins me and pulls me to the edge of the island. With a sultry smile, I lap up the chocolate sauce smeared on his neck and suck the flesh. Talon hisses and grips my hips, grinding himself against my throbbing pussy.

"Please tell me you have a condom nearby." He groans, biting and tugging on my bottom lip.

"In my bedroom," I answer breathily and wrap my legs around his waist, drawing him closer until he's pressed up against my entrance. "You don't need one. I'm on the pill and I trust you."

Talon baulks and stares at me. "Rein—" Before he starts to protest, I press my fingers to his lips, silencing him.

"I want to feel you," I whisper, brushing my fingers against his full lips. "Every inch, every curve, every drop." Talon eyes close and his burly chest rises and falls quicker. He's hesitant, I can sense how tense he is, but he doesn't make a move to stop me when I draw him closer, not even when the crown slips in. He presses his forehead to mine, his breath hastening. Is it irresponsible? Absolutely. We don't really know anything about one another, but something deep inside my gut tells me I can trust him.

"Fuck." I kiss him softly, sensually, while I tighten my legs around him, pulling him in deeper. Talon growls deep in his throat. "Snowflake, what are you doing? This is so reckless."

"It is, but it feels so damn good."

"Christ, it does." He moans, easing himself deeper into me. "Too fucking good." Our lips fuse together, and it seems Talon gave up fighting because he pushes himself in to the hilt with a throaty groan.

He's the first man I've ever allowed to go bareback, and I'm pleased I did, because it felt in-fucking-credible.

We fucked like two wild animals, first on the counter then again in the shower before we collapsed on the bed, well and truly worn out.

I wake up at four in the morning expecting to be alone but smile when I find myself cocooned in his strong arms.

I know one thing for certain.

I'm not ready for this to end.

Chapter 3
Talon

WICKED GAME - DAISY GRAY

"You fucking dickwaffle…" I roll my eyes in exasperation when I pull the door open and see JT standing there, a frown fixed on his face.

"Hello to you too, mate," I utter dryly, pinching the bridge of my nose tiredly.

"Hello? *Fucking* hello?" he gripes and storms into my apartment. I watch him and push the door shut with a shake of my head. "Where have you been? I've not heard from you in almost a week."

"Please, do come in," I drawl dryly. "Gee, I'm sorry, Mum, I've been busy," I throw back with a chuckle, and he glares at me, unmistakably unamused at my mocking response. Jase pauses halfway through taking his jacket and tan cashmere scarf off and glowers at me.

"Too busy to pick up the phone and reply to a text, so I know you're alive, you dick?"

I frown. "Why wouldn't I be alive?"

Jase throws himself down on my sofa with a rather dramatic sigh. "Oh, well, let's see, shall we?" He leans forward, placing his elbows to his knees and lifts his eyes heavenward. "Could it maybe be because you almost drank yourself into an early grave not that long ago?" I roll my eyes and take the seat on the other end of the sofa with a drawn-out sigh. "You've not returned my calls or texts. I was worried when I came by your place last night and you weren't in. Your concierge said you never came home." His eyes rake over me, his frown deepening. "You look…" He trails off and his head tilts to the left while he observes me. "Wait a minute, I was going to say you look like dog shit, but I *know* that look."

I shove a hand through my hair and veer my gaze from my best mate's probing one. "JT…"

"You finally got pussy!"

Oh, fark me dead.

I gape at him when he suddenly springs up from his seat like someone lit a firework up his backside. "I'm right, I'm fucking right!" He grins wildly, pointing his long index finger in my direction animatedly. "Oh man! That look right there isn't work fatigue, no sir, that right there is the 'I've been up until the ass crack of dawn screwing some chick till she's legless' kind of tired."

"I don't know what you're talking about," I deny, shaking my head. The shit eating grin on JT's face tells me he's not buying a word of what I'm selling.

"Don't lie to me, you fuck. You think I can't recognise your fucked-out look by now? I spent four years involuntarily staring at that look back in college."

I bite back the urge to smile and rub my hands over my face instead. "Who is she?"

"No one."

"Tal…" I look up at him and he stares back with his brows raised. "Stop acting like a square and spill. I want every sordid detail. You owe me this at the very least for making me hound your ass every day of the week to get your dick wet."

"Must you be so crude?" I scowl at him and he laughs, walking over to the kitchen.

"Must you be such a pussy?" he throws back while he opens the fridge and rifles through in search of something to–likely–eat. I roll my eyes and rub the back of my neck. What on earth am I supposed to tell him? He won't stop hounding me now he's gotten a whiff of my not so *virtuous* activities. I swear, the kid's got a razor-sharp radar when it comes to sensing fuckery in vicinity. "I'm going grey here, you jackass." I catch the green apple that comes flying in my direction when he hurls it at me. "Who is this mystical creature that has *finally* managed to lure you into her enchanting fissure?"

I bite into the apple and look at him quizzically. "*Enchanting fissure?*" I drawl sardonically. "Are you all right, mate?"

JT laughs and plonks himself down on my sofa and crosses his left leg over his right knee. "You said I was being crude. What, is it not urbane enough for you?"

I chuckle and throw a cushion at him. "Fuck off, you dip shit. Not all of us are root rats like you."

"Ain't a damn thing wrong with having a dynamic sexual appetite, my friend," JT drawls, wagging his brows at me as he takes a long swig of his—or rather *my*–banana and berry smoothie that I was saving to drink after my gym session.

I remember my days of chasing skirt before I met Taylor and realised for me it's more about the quality than the quantity. There was a period in sophomore year in high school where I had a different girl in my bed every other night. I foolishly believed life couldn't get any better and I was some sort of prodigy. I often reflect back on those times and cringe. I didn't think I would ever feel this way again after Taylor, but each day that passes, Rein is sinking deeper and deeper under my skin, and I can't seem to do a damn thing to impede or control this fixation I seem to have with her.

"Hey, are you even listening to me?"

I snap out of my trance when JT nudges my knee with his foot to get my attention. "Would you like to braid my hair or paint my nails while I tell you all about my sexual endeavours?" I utter in exasperation.

JT pins me with a disgruntled look. "What's her name?"

"None of your business."

"Where did you meet?"

I groan and throw my arm over my face. "Fucking hell, mate, she's a co-worker. Happy? Will you give that trap of yours a rest now?"

JT winces. "Oh, I see. Was she not good? Because for someone who spent hours *fucking*, you sure are cranky, Sexy Saxy."

"Jesus, you're killing my high, you fucking dicklicker."

JT's eyes gleam with intrigue. "Your high? So she was *that* good."

I sit up and glare at him. "Get the hell out before I throttle you."

JT laughs and dodges the pillow I hurl at him. "I'm happy to share some tips if you've gotten rusty, bro—ow!" I lean over and give his leg a swift punch, and he groans, rubbing his thigh.

"This isn't an episode of Sweet Valley High; we're not going to sit here and confer the ins and outs of my sex life. Unlike you, I have better things to do, so if you could kindly fuck off it would be greatly appreciated," I declare and stand up.

"Well, one of those things better be the gym because I drove all the way over here to pump some iron, dude," JT announces and takes a large gulp of the smoothie.

Give me strength.

IT'S OFFICIALLY FINALS WEEK AND I CAN TASTE THE STRESS LINGERING in the air as I walk through the corridor towards my office come Monday morning. It brings back so many memories of my days not that long ago, cramming in study sessions–my head buried in books.

"Morning, Professor Saxton." Students greet me as I walk by them. I smile courteously and nod, making my way to my office. My eyes scan the corridors in search of Rein, hoping I'll get a glimpse of her, but she's nowhere to be seen. I won't see her until finals week is over now, which is probably a blessing in disguise. Since that night I spent in her apartment, I had to practically tear myself away. I'm simply bewitched by her. Every dip, curve and crevice of her gorgeous body. The astounding taste and vastly addictive scent of her is driving me to insanity.

I was once a man that had his shit together, and now, I'm obsessing over a fucking student. What has become of me? What in hell has *she* done to me?

Walking into my office, I set my Starbucks coffee and briefcase on my desk and throw myself into my chair with an audible groan. I release the latch and lean back, staring up at the brilliant white ceiling.

"We've got to put a stop to this, Snowflake."

"Talon, why do we have to? No one will find out as long as we're careful."

"It's unethical, Rein, and as good and right as it may feel to the two of us, it's so wrong. You're my student and every second we spend together puts us both at a great risk."

"I know, but the fact I can't have you just makes me want you that much more. I know that sounds juvenile, but I don't want this to end."

"I don't either, Snowflake, but if we both continue down this path, we'll eventually get caught and everything will go up in flames. I can't nor will I risk our futures for something that's barely a relationship..."

"Professor Saxton?"

I sit up, my eyes flitting over to a student poking his head in the door. "Yes, uh… Mr Tomkins."

"Sorry, Professor. I did knock a couple of times."

"Right, my apologies. My mind got away from me. Please come on in and have a seat." I gesture to the seat opposite my desk and place my forearms on the desk. "What can I do for you, Mr Tomkins?"

"I have some follow up questions on the material you handed out in our last class…"

Fuck me, it's going to be a long and tedious week.

I'M GOING STIR CRAZY. I'M RESTLESS, UNABLE TO FOCUS, AND IT'S really grating on my last nerve. I'm running out of things to do to keep my mind occupied so I don't think about Rein, but whatever the fuck it is she's done to me, ninety-five percent of my day is spent thinking about her. I've lost count of how many times I almost called or texted her throughout this week. I'm obsessed, and it's terrifying me. The harder I fight to keep my promise and stay away from her the more I want her. Just as I presumed, she's not been around campus. It's likely she's hauled up in the library or back at her place, studying for her end of year exams.

My phone buzzes beside me on the desk and I snatch it at lightening speed. My stomach goes all giddy when I see the snowflake emoji flashing on my screen.

Snowflake:
I need help!

I lean forward, brows drawn together while I stare at the text. Dread twists my gut. I hold my finger down on her name and the option comes up to call her, so I do.

It rings, once, twice, and on the third, she answers. "Professor."

"Rein, are you all right?"

"Um, no, not really."

I stand and start pacing the living room like a lunatic. "What's the matter?"

Rein heaves a deep sigh, her voice heavy when she speaks. "I'm so sorry, I know we agreed to stay away, but I'm really stuck, and I've been trying to figure this thing out for three days straight and it's due on Monday and I just… I can't do it, Talon."

I stop pacing. "Rein, hey, slow down. Tell me where you are."

"I'm in that little pottery studio just off campus," she replies.

"Stay put, I'll be right there." I hang up the phone, grab my jacket and briefcase, and hightail it out of my office. The pottery studio is a ten-minute walk from campus–I made it there in eight. When I reach the studio, I see Rein standing over a lump of clay, staring at it, her face presenting her current state of frustration and hopelessness.

Those gorgeous eyes lift to meet mine when I push the door open and walk into the studio. I exhale slowly, my eyes sweeping over her attired in a plain black vest top and tan overalls strapped up on one side. Her hands and wrists are covered in clay. I set my briefcase on the side and walk over to her while she looks at me beseechingly. "Are you okay?"

Rein shakes her head and points to the clay sitting on the pottery wheel. "No, I can't say that I am," she utters with a one shoulder shrug and rubs her arm over her forehead. "I can't do it. I've tried, it's just either not coming together how I envisioned it, or it keeps collapsing on me and I don't know what I'm doing wrong. I should be painting it by now, but it's just not coming together, and I need to give this in on Monday morning," Rein replies in a flurry, all in one breath. "I'm going to have a big fat pile of whatever the fuck that is to hand in and Mr Stevenson is going to fail me."

"Whoa, whoa, come here." I take hold of her upper arms and gaze down into her upturned face. "Take a breath, Snowflake, you're not going to fail, all right?"

Rein stares up at me and shakes her head sullenly. "I already have, Professor. I have five days to finish this vase, and even if by some miracle I manage to finish it, I still have to wait for it to dry before I can put it in the kiln and paint it. It's impossible."

"Hey, stop, there is no such thing as impossible. You're anything but a quitter, Snowflake," I assure her, and she closes her eyes, drawing her bottom lip between her teeth. "Slow down, take a deep breath and refocus. You're rushing and this is likely why the mould keeps collapsing on you. Pottery takes patience and precision. Working while you're frustrated isn't going to help. You can't rush art, darlin', you should know this by now."

Rein's eyes slowly open and she gazes up at me. The annoyance she felt moments ago slowly drains away, leaving her eyes clear and dazzling, just as I adore them. "Do you have any pointers that you could maybe share?"

I smile and nod. "I'd be happy to help *guide* you until you get your sculpture moulded into the shape you desire."

Rein's eyes light up and she smiles wickedly. "So, you'll help me *erect* it then?" she purrs suggestively, and I resist the strong urge to yank her up against me and bruise her soft full lips with an arduous kiss. Instead, I wet my lips and stare deep into her eyes.

"I can tell you with absolute certainty and from personal experience that you, Miss Valdez, have no problem and are more than capable of *erecting* things," I assure her gallantly and marvel at the gorgeous glow of her cheeks when she blushes.

I'm enamoured by you.

Rein cocks her head to the side and gazes up at me through her lashes. "Some things are a lot more effortless to erect than others, Professor. It all differs on the subject at hand, does it not?"

"That it does, Miss Valdez," I answer, reaching up and brushing a loose strand of her hair away from her angelic face. "I know you're more than capable of doing this, but I'll be happy to lend a helping hand to get you underway."

When Rein's lips curl into a brilliant smile, I can't fight back my own. We stand there for a good minute just staring at one another, smiling eloquently. "Shall we?" I say, shrugging off my jacket and setting it aside on the chair by the desk.

Rein clears her throat and nods. "Uhm, sure." Her eyes take in my attire, and she frowns a little. "Wait, you're going to ruin your suit."

"Good thing I have a closet full of them then," I reply readily while rolling up the sleeves to my light grey shirt. Rein watches me raptly, and my eyes remain fixed on hers whilst I loosen my tie and pull it off, draping it on the chair with my jacket and unbutton the top two buttons to my shirt. "Stop staring at me like that and take your seat, Snowflake."

Rein blinks, snapping out of the stupor she's emmeshed in and nods with a nervous chuckle. "Right." I grab a short stool on wheels, sit on it, and roll to sit opposite her. This is profoundly risky given we're still within close proximity to campus. "Doesn't this studio close at seven?"

Rein nods, wetting her hands. "Yes, technically it is supposed to, but I managed to beg and plead with David to let me stay back so I can finish. It's also his wife's birthday, so he was in a dire rush and therefore didn't have time to protest too much."

I nod and look around the small studio. "Putting those persuasion skills to good use as per, I see."

Rein smiles softly and lifts her eyes from the spinning wheel to look at me. "I can't help that I'm ever so charming, Professor."

My eyes find hers, and I smile, wetting my hands also. "I'm the last person you need to convince on that note, Snowflake." Rein titters softly in response. She picks up a lump of stoneware clay and drops it on the spinning wheel. "Tell me what you've got envisioned for your sculpture."

"Well…" She sighs, wetting the clay and wrapping her fingers delicately around it until it smooths out and centres. "I'm thinking a spherical shaped vase with a narrow lip." I nod in understanding while I observe her shaping the clay dexterously, her dainty fingers lifting the clay until it's a cylinder shape. "I don't know where I'm going wrong. I get the shape right, but when I go to narrow the neck to create the lip, it collapses on me."

"I see." I hum and observe her closely. "Could be a number of reasons. Spherical shapes need a strong structure, that could be the reason it's collapsing on you. You see, your base is not thick enough, it needs to be sturdy enough to hold the weight as you flare it out."

Rein bites her lip and creates a ledge at the bottom and slowly pulls the clay up. "Is that better?"

"No, it's still not thick enough." I wet my hands again and place my fingers on top of hers, guiding her fingers to the base of the vase. Our eyes lift at the same time when our hands touch and she holds my gaze, lips slightly parted. Between her gaze and the feel of her fingers interlacing with mine, my stomach goes tight as my nerves bunch together.

HOOK, LINE, PROFESSOR

Focus, Talon. Now is not the time for larking around. You're here for one reason and one reason only—to help her out.

What in the high heavens am I doing? I shouldn't even be here. I have no obligation to be. I don't teach pottery for fuck's sake, this isn't even for my class. I'm just digging myself deeper into a hole I'm already hopelessly immersed in.

"That should do it. Now, try flare it out," I instruct with an encouraging smile, and she exhales, chewing on her lip nervously. She hesitates. "Rein don't be nervous. Keep your hands steady and slowly flare it out using your knuckle. You've got this."

"What if it falls apart again?"

I take hold of her hands and gaze into her captivating eyes. "Then you try again, because based on my perception over the years I've taught you, you're no quitter."

Rein nods meekly. I let go of her hands and watch as she hesitantly reaches one hand inside the vase to widen it. "That's good, not too much pressure, you don't want it too thin."

The concentration on her face and the way her fingers move over the clay is making me feel a little hot under the collar. I grin when she nervously brushes the back of her hand against her forehead and leaves a stain. "That looks great, Snowflake, just lift the shoulder up a little bit and narrow the top so you can shape the neck and lip." Rein does as she's instructed and shapes her vase like a pro. "Atta girl."

"I can't do the neck and lip, Talon, I'm scared it's going to collapse again. My heart can't take watching it fall apart again," she asserts dejectedly, shaking her hands. I notice the stress written all over her face and roll my stool over till I'm sitting behind her.

I brush her hair over to the other shoulder. "Don't be afraid," I whisper in her ear, my hands trailing down her forearms till my fingers curl around her deft wrists. Rein sinks back against me; a slow frustrated breath flows past her full lips. "You'll never truly grasp how exceptional you are if you keep allowing your fear to cripple you and hold you back," I murmur in her ear while I guide her hands toward the vase. They tremble faintly so I give them a gentle squeeze. "Take a deep breath and focus."

I let go of her hands and observe as she wets her hands and carefully stretches out the neck of the vase. "Very good, now, slow down the wheel and use the pin to clean up the lip." I hand her the pin and she slices off the top, leaving an even and smooth cut. Rein pulls her hands back and stares at the vase for a full minute, holding her breath as if waiting for it to fall apart.

Okay. "Oh my God, it's... it's not collapsing."

I smile and lick my lips, leaning a little closer to examine her creation. "Mhm, amazing what a little perseverance can result in, isn't it, Snowflake?" I murmur against the shell of her ear. I grin when I feel her visibly quiver and goosebumps rise over her smooth olive skin.

"I'm sure you've already noticed, Professor, but patience has never been one of my virtues," she voices brazenly, turning her head a little to gaze back at me. Like a magnet, my eyes are instantly drawn to her mouth, and I almost lean in to kiss her but catch myself just in time. "Especially in light of something I desperately want."

I swallow thickly, my throat suddenly going as dry as a bone.

"I certainly have noticed," I affirm, raising my eyes to meet hers. "Though I can absolutely relate, you make it damn impossible to show forbearance, Rein Valdez. I've always been a patient man, until you came along and stripped away every ounce of my perseverance one bit at a time with your rapaciousness."

"If you're waiting for an apology, I wouldn't hold your breath, Professor," Rein expresses, her eyes slowly ascending to my lips.

"What I want more than anything right now is to give you a lengthy Aussie kiss," I proclaim, lowering my tone, my lips inching closer and closer to hers.

"An Aussie kiss?" she queries with a breathy whisper, her brows knitting faintly. "What's that?"

A flame ignites deep in my gut and starts to gradually consume me. Whether it's from the humidity of the studio or the affect Rein is having on me, I feel like I'm burning from the inside. "It's just like a French kiss…" I drawl raspingly. "But down under."

Rein's eyes close and she releases a slow lustful sigh. When she opens her eyes, they're radiating such desire it singes me down to my deepest core. "Do you mean…" She trails off, and taking my hand, she slowly pushes it between her legs and grinds her pussy against my fingers. "Right here, Professor?"

I groan and bite down on my lip so hard I almost draw blood. "Yes, right fucking there, Snowflake." I growl, leaning in to bite that luscious bottom lip, but Rein draws back a little.

"Ah, ah, not so fast there, Professor."

I slowly raise my eyes from her pouty mouth to meet her tantalising gaze. "I thought you said the other night was going to be the last time and you wanted out?"

I did. I fucking do, but I'm incapable of leaving you alone.

Rein stares at me, her eyes searching mine while I scramble to find the right words to say and attempt to keep fighting the losing battle within myself. Desperately trying to convince myself that I have the strength to walk away when fuck… it's clear that I don't. "I still do. My view on the matter still remains the same as does the risks," I admit openly and wet my lips before continuing. "However, that doesn't prevent me from wanting you, Rein. I can't seem to control this irrepressible attraction I have towards you anymore than you can. It seems the harder I fight to stay away and let you be, the more I find myself gravitating to you."

"Then stop fighting it, Talon," Rein expresses melodiously, her lips grazing mine ever so lightly when she speaks.

My eyes close and I swallow thickly. "Do you think I don't want to? Or that I haven't spent countless hours and days fantasising about how good it would feel if I just surrendered and stopped looking for something, *anything* to rationalise my actions?" I affirm and sweep my nose over hers. "Believe me, Snowflake, you have no fucking idea how badly I want to succumb to these impious desires and make you mine, but that's just never going to be a possibility."

"It could be. Maybe we should just stop fighting and let whatever this is run its course, because it's glaringly obvious that neither of us are capable of staying away," Rein states evenly.

"Snowflake, something that starts this hot tends to burn out just as fast." Rein grinds herself against my fingers.

"Then let's enjoy it while it's still hot, Professor," Rein whispers, sweeping her lips over mine teasingly.

I'm going straight to hell.

Even if I tried to put into words this incessant need that is engulfing me at an alarming speed, I couldn't. This striking woman does something to me, something that makes me want to abandon every ounce of self-possession and claim her. "You're wicked, Rein Valdez." I almost growl, cupping her pussy through her denim overalls and sucking her bottom lip till she moans wantonly.

"Oh, you've not seen anything yet, Professor."

Oh, fucking Christ, I'm done. I've got absolutely no fight left in me.

To hell with my ethics and being responsible.

I want what I want, and Rein Valdez is *mine*.

Chapter 4
Rein

PRETTY - ASTRID S, DAGNY

"REIN VALDEZ, I know you're in there! You better open this door right this second!"

With a gasp, I pull the covers down and lift my head to look at the bedroom door wide eyed and panting.

"Oh shit."

Talon's head pops up from between my legs, his blue eyes wide with panic. "What the fuck?"

We stare at one another in alarm for a good thirty seconds, neither of us able to move or even think straight. "REIN?! I will scream this apartment down. You better let me in!"

"Shit. Shit, Talon, get up." I sit up hastily. Talon and I scramble off the bed, frantically searching the room for our clothes that we discarded haphazardly all over the place in the midst of our passion.

"It's past midnight. What the hell is she doing here? It's way past curfew," Talon questions, pulling his boxers on—back to front, might I add.

I pull my robe on, my heart racing a mile a minute as I pick up Talon's black shirt and trousers and throw them at him.

"Oh wait, give me a moment to tap into my psychic abilities so I can read her mind and tell you. How am I supposed to know why she's here, Talon? My mind was more than a little preoccupied while you were begging me to ride your tongue, in case you've forgotten."

Talon stops halfway through pulling his shirt on and pins me with a stern yet sexy glare. "Which I'd like to get back to if you could kindly get rid of your friend before she lures the entire CPD precinct to your fucking door." He growls, gesturing towards the door that Paris is currently–and relentlessly–pounding her fist into.

The blood rushing through my veins heats up the longer I stare into those cerulean blue eyes that are burning hot with need. "Relax, I'll get rid of her, just go hide and make sure you take your clothes with you."

I watch Talon snatch up his shoes and walk out of the room while muttering incoherently under his breath all the way to the bathroom. Fucking hell, Paris. I just got clam jammed by my best friend. I could honestly kill her. I was right there just about to go over that sweet edge.

"Keep your wig on, I'm coming!" *Well, I was, but sure as shit I'm not anymore.* I muse bitterly and voice my frustration as I walk to the door. When I unlock it and pull the door open, my body that was pulsing with need moments ago is now thudding with agitation as I see Paris standing there, her fist in the air. Her honey-coloured eyes sweep over me, and I almost shrink back under her prodding gaze.

"Well, smack my ass and call me Sandy, you are alive." Paris doesn't even wait for a response before she storms into the apartment. I watch her, my mouth agape as she breezes past me, unwrapping her outrageous overpriced Burberry scarf from around her neck.

"Oh, please, do come on in, *Sandy*. I mean, who cares that it's the middle of the night and you've probably pissed off the entire building with your incessant pounding and shrieking."

Paris tosses her tie and bag on the sofa with a huff before she turns to face me. "Be thankful I didn't bring the entire police force to your damn door. Where the hell have you been? I've been calling you, texting you, and you've not responded to a single one, bitch!" Paris fumes, placing her hands on her hips and glaring at me furiously. "Look at me, I've aged, you made me age ten years this past week!"

I roll my eyes. "Way to be melodramatic, P. Would you like an award to go with that scene you just caused?" I drawl sardonically.

"I am not being melodrama... wait a damn minute, sis." Her eyes narrow and she shuffles towards me slowly. "Let's back the hell up for sec. Why are you so flushed?" Paris queries, narrowing her eyes at me before they dart across the apartment, and then she gasps. "Oh my gosh, were you... you were totally getting railed, weren't you? Is someone here?"

Kill me now.

Panic rises in my gut at rapid speed, and I shake my head, my cheeks aflame. *Stay calm, Rein. If she gets a whiff of a lie, she will just keep digging and you'll be fucked.*

"No! Don't be ridiculous," I refute, wrapping my arms around my stomach when my robe begins to loosen at the front. "Unfortunately, I was in bed *alone*, handling *business* when you so rudely decided to interrupt."

Paris' eyes grow wide, and her jaw drops a little, her hand coming up to cover her mouth while she fights back the urge to snigger. "Oh! My bad. That's why you took so long to answer the door. You were pattin' the bunny," she coos, amused.

I'm so beyond mortified right now. My cheeks are so hot I'm almost certain you can cook an egg on my face. I suppose this does beat her finding out that I'm screwing my professor. I dread to think how she would react if she knew I was sleeping with Professor Saxton. "Yes," I hiss through gritted teeth. "So, thank you very much for the cliterference."

Paris giggles behind her hand, her eyes gleaming. "Maybe next time you should answer my calls and messages then, sugar tits. Let this be a lesson to you," Paris utters flippantly and throws her hair over her shoulder proudly.

"How about next time you get the urge to show up at my door like some crazed loon you come at a more reasonable hour?" I suggest with a scowl. My eyes drift over her shoulder when I see the bathroom door open and Talon glares at me through the gap. I press my lips together to suppress the smile tugging at my lips. He's so going to make me pay for this later.

Paris waves her hand dismissively. "Girl, please, you've walked in on me doing much worse."

This is true. I once walked in on her having a full-on threesome with two other girls while a frat boy watched. I almost choked on my uvula.

I grimace just recalling that memory. Not one of her finest moments. This was back in our first year in Oakhill. I had only just met her, and she was going through some wild phase at the time. Of course, being friends with Sydney and her cronies did her no favours at all during that time. She went off the rails. It was Hunter and I that helped her through it and got her back on the right path. Thankfully, she's in a much better place now.

It just goes to show that money isn't everything. It can buy you a lot of things, but happiness isn't one of them. It won't ever replace the love and affection you need from your parents. All Paris needed was to know that someone cared for her. However, both Rome—her brother—and Paris were neglected by their parents growing up. They were sent to the most prestigious private schools, had all the best things money could buy, but no amount of money or materialism could replace the love and affection they were missing from their parents.

Looking in from the outside, you would assume she has it all, until she allows you into her life and you see the real her and how unloved and abandoned she really is, and it makes you thankful that you have people in your life that love you unconditionally.

"Thank you for reminding me." I shudder inwardly. "Well, now that you see I am alive, you can go before Syd snitches on you for sneaking out in the middle of the night past curfew."

Paris rolls her eyes with a shrug. "Syd can go fuck herself." I frown when she smiles at me adorably while batting her lashes. "I could just stay here and we can have a sleep over like we used to?"

Oh crap.

Paris, for the love of God, don't do this to me.

I look fleetingly towards the bathroom and see Talon shaking his head slowly, his eyes shooting beams of rage straight in her direction. "P, that sounds great, but can we do it another time? I am honestly so exhausted, and between finals and work, I am beaten down, babe."

Paris pouts like a putout child, clearly dissatisfied, and in return I give her my best beseeching look. "Fine, you boring old hag. I'll go." She huffs and picks up her bag and scarf then turns to point her index finger at me. "But we're meeting tomorrow for brunch, and this time I won't take no for an answer, and so help me Godiva, if you even try giving me that puppy look, I'll be inclined to slap it right off your beautiful face, ya hear?"

I chuckle and nod, holding my hands up, palms facing her in surrender. "I hear ya, loud and clear. Tomorrow brunch, just text me the time and place and I'll be there."

"Okay, fine." She beams loosely, wrapping her scarf around her neck. "I'll go and let you get back to playing some *clitar hero.*"

I throw my head back and laugh while I walk her to the front door. "Fat chance of that happening now you've killed my vibe."

Paris gives me an impish look. "Need a hand?"

I open the door and push her cackling arse out of it. "You can get the hell out of here, you daft cow."

"Hey, it's nothing I haven't seen before–"

"Please stop talking."

Paris giggles while she walks out of the door. "Love you forever, sugar tits."

"Love you always, bitch tits," I reply and wave before closing the door and leaning against it. I close my eyes and release a slow breath of relief.

Shit, that was a close call.

The bathroom door opens and Talon steps out wearing his black trousers and navy-blue shirt that makes his eyes stand out, giving them a deeper hue of blue. His shirt and trousers are both still unbuttoned, a black tie hanging loosely around his neck, leaving his smooth, strapping chest and rock-hard abs exposed to my appreciative scrutiny. My eyes greedily roam over him, taking in every delightful inch of rippling muscle. The displeasure radiating in his gaze only heightens my already unruly desire and has my sex stirring and moistening on the double.

Good grief. How does one man make appearing angry so alluring? I cock my head to the side and push off the door before I saunter over to him on the tips of my toes. "Going somewhere, Professor?"

Talon watches me steadily as I near him. It doesn't take a genius to see that he's troubled about us almost getting caught, and he's gearing himself up to bolt out of the door and put an end to it all. "Rein, we almost got caught. That was a little too close for comfort. We're being careless. I think it's time to cool things off for a while."

My heart sinks.

I step closer until we're toe to toe and gaze up at him. "But we didn't," I answer, resting my hands against his well-defined abs. Talon's eyes close for the briefest second and he licks his lips, his chest rising when he inhales deeply. "We always knew going in that there were risks involved when we started this, right?"

His eyes open and he stares down at me, his jaw set tight, his gaze still apprehensive but he nods. "We've been lucky so far." He sighs, draping his jacket over the back of the chair and turning to face me again. Talon takes a hold of my upper arms and draws me a touch closer. "Perhaps this is a sign that our luck is starting to run out. The smart thing to do here is walk away, Snowflake."

I curl my fingers around the tie hanging around his neck and push up on my toes, pressing my body flush up against him. "Maybe you're right, Professor," I purr, drawing his face closer to mine with a gentle tug on his tie. "Maybe we should do the right thing and walk away," I whisper sultrily, my lips feathering his with every word. "I'm sure we can go back to ignoring this intense attraction we have towards one another and just forget how witlessly good it feels whenever we're together, right?" Talon's eyes close, his Adam's apple rises and falls when he swallows, his grip on my arms tightening. My stomach knots when I feel his dick swell in his boxers, and he grinds himself against my hip.

"Fuck, Rein," Talon hisses urgently and leans in to kiss me, but I pull my head back a little.

"Do you have the strength to walk away, Professor?"

Talon's large hands skim down my arms to my bum which he grasps handfuls of and gives both cheeks a firm squeeze. "You damn well know I don't, Snowflake."

"Then let's not waste another second procrastinating, Professor," I murmur, sucking teasingly on the soft pillow of his lower lip. "Take me back to bed and spend the night composing a sonnet all over my pussy with that wicked tongue of yours."

Talon groans throatily. He slides the robe off my body and grabs my face with his left hand and stares deep into my eyes. "I'm going to fuck this beautiful face till I cum all over it," he growls.

My pussy pulsates wantonly. I only manage a nod just before he sweeps down and bruises my lips with a hungry kiss that drains every drop of oxygen from my lungs. I eagerly push his shirt over his shoulders and drag it down till it falls at his feet. I've never been so desperate to feel someone's heated flesh up against my own. I want to be pinned down by his weight while he ploughs himself savagely into me, making me scream until my throat burns and I lose my voice. "Get on your knees."

I don't respond well to being ordered around or controlled. In fact, I damn well hate it. Any other man I would have told to go jump up their own arse, but Talon, he makes me want to submit and surrender myself over to his every whim. I suppose that's the power of good dick. Sounds awful, I know, don't judge me too harshly, but my God, the man can fuck and I'm here for it—every filthy second of it.

I kneel in front of him and peel his trousers and boxers down, freeing his fully erect manhood from its confines. Talon steps out and kicks them to the side whilst I stare up at him in awe. I lick my lips keenly, my eyes gorging on his hefty cock. It's no surprise that a man of his stature packs quite the love stick. Long, girthy and clean. I'm just itching to lick that pearl of precum glistening on the tip of his dick. Talon grasps my chin and tilts my head up so I can meet his gaze. His eyes are dark and hooded with lust.

"Do you see what you do to me, Snowflake? Do you see how fucking hard I am for you? With every sordid thought I have of you, you make my dick weep all fucking day, just like this, baby," Talon rasps, brushing the pad of his thumb over my lips, which I part and give the tip of his thumb a teasing lick. Talon sucks in a slow breath through his teeth, his eyes rolling to the back of his head. "Fuck."

Talon removes his thumb from my mouth and grasps the base of his dick and rubs the thick rim of the head over my lips. I part my lips and flick my tongue against the ridge and give him a slow lick up to his slit, lapping up the sticky precum with a breathy moan. "Ahh, fuck. You like that? You like the taste of me, baby?" Talon moans, curling his fingers in my hair and feeding his cock into my mouth one succulent inch at a time. "That's it, baby, take my cock. Look at me, I want those gorgeous eyes on me while I fuck your mouth." I moan and lift my eyes to his. The lust in those blue orbs lights an inferno deep in my belly. "Good fucking girl."

His moans alone are enough to drive me senseless. Just listening to him panting, moaning, and talking to me in that racy manner, I'm ready to come apart for him before he's even laid a finger on me. I want to hear more; I *need* to hear him lose his fucking mind while he fucks my mouth and makes an absolute mess of me.

Talon's fingers tighten in my hair, and he watches avidly while his cock slides in and out of my mouth. The look of carnality on his handsome face with each stroke makes my pussy ache that much more. I swallow his cock greedily, matching his tempo until I feel his body tense and his cock grow harder, thicker and start to throb as he chases down his orgasm.

The head of his dick hits the back of my throat and he presses his eyes tightly shut as I suck him deeply towards the brink of his release. "Ahh, fuck, God, baby, I'm coming. You want my cum, don't you? You're going to drink up every last drop of my seed like a good girl." Talon groans, losing his breath, his entire body shaking as he comes undone. "Oh fuck, fuck, Rein!" He explodes, firing spurt after spurt of his hot seed down my throat. I lap up every last drop and lick him clean after with a gratified moan of my own. Talon hisses and bites down hard on his lower lip when I give him one last greedy suck and release him with a pop. I lick my lips, sated, my eyes hot on his.

"Get up." He growls lowly, his eyes almost black with lust. Exhilaration coils deep in my groin. I barely make it to my feet before he grabs me and throws me over his shoulder as if I weigh nothing but a bag of potatoes. I can't complain, the view of his taut bum is a nice distraction, until Talon grasps a handful of my left bum cheek with his free hand and bites the other while he carries me to the bedroom. I'm thrown down on the bed and he towers over me, looking like an enchanting Greek God and the leading star of my every wet dream, ready to ravish me.

"Stop staring and mount me, you beauteous beast," I purr sultrily and spread my legs for him suggestively.

Talon's eyes lower to my sex and he exhales slowly. I watch him readily as he slowly crawls up on the bed and over me. "You and that sinfully wicked mouth of yours is driving me fucking insane, Snowflake," he voices as he lowers his mouth to mine, his lips dextrously brushing mine apart before he sinks his velvet tongue into my mouth and sucks on my tongue, making me moan lasciviously into his.

"The feeling is absolutely mutual, Professor." I breathe when Talon bites and tugs my bottom lip. He rolls us over until I'm on top of him, my naked body draped over his. I pull my head back and gaze down at him. Our eyes interlock and Talon brushes his fingers through my hair, pushing it away from my face.

"Take a seat on your throne and allow me to worship the masterpiece that is your sweet cunt, Miss Valdez."

Oh, sweet Jesus, the mouth on him.

I smile down at him and he grins back wickedly. The smile accompanied by the insatiable look in his eyes tells me he is about to wreak absolute havoc to my body, and I'm readily welcoming every salacious second of it.

"I've always detested that word, but hearing it from you, I honestly can't hear enough of it."

Talon smiles and curls his fingers at my nape and draws my mouth to his. "I can't get enough of *you*," he murmurs gruffly and glides his tongue past my lips to teasingly fondle my tongue. "I'm going to drink up every drop of your tasty girl cum. I want your thighs trembling while you ride my face and fucking suffocate me, Snowflake, so get on up here and satiate my appetite."

With a moan, I crawl up over his exquisite body till I'm straddling his face. Talon grips my hips, his eyes burning into mine as he takes that first, slow lick through my folds. My mouth hangs open, and a delicious shiver travels through my body from my groin all the way to the top of my head, causing the hairs to stand on end. "Yes."

I can say with absolute certainty that I have never had *anyone* devour my pussy the way Talon does. With every lick and every deliberate suck, he enjoys every second of eating pussy. I'm not even getting into the sexy, appreciative noises he makes while doing so. Deep, throaty groans while his tongue glides through my cleft, and then he circles his tongue around my clit. "Talon, holy fucking shit, the things you do with that mouth. God yes," I whimper, grinding my pussy back and forth against his tongue, riding it until I find a steady tempo. I can feel that sweet pressure in my groin building and building with every suction and flick of his tongue against my swollen nub.

I come undone when he does this thing where he spreads my pussy lips apart, exposing my clit, and he sucks it into his mouth and his tongue flickers over it again and again, sending me soaring over the edge into blissful rapture. "Talon, fuck, yes, yes, baby, I'm coming!" I curl my fingers into the bedsheet with a death grip and I let out a strangled whimper as I shatter all over his face. Stars explode behind my eyelids, and I momentarily forget how to breathe, but fuck, I don't care. I've never felt such intense pleasure as wave after wave of my orgasm makes my body shake frenziedly. A gush of liquid heat trickles from my pussy and he drinks up every drop of it with a greedy growl, lapping at it incessantly like a man that's been deprived, starved, and he can't seem to appease his unquenchable thirst.

Talon promised he would make a mess of me, and fuck me, he did. My arms tremble as I fight to keep myself upright, so I don't collapse on top of him. I attempt to roll off, but he tightens his hold on my hips and keeps me in place while he brushes feather light kisses and kittenish licks against my sensitive mound that's still quivering from his onslaught. Panting to catch my breath, I peel my eyes open and stare down into those mesmerising eyes that are ablaze and gazing up at me with lust.

"That tongue of yours is lethal, Professor." I pant, biting down on my bottom lip. Talon nuzzles my inner thigh and nips at the flesh, the corner of his lip lifting into an errant smirk.

"So is the taste of you," he murmurs, giving my bum a firm squeeze and licking through my slit while he stares up at me. I hiss and judder when he flicks his tongue against my swollen nub.

Talon grips my hips and in one swift move rolls me onto my back. I'm pinned down to the mattress, his gorgeous body covering mine. "Talon..." I whisper, parting my lips for him when he leans down to kiss me.

"Tell me."

"I want to feel the weight of you on top of me." I graze my fingertips down his muscular arms, over his biceps, and lace my fingers with his and pull his arms up over my head until his body is entirely pressed against mine, cocooning me.

"I'll crush you, Snowflake."

"I don't care." I breathe against his lips and rock my hips up.

"Wrap those thick sexy thighs around me," he commands, his voice deep and hoarse, every word a slow drawl. The vibration of his vocal chords resonates through my entire body. When I circle my legs around him, Talon presses the crown of his cock against my entrance. My hips instinctively roll up, impatient, eager to be filled by his girthy member. I bite down on my lip and stifle a moan when he slowly feeds his cock into me. "Oh no, Snowflake. Don't you dare stifle those sexy moans. I love it when you moan for me, drives me fucking crazy. I want to hear every whimper, every gasp. I want you to scream loud enough to wake the fucking dead as you shatter all around me," Talon rasps, rocking his hips into mine, his fingers tightening around mine.

"Yes, Professor." I moan.

"Good girl." His lips brush mine apart. "That's it, baby, just like that." He groans, pushing himself deeper into me.

"Oh, Talon, yes." I whimper when he starts to thrust into me.

"Does it feel good, baby?" Talon moans, driving himself into me, his thrusts growing harder and more urgent. "God, you feel so good —so *fucking* tight. The way you're gripping my cock. You fit around me so perfectly, like your pussy was made just for me."

The combination of the bed creaking–which amplifies with every ferocious thrust–and the way he's talking to me heightens my state of arousal that much more. Flesh hitting flesh, our moans and cries of pleasure reverberating around the room. The headboard thumps almost violently against the wall, and I'm sure the neighbours on each side and the ones below us can hear. "Oh, Snowflake, fuck yes, milk that fucking cock, baby." Talon growls, dipping his head. He bruises my lips with a breath-taking kiss that leaves my lungs blazing and my pussy throbbing frenziedly.

"Oh my God, yes, Talon, fuck, I'm going to come." I whimper, thrusting my hips up urgently. That knee-weakening pressure builds and builds with each stroke of his cock against my G-spot until I go flying over the edge. My pussy clamps down around him and he moans audibly. "Come with me."

"Fucking Christ…" He growls, panting, his thrusts becoming short and hard as he nears his orgasm "Rein. Ah, ah, yes, yes, I'm coming, baby, I'm fucking coming."

Pumping his cock into me, the throbbing of his dick sets off my orgasm and I go over with him, exploding all around him with an ear piecing cry. "Ohh fuck!"

"Oh God, yes, yes, Talon!" I pant, digging my nails into his muscular back while my body jerks and convulses against his with the sweet rapture that crashes over me.

We lay together, our hearts racing, breathless, our foreheads pressed together while our orgasms slowly ebb away.

As I lay in his arms, counting every beat of his heart against my own, the realisation hits me that there is no other place I'd rather be.

And that petrifies the ever-loving shit out of me.

Chapter 5
Talon

SEX THERAPY- ROBIN THICKE

MAN, I love winter break.

Three whole weeks of peace. No assignments, no emails, no classes to prep for. And best of all, no evading indecent advances from Polly… absolute fucking heaven. On that last day of term, the moment I step off campus grounds, I switch off from work mode and hop right into vacation mode. Granted, Christmas is a hectic time of year, especially with my mother persistently coercing me into going back home for the holidays.

That reminds me, I still need to do my Christmas shopping. Shopping for my dad is easy—a bottle of single malt, some Cubans, and a pair of unique socks. That's become our thing over the years. We find the most absurd pair of socks to gift one another for Christmas. The whackier the better. My mother, on the other hand, I struggle with picking out a gift for. Taylor would pick out the gifts for her, so I didn't have to worry about it. And considering I skipped out on the last two holidays, not being able to face anyone after Tay died, which I now feel terrible about, I'll absolutely need to make the effort this year.

Question is, what on earth am I supposed to buy her? I have a week before I fly home.

I fire up my MacBook and run a search for Christmas gift ideas for mums. I click the first link–eighty-four gift ideas for mother dearest. Chocolate gift basket? No, she's not a huge fan of chocolate. A wine subscription? Nope. What about a Fitbit? She is very much into her fitness. Wait, I think my dad already got her one for her birthday last year.

Damn.

Frustrated, I slap my laptop shut and sink further into my sofa. I cover my face with my hands and groan. I'm hopeless at this. Perhaps I can ask Rein to help me pick something out?

I've not seen or spoken to her in a few days. She's been keeping herself busy working double shifts at Zen's. The last time we spoke was three days ago. I called her after her shift and we spoke till the early hours, even though she was utterly exhausted. As per usual though, she continues to drive me troppo with her disobedience. She refused to hang up until she eventually fell asleep on the phone.

Fuck me, I really miss her.

I keep telling myself that I need to find some way to sever this enigmatic connection I have with Rein, because we're both heading down a very perilous path. I keep putting it off. I have to do the right thing and walk away, but for the life of me, I can't seem to do it. It's become a fixation.

I stare down at the blue plastic folder in my hand and rub the nape of my neck with a weighty sigh. How am I supposed to walk away from her when I can't bear to be apart from her for more than a couple of days? A surge of aggravation washes over me. I toss the file on the coffee table and lean back against the sofa, staring up at the ceiling. "Fuck."

What am I doing? What the actual fuck am I doing? I have to end this, and I have to end it right now before I get sucked in any deeper and destroy her. This isn't me. I've never been this selfish and inconsiderate *ever*.

You still have time, Talon. You'll have three weeks where you won't be forced into seeing her around school. You're going to be heading home in a few days, the timing is perfect. It's time. You have to let her go for both your sakes. This absurdity has gone on long enough.

I close my eyes for a long moment and let those thoughts sink in. With an audible growl, I lean forward and thrust my fingers through my already dishevelled hair and mentally prepare myself to go over to her place and end this... entanglement.

It's two in the afternoon. Rein doesn't usually start work till four thirty, so that gives me two hours get my shit together and head over to her apartment. Exhaling, I pull open the storage drawer at the base of my oak coffee table and drop the file inside before closing it and getting up to my feet. My stomach ties itself in a giant knot deep in my gut as dread fills me.

I fucking hate this.

Thirty minutes later, I'm standing outside her door, my heart heavy and palms sweaty. While I'm staring at the dark wooden door in front of me, I'm trying to envisage her reaction. Every cell in my body is juddering tautly and I almost turn and bolt, but I force myself to stay put and rap my knuckles on the door a couple of times.

I hold my breath while I wait for her to answer the door with my eyes closed and inwardly praying she's not home. I sound like a right drip, I'm fully aware, but ending something that feels so fucking good–so goddamn right–feels like a downright crime. The last thing I want to do is hurt her. I strain my ears and feel my heart drop when the chain unlocks from the inside and the door opens.

Rein stands at the door, or rather leans against it for support, and looks up at me, her expression pained and eyes rimmed red. "Talon?"

What the fuck? She looks dog-tired, though annoyingly still very beautiful, even with her hair in a messy bun piled on the top of her head and clad in an oversized grey sweatshirt with Oakhill University's logo printed on the front. "Snowflake, were you sleeping?"

Rein shakes her head and winces. "No, no, I wasn't. I've been up for a while actually. I've just been curled up in bed," she explains with a sigh and shifts onto her right foot, pulling the door open to allow me to pass by her.

I feel my brows fuse as my eyes rake over her tousled appearance. "Are you all right?" I question, concerned.

"Damn, do I look *that* horrific?" she drawls dryly and pushes the door shut before she leans against it, her left hand resting on her abdomen.

I take a step towards her, and she looks up at me. I brush my thumb along her jaw line and she leans into my touch, sighing softly, as if comforted. "Not at all. Even on your worst day you would still look exquisite, Snowflake," I assure her, and the corner of her lip curls ever so slightly. "Are you unwell?"

Rein shakes her head and shrugs. "No, I'm fine. It's nothing a couple of painkillers can't fix," she voices and pushes off the door. "If I can remember where I put them, that is."

Before she passes by me, I grab hold of her arm and draw her to me. "Why do you need painkillers? What's the problem?" I question curiously, and she chews on her bottom lip, her eyes narrowing while she looks up at me.

"Nothing."

"Rein..." I press grimly.

Rein sighs audibly with a roll of her eyes and rubs her forehead while she veers her gaze from mine as though she's a little embarrassed. "Fine. If you must know, cramps." Ah, I see, she's menstruating. "Sorry to inform you, but if you came knocking expecting to get lucky, I'm afraid I'm out of commission for the next five days, Professor." Her tone is derisive. "Unlike some, I don't fuck while I'm riding the rag." Whoa, someone turned up the dial on the bitch-o-meter. Though, I can't lie, I'm not loving the insinuation that I'm some sexual degenerate only around or interested in humping her every second of the day. What does she take me for? While it may not seem like it when I'm around her, fucking hell, I do possess some level of self-control.

I let the remark go right over my head. I get it, she's grouchy and likely in a lot of pain given that she's cradling her stomach like she's about to keel over at any moment.

I can't break things off with her when she's in this state. I can't risk upsetting her, and quite frankly, I'm a little scared she might wind up ripping my nuts off with the mood she's currently in. "That's rather presumptuous. Believe it or not, I dropped by to check in on you, Rein. While I may have an overcharged libido and I enjoy sex as any red-blooded man does, I am more than capable of keeping my cock dry for longer than five minutes. This might shock you, but I do happen to possess a few more qualities than those that are fulfilled with what's concealed between my legs."

Rein's eyes soften and her shoulders slump a little. My eyes fleetingly lower to her mouth when her lips part. "I'm sure you do, but you can understand that it's hard to appreciate those qualities when you won't let me in to see them, Talon."

"It's better this way, Snowflake," I tell her, taking a gentle hold of her chin. "No expectation, no disappointment for either of us."

Reins stares up at me, those gorgeous eyes bewitching me yet again, and I hold her penetrating gaze, inch for inch. "A part of me really gets off on this air of mystery you've got about you, but at the same time, I've got this whirring curiosity that is itching to know more about the man with whom I've been spending countless days and nights executing unspeakable acts."

With a smile, I sweep the back of my fingers over her soft cheek and tuck a loose strand of her hair behind her ear. "I prefer you stay curious. We happen to live in a world where people are often overexposed. The greatest thing you can do for yourself is to always maintain your mystery. I prefer to give people the option to make their own judgements about me rather than having to explicate myself to them constantly."

Rein raises a brow, her eyes narrowing at the corners while she observes me. "Even if they deem you a hard-nosed tyrant?"

I wet my lips and smirk. "I didn't get to where I am today by being loved. The way I see it, if nobody is fearful of me, I've failed. I'm inconsequential."

Rein's face consorts to one of bewilderment. "So, you like that most of your students are fearful of you?"

I shrug. "I've learnt that fearful pupils will perform how you want them to, immediately and without question. Unfortunately, being nice isn't correlated with achieving desired goals, and as I've told you before, I'm all about obtaining the best out of my students. They may complain and bitch about me now, but in the long run when they've got their degree's and are doing the jobs they love, they'll look back and thank me for not spoon feeding them. Therefore, if I need to be the arsehole to get the absolute best out of them, then so be it," I explain, letting go of her chin.

"You've done a fine job of instilling fear into your pupils, this is true, though, while they may be a little fearful of you, I think it would surprise you to know that most regard you highly. Personally, I was never afraid of you. Intimidated and infuriated sure, but scared? Not for a second."

"Intimidated?" I reiterate, genuinely surprised. Damn, I had no idea she found me intimidating. Colour me impressed; she hid that well. "I would have never guessed–you never showed it. You always came across as quite tenacious and brazen whenever you were around me."

Rein shrugs and nibbles on her bottom lip. "You baffled me mostly. I couldn't decipher my feelings toward you. By day, I was sure I hated you, but at night, when I was all alone in bed, you were all I ever fantasised about."

There's no repressing the shit eating grin that spreads widely across my face at her affirmation. I'm all too familiar with that feeling also, but fuck, the way her cheeks are reddening under my intent stare is making my dick demandingly pulsate against the zipper of my jeans. I promised myself I would behave. I need to put a stop to this once and for all, but here I am five minutes in and rocking a raging hard on, ready to spread her out and...

Fucking hell, stop it, Talon. Get a damn grip on yourself.

Damn, I have the strongest urge to pull her to me and kiss her, devouring every crevice of her mouth till my lungs burn in protest.

You're an idiot.

"I assure you, Snowflake, you were not alone on that note. I've lost count the numerous nights I spent beating my dick raw to the very thought of you. Each thought lewder than the last."

Rein watches me, eyes aflame and interlocked piercingly with my own. She licks her lips beguilingly, drawing my eyes down to the soft pillows of her lips, intensifying the already burning need I'm currently battling to not cave and kiss her.

There it is again, that irrepressible magnetic force drawing me to her. We're standing toe to toe. I'm staring down into her upturned face. She's gone and sucked me into a trance again with those captivating eyes of hers. "The imagery alone of you lying in bed naked and stroking yourself is sexy in itself, Professor, but knowing you're thinking about *me* while doing so is..."

"Sinful," I whisper, tucking my finger under her chin and tilting her head back a little so our lips are aligned. Rein's eyes close and her lips part, her breathing slowing. I lower my eyes and stare at her mouth, my lips slowly inching closer, so close I can practically taste her. "Morally wrong, but I couldn't help it. I still can't. My body craves you like you wouldn't believe. You, Snowflake, have become an unappeasable addiction; one I'll never fully recover from," I murmur as I brush her lips apart with my own. Rein's tongue teasingly skims along my bottom lip, and I come undone. I feel the last sliver of my control slip away from me.

You're a weak son of a bitch, Saxton.

When it comes to her, I am weak, she's my fatal flaw and I couldn't give a flying fuck. Especially with the way her lips feel against mine, so perfect and succulent, or the breathy moan that escapes her when my tongue glides over hers. Have you ever been so wildly attracted to someone that you can actually feel it slowly driving you insane? That's how Rein makes me feel. I can have her pressed closely and tightly against me and I'll still want her closer. I'll still beg her to pull me closer.

I curl my fingers at her nape, ready to devour her mouth when her phone ringing loudly nearby interrupts the moment. Our eyes open at the same time, lips still pressed together. We stay like that for a full second before she draws her head back slightly. "I should get that." She sighs, her tone tight. I nod and let go of my hold on her neck when she starts to pull away.

My eyes follow her until she disappears in the direction of the bedroom. "Shit," I grouse irritably while I rub the nape of my neck. For a split second, I contemplate getting the fuck out of her apartment before she comes back. No, there's no fucking way. I can't do that. What a fucking moronic thing to do. Kiss her then bolt like some spineless dipshit.

I can hear her talking to someone on the phone in her bedroom and I strain my ears to listen. "Abuela, I know, I miss you too. I wish I could be there with you guys for Christmas, but it's just not possible this year," Rein states sullenly.

I lean against the wall behind the door, not wanting to interrupt her phone call. She must be talking to her family back in London. "I'll be fine. I'll be busy working anyway, so I won't be all alone. Yes, I am eating. Sí, Abuela, lo prometo. I did, tía Dani sent me a photo of all the flowers on the grave. Okay. Give my love to tía, I'll facetime you both tomorrow, okay? Te quiero más," Rein replies, her voice heavy before she hangs up and sets her phone on the bedside table with a sigh.

The saddened look that falls upon on her beautiful face makes me ache deeply. The tears that roll down her cheeks feel like a hot knife piercing right through my heart. I know first-hand how hard it is being so far away from home and the people you love, especially during the holidays.

I watch her pull her knees to her chest and bury her face into her arms while she sobs. Before I can even react, my feet are already moving towards her, like an invisible force towing me to her. The bed dips under my weight when I sit in front of her.

Rein lifts her head and looks at me, eyes rimmed red and glistening with tears. I brush away the endless tears that keep streaming down her cheeks with my thumb. We don't need to utter a single word, I know what she needs and I don't hesitate, not for a second, before I pull her into my arms and she sinks against me. Her body shakes in my hold with every heart wrenching sob that escapes her. I bury my nose in her hair and hold her until her sobs eventually ebb away and only occasional sniffles remain.

I couldn't tell you how long we remained in that position, but I knew one thing for certain, my feelings for her have gone beyond just sexual attraction.

You're fucking falling for her.

I force away the panic that starts to fill me. Rein lifts her head off my chest, and she looks at me, her brows drawn together slightly as she chews on her bottom lip and lowers her gaze. "I'm sorry. I didn't mean to…" I lift her head back up so I can see those beautiful eyes of hers.

"Don't apologise," I interject and use the back of my fingers to dry the wetness around her eyes. "You're allowed to feel homesick, darlin'. I get it, I've been there, and it sucks, but you are not alone, all right?"

Rein nods, her eyes watering all over again. "I just miss them so much. We go and visit my mum's grave for birthdays, for Christmas, and twice I've missed it now. I just feel so bad for being so far away from them. I know they're proud of me for pursuing my dream, but I can't help but feel like I abandoned them by running away," she admits miserably.

"You didn't run away."

"I did," she declares woefully. "Every school I applied to in London I got accepted into, but I chose to come out here. I chose the furthest school because the thought of living in that house without my mum, surrounded with all her memories… it was suffocating me." I stare at her silently for a long moment. "I abandoned them at a time when they needed me, and I've been terrified of going back."

"Rein, we lose a part of ourselves when we lose someone we love. You never truly stop missing them. You just eventually learn to live with the giant gaping hole their absence has left behind, and there's no running away from that. Even if you run to the other end of the world, that ache in your chest will ease sooner or later, but that gaping hole, it will always be there in the shape of the one you lost, a shape that can never be filled by anyone else," I explain, cupping her face with my large hands and gazing into her tear-filled eyes. "Out of sight doesn't always mean out of mind, and perhaps there's another reason your *heart* led you here."

Rein doesn't say anything for a beat. She looks pensive while she holds my gaze. I find myself deeply curious, wondering what's going through her mind in this very moment. "Maybe," she finally says and shifts to get off me. I watch her closely; she exhales and places her hand on her abdomen again. "I need to, uh, get ready for work"

"Ah ah, you're not going to work, not like this." I take her hand and pull her back to me. "You're exhausted and evidently in a lot of pain. You can barely stand straight for goodness' sake. How are you planning to work?"

"Talon, I'm fine. I'm not going to skip out on work because I'm on my period. I'll take some pain killers and I'll be all right," she protests and gasps when I stand up and sweep her into my arms–bridal style–and drop her on the bed. "What are you—" I pin her arms down over her head and stare down into her face.

"Hush. Work will still be there tomorrow. You've been working yourself silly. Today, you're staying in bed and getting some rest. Understand?" I edict, and she blinks up at me, her eyes lit up and her brow raised, looking like she's ready to argue. "Keep staring at me like that and see what it gets you," I tell her firmly, and she sighs, her body relaxing as she sinks into the mattress. "Good girl." I brush a chaste kiss to her pouting lips and pull back. "I'm going to run to the store and get you some painkillers. Do you need anything else?"

"No."

With a nod, I get off the bed and go to walk out of the bedroom. "Talon?" I stop and look back at her over my shoulder. "Thank you."

I smile at her. "Stay in bed. I'm taking your keys."

"Okay, I'm at the store. What should I be looking for here?" I question, walking through the aisle.

"Well, what does she like? What's her favourite flavour of ice cream?"

I stop in the middle of the aisle with a scowl. "I don't know, Mum. How am I supposed to know that?"

"Oh, sweet heavens, boy, how can you not know what flavour of ice cream your girlfriend likes?" my mother gibes on the other end of the phone. "I thought I raised you better than that?"

"Well, first of all, she's not my girlfriend," I utter with a roll of my eyes. "We're just friends, as I have already stated countless times." I walk past a box of donuts and track back to pick one up and place it in the basket.

"And yet, here you are shopping for period supplies for a girl that's just a *friend*. I wasn't born yesterday, Tal. This girl clearly means something to you. I don't understand why you're so dead set on staying alone. I like her, and it's clear she's good for you, darlin'. And the energy between the two of you is so palpable."

"Mum." I pinch the bridge of my nose. I'm really starting to regret calling for her help. "Mum, please, are you going to help me or not?"

I hear my mother exhale on the other end and mutter incoherently under her breath. "Yes, fine, just pick up anything chocolate. You may not have paid attention, but lucky for you, I'm quite observant. She seems to have a sweet tooth, and us women have an unwavering love for chocolate." I open the fridge and pick up a tub of triple chocolate and brownie ice cream.

"Okay, chocolate ice cream and donuts. What else? What about the pain? She seems to be in quite a bit of pain."

"A warm bath, Advil, and a hot water bottle will do the trick for the cramps. Oh, and also, see if you can find some lavender oil and massage it into her lower back and lower abdomen, it will help with the cramps and relax her."

"Lavender oil? Where am I supposed to get that from? I don't think they sell it here," I question, wandering around aimlessly through the store.

"Talon, don't be a flaming' galah. They sell it at any supermarket. Just check in the candle and aromatherapy section. All right, I've got to go, my next client just pulled up. Give my love to Rein. Love ya, cheerio." I look at the phone when the line goes dead.

"Yeah, love you too." I sigh and slide the phone back in my pocket. "Hot water bottle and lavender oil…"

It took me over an hour to pick up all the supplies and find a store that sold lavender oil. When I walk into the apartment, I see Rein pacing up and down the living room. With a frown, I put the bags down and walk over to her. "Rein, I told you to stay in bed. What are you doing?"

"I can't stay in bed. Moving around helps me not to think about the spine splitting pain I'm currently in," she grouses irritably. "Please tell me you have some pain killers because I'm about to split in two," she questions beseechingly while she continues to pace back and forth. I can detect the pain in her voice when she speaks.

"Surely it's not normal for you to be in so much pain? Maybe we should take you to the hospital or something?" I suggest, walking over to her with a glass of water and two painkillers in hand. "Here."

Rein takes the pills and washes them down with the water and groans. "There's nothing they can do. I just happen to be in the small percentage of women that suffer with severe period cramps. The first day is the worst, then it eases off. But right now, it feels like someone is stabbing me in the gut repeatedly with the sharpest, hottest knife in the world while another is bashing my back in with a steel mallet."

I wince and inwardly shudder. I've never been so pleased to be a man, because that sounds fucking excruciating. I figure it would hurt; I mean, you're shredding the lining to your womb, but to that extreme? Taylor never complained about her periods, she wouldn't even take a pain killer.

"Come on, Snowflake, you can't keep pacing back and forth all day. You should be resting. Let's see if we can ease off some of that pain until your pain killers kick in." I take her hand in mine and lead her to the bedroom.

"What's with all the bags?"

"Supplies."

Rein frowns. "Supplies?" she intones, sitting at the edge of the bed and wrapping her arms around her stomach while hunching over. "What kind of supplies?"

"Ones that will hopefully make you feel better. Lay back. I'm going to run you a hot bath." I drop a kiss on her forehead before I scoot her back on the bed. Rein watches me, moving around the room while she curls up on top of the bed in the foetal position.

"Talon, I'm sure you have better things to do. You really don't have to stay and babysit me. I can take care of myself," I hear her say from the bedroom. I smile and shake my head as I reach over the bathtub in the ensuite to run the water.

"I know you can take care of yourself, and I am in no way babysitting you. Maybe I just happen to like taking care of you, Snowflake," I reply, watching her from across the room while leaning against the doorframe of the bathroom and crossing my arms over my chest.

"I'm not used to being taken care of. If you're not careful, I might start to become too reliant on you, Professor." She sighs, hugging the pillow. "Though I must admit it is refreshing. Usually, when men hear the word period, they take off running like we're wicked witches from the east that are planning to make them drink the blood in their sleep or some shit," she explains with an exasperated roll of her eyes. "Hunter wouldn't come near me while I was on my period, let alone take care of me."

Not surprising. What does a dipshit like Hunter know of taking care of a woman? Even the mere mention of the little tosser's name makes me want to throttle him. "Probably for the best considering he didn't know his arse from his elbow."

"You do make a valid point." I walk over to her and hold out my hand to help her up and out of bed. I guide her toward the bathroom, the smell of lavender lingering in the air. "What's that smell?"

"Lavender. According to the grapevine it helps soothe menstrual cramps—so says my mother and the clerk at the store. I put a couple of drops in your bath to help relax you. They also said to rub some on your lower back and lower abdomen too after the bath… why are you looking at me like you're about to burst into tears?" I ask when I see her eyes go all wide and doe like.

"You… you called your mum?"

Oh damn. Went and walked right into that one. I rub the back of my neck awkwardly and wince. God, this girl turns me into a right stupe. "Perhaps."

"Talon, that's…" she starts to say, her lower lip trembling ever so slightly. Oh crap, well done you numbnut. I really hope she doesn't start weeping again. "I really don't know what to say. Why are you so good to me?"

Christ, Rein, if you knew the truth you would despise me. I hold her gaze and brush the backs of my fingers against her soft cheek affectionately. "Because you deserve it."

Rein leans into my touch, her eyes closing for a second before they flutter open again. "I always knew there was more to you. I'm pleased I was right. You're a good man, Talon," she affirms earnestly, her fingers curling around my wrist. We share a moment where we just gaze at one another longingly, and if it weren't for my guilty conscience eating away at me, I would lean in and finish that kiss we almost shared earlier.

I'm not a good man. I was, *once*, but somewhere along the way, I lost my integrity. I've become a version of myself that I truly can't stand to look at in the mirror. I'm a pitiful shadow of the man I was not so long ago. Sure, I had my flaws but at least I had some sense of decency. It's no secret that I've been struggling to find myself since Taylor died, but that all changed when Rein came crashing into my life, *literally*. I refuse to believe that our meeting is simply a coincidence—it can't be, it feels too cosmic. A big part of me is desperate to believe that she's my second chance at finding some form of happiness, because in a perfect world, I can absolutely see myself being happy with her. Then again, second chances don't always mean happy endings–sometimes it's an opportunity to make right what you fucked up the last time.

"Go enjoy your bath, Snowflake," I tell her, gesturing towards the bathroom with my brows. I see the disappointment grow in her eyes that little bit more each time she tries to get me to open up to her but winds up walking straight into that impenetrable wall I have around me. Well, it's evidently not so impenetrable any longer, because she's somehow gone and managed to worm her way in despite my greatest efforts to keep her out.

It seems the bath worked because Rein came out thirty minutes later looking more comfortable and less irritable. She's currently laid out on her front, topless, her head resting on her arms with her eyes closed while I lay on my side beside her, my head propped up on one hand while the other soothingly massages the lavender oil into her lower back. The sexy, breathy moans emitting from her as I gently work my fingers into her lower back is honestly testing my sanity. "Mm, that feels so good."

"Turn over and I'll do your stomach." Rein opens her eyes and looks up at me, her lips curling into a lovely smile that causes a warmth to spread across my chest. She obeys and rolls onto her back. I gaze down into her pretty face. Our eyes interlock, and for a moment, we stay that way. Her pupils dilate and her eyes go dark with lust. When she parts those luscious lips and slowly licks them, my dick responds perilously, the throbbing matching every slow but brutal rhythm of my heart.

My throat goes dry, and I swallow thickly. Fuck, I want to devour that mouth of hers. My eyes travel down her torso–her perfect tits bare, nipples hard and pleading to be sucked on. I focus on pouring a generous amount oil on her stomach. As I go to pull the bottle back and set it aside, Rein stops me. Her slender fingers wrap around my wrist, and she tilts the bottle and pours oil over her breasts.

Lord have fucking mercy.

My eyes find hers again. "Do you know what else is effective for menstrual cramps, Professor?"

I swallow hard and clear my throat. "What?"

"An orgasm," she whispers, taking the bottle from my hand, closing the cap, and dropping it on the bed, all the while her eyes never leaving mine. "Touch me, play with my body and make me feel good the way only *you* can, Professor."

My head whirls with razing desire. "Where do you need me to touch you, baby?" Rein bites her lip and reaches up. Her fingers brush along my cheek, her lips slowly inching closer to mine. "Here?" I question, brushing my index finger over a hardened nipple. Rein moans, her back instantly curving up into my touch, readily commanding more.

"Yes." She whimpers, and her beautiful body quivers enchantingly when I pinch and roll her nipple between my thumb and forefinger and give it a gentle tug. I massage the oil into her breasts, giving them an appreciative squeeze and then rub the oil over her torso and slowly move down her stomach.

"What about here?" I whisper, lazily grazing my fingertips up her inner thigh.

She quivers. "God, yes." I can't contain my smile when she rocks her hips up. She's just burning for me to play with her slick pussy. I've heard women feel randier when they're on their periods, because of the increased level of hormones in their body, which in some triggers a rise in libido.

I'm fucking fascinated with the magnificence of a woman's body and all it can do and endure. Take a woman's pussy for example, so many pleasure zones to explore–its mind blowing. An exquisite work of art, a fucking masterpiece that is worthy of the reverence. Especially Rein's. I can play with her pussy for hours, tirelessly just to soak up every moan and whimper or the way her body trembles and quakes differently with each body part you touch.

"Look how wet you are." I groan, spreading her pussy lips apart and marvel at her slick juices lusciously glistening. The beast within me salivates at the sight and scent of her arousal. How I would love to feast on that cunt and lap up all that honey.

I pull the hood back, exposing her engorged nub. "Fuck me, your clit is so swollen," I state gruffly while I rub the pad of my thumb over her clit softly. "Oh, baby, you're so worked up for me that I don't even have to try. I can just tease you to orgasm." Rein gasps, her hips lifting off the bed upon contact, and she rocks herself against my thumb. "Mm, that's my greedy girl." I pull my thumb back and give her pussy a slap. I smirk when she whimpers audibly. Her beautiful thick thighs close around my hand, and she bucks her hips up, grinding herself against my fingers. "You love having your pussy slapped, don't you, Snowflake?"

"Yes." Rein pants, her chest rising and falling quicky, her pretty face flushed.

"Yes what?"

"Yes, Professor."

I slap her pussy again and grind the heel of my hand against her clit. "Good girl."

"Oh fuck!" she cries out, gyrating her hips to match my rhythm.

"Goddamn, you're beautiful."

"Kiss me, Professor, please." She pants, her head tilting up, her lips zealously seeking out my own as I continue to tease her clit with my thumb in slow, lazy circles.

I eagerly comply, and without missing a beat, I kiss her hard and hungry. Our tongues clash in a frenzy and glide over one another. I suck on her tongue and swallow her moans of pleasure. "Are you going to come for me, baby? Oh, yes you are, you're so close. You're trembling." I growl, biting and sucking on her bottom lip while I stroke her closer and closer to her orgasm. "Come on, beautiful girl, give it to me. Let me watch you come undone."

And fuck, she doesn't disappoint. Rein grips the bedsheet above her head with a death grip as she soars towards the brink of her release. Her body shakes underneath mine, her mouth hangs open, her chest rising and falling with every desperate breath. "Ay, dios mio, arruinarme papi, hazme tuya!" she whimpers in Spanish. Whoa. Holy shit, I didn't understand a word of what she said other than the 'papi,' which I know means daddy, but fuck it sounds so sexy. I'm ready and willing to fuck her brains out, period or not. Rein arches up when I pinch her clit, and she comes with a shudder. "Oh yes, yes, Talon!"

I watch avidly as she rides out her orgasm. She shakes with each wave, her pussy pulsing against my fingers until it ebbs away and she collapses onto the bed in a hot, sweaty, breathless mess. I gaze down into her flushed face as I continue to stroke her softly, her pussy drenching my fingers while she basks in her post orgasmic bliss.

"Feel better?"

"Mm," Rein moans, pulling me down by the collar of my T-shirt and kissing me passionately. "You're the best kind of pain relief I've ever had."

I smile against her lips and draw back a little to look down into her glowing face. "Pleased to be of service." I grip her waist and lift her on top of me. "Now, I'm going to need you to translate what that little Spanish outburst was while you were coming."

Rein's cheeks turn a brighter shade of red, and I grin. "Spanish? I don't know what you're talking about," she utters dismissively and tries to slip off me, but I tighten my grip on her waist and stare up into her eyes.

"Snowflake, we both know I'll get it out of you one way or the other, so come on, tell me," I assert.

Rein heaves a sigh and chews on her bottom lip contemplatively. "Fine, I said, oh God yes, ruin me, daddy, make me yours."

My brows rise with intrigue. Well, this is certainly new. No one has ever referred to me as their 'daddy' before. I curl my fingers at her nape and draw her face closer to mine. I wet my lips before I speak. "Daddy, huh?"

Rein's eyes widen and she nods, pulling her bottom lip between her teeth. "Yeah, is that okay?"

"Let's find out," I burr gruffly. Drawing her pouty mouth to mine, I kiss her slow and deep.

I ended up spending the remainder of the day with her in her bed. We pigged out on Chinese food, ate an entire tub of ice cream, and wolfed down a box of donuts all while we talked about our childhoods. Rein then decided it would be a great idea to binge watch all the Avenger movies—least that was the plan until she fell asleep, peacefully cocooned in my arms not even halfway through the first movie. Not that I minded, it felt really nice. I can't recall the last time I felt so relaxed and at ease around anyone, let alone a woman.

I don't make it much further into the movie until my eyes start to grow heavy and I drift off into one of the best nights of sleep I've had in a very long time.

Chapter 6
Rein

I SEE RED (SLOWED) - EVERYBODY LOVES AN OUTLAW

"Rei Rei? Heeeello?" Paris waves her hand in my face. "Earth to Rein. Bitch, are your antennas on the frisk again?" she complains, giving my ear a flick. I start out of my thoughts and sit upright in my seat before I slap her hand away with a pout.

"Ouch, what the hell, P?" I grumble, rubbing my ear. Paris grins satisfied she's gotten my attention and sinks back into her chair. "What's with the abuse?"

"Well, that woke you up didn't it, sugar tits?" She shrugs impassively, picking up her iced Frappuccino and taking a long sip through her straw. "I've been talking to myself for the past ten minutes. What on earth were you daydreaming about? You were drooling; look, you even made a puddle on the table," she states after she swallows her cold brew.

I bring my fingers to my lips and glance down at the table. It's clean, no sign of drool anywhere. Paris giggles when I scowl at her. "Very funny," I say deadpan with an exasperated roll of my eyes.

"What's up with you, Chica?"

I take a long sip of my vanilla latte and glance around the

coffee shop we are currently sitting in. It's bustling with people, some in groups laughing and conversing, some sitting alone with their laptops. "Nothing, I'm fine. I was just thinking about... work."

Paris narrows her eyes at me, clearly not buying a word of what I'm saying. "Since when does work put you in such a trance and make you slobber?"

"Jesus, I wasn't slobbering," I protest, throwing a sugar sachet at her. "Oh, that reminds me." I unzip my purse and take out the brown envelope and hand it to her.

Paris takes it with a frown. "What's this?"

"The first instalment of the money I owe you. I'll pay you with whatever extra cash I have left over at the end of every month, if that's okay?"

Paris sighs and her face drops, a saddened look radiating in her pretty honey-coloured eyes. She sets the envelope on the table. "Rein, you really don't have to pay me back. Just keep the money for a rainy day," she says, sliding the envelope across the table towards me. I shake my head and push it back to her.

"Thank you, but I can't," I decline politely. "I only took the money with the agreement that I pay you back. I'm so grateful for you, P. I honestly don't know where I would be without you."

Paris takes a hold of my hands and smiles warmly at me. "I'm grateful for you too. You're not just my best friend, Rei Rei, you're the sister I've always wanted. You're my family."

A surge of guilt floods me. She would be devastated if she knew I'd been lying to her. I force a smile on my face and give her hands a squeeze.

"Ditto."

I look at the time and sigh. "Well, this has been fun, as always, but I have to go. I've got an appointment."

"Appointment?" Paris questions curiously.

"Yes, at Belle's." Belle's is our go to beauty salon to get our mani-pedi's and waxing done.

Paris frowns. "Belle's?"

"Yes," I say slowly, pinning her with a dubious look. "Are you just going to keep repeating everything I say?"

"Bitch, what are you going to Belle's for? And more importantly, why is it without me?"

"You know... upkeep," I mumble, standing up from my seat and averting my gaze from her probing one in hopes that maybe she won't keep poking for more information.

Paris tosses her silky hair over her shoulder. "Oh no, hoe, you can sit your ass back down. I have some follow up questions."

I roll my eyes. Kill me now. "Could you maybe email them to me?" I offer with a sheepish smile, and she stares at me blankly. "Fine, make it quick." I sit back down on the chair.

"Who is he?" My heart drops. Damn, I forget this girl knows me a little too well. I shift in my chair and clear my throat before I open my mouth to answer. "And before you even consider trying to lie to me, may I remind you that you stink at it and I've known that you're secretly screwing someone for weeks now, so spill it." I gape at her, stunned, and she nods, sipping her drink.

"How did you..."

Paris sets her drink down and smirks at me wickedly while she plays with her straw. "I didn't, you just confirmed it. Reverse psychology, bish." She leans back in her chair, crosses her arms over her chest, and stares at me expectantly. "I'm listening."

Goddamn it, she's sneaky.

I exhale and chew on the inside of my cheek contemplatively. What the fuck am I supposed to tell her? "Uhm, well, I am seeing someone... sort of," I admit and lean forward a little, and so does she, her eyes glowing with interest. "P, I've been itching to tell you, but it's just something that happened and we decided to keep it between us because it's just casual. I don't want anyone finding out, so please keep it to yourself, and I am begging you, don't start planning your double dates and demanding to meet him, because that's not going to happen, okay? It's just sex," I assert coolly, and she narrows her eyes at me.

"If it's so casual, why all the secrecy?" she questions, and her eyes suddenly widen to the size of saucers and she gasps. "Is he married?" she shrieks.

"Shhh!" I look around the coffee shop and my cheeks burn hot when near enough every person in there turns to look at us, each one with a different facial expression.

Oh great, now people think I'm a homewrecker.

Shit.

I laugh nervously and give Paris' hand a firm squeeze. "It's not what you think, people. She's preparing for an audition, nothing to see here." I gesture with my hand. "You can turn around now." Paris' nose crinkles and she gives me an apologetic look. "Jesus Christ, P, dial it down, will you? He's not married, okay? Don't be ridiculous, and do you honestly think I'm the type of girl that will ever go for another woman's husband?" I shake my head and get up, picking up my bag to leave.

"Rein, wait." Paris follows me out of the coffee shop. I should have just kept my mouth shut. "I'm sorry, of course *you're* not. Look, guys can be shady as fuck, and when they're adamant on keeping you a secret, that's a red flag, babe."

With a sigh, I spin and look at her. "Maybe with some men, sure, but he's not like that. The man went out and got me supplies while I was on my period to make me feel better and didn't leave my side until he was sure I was okay."

Paris' jaw drops and her eyes go meltingly soft. "Shut up, he sounds like a fucking dreamboat."

I sigh with a nod. "Not everyone likes to put their lives on display for all to see, some people like to keep things private, and you know what, it's actually really nice being with someone who is mature and respectful."

Paris observes me closely for a beat and a slow smile stretches across her pretty face. "Oh my, you really like him," she states, practically giddy, which causes my stomach to churn anxiously.

Like him? I'm fucking arse over heel in lust with the man.

"P, I'm going to miss my appointment," I reply, ignoring her comment. I turn and walk off down the bustling high street and she follows me. It's bloody freezing out. I wrap my jacket tighter around my body and almost slip on the icy surface of the ground in my haste to get away from Paris and her inquisition. Paris shrieks and we grab onto each other before we both slip and fall flat on our arses.

"Jesus. Slow down, betch, I'm not looking to break my neck," she complains, hooking her arm into mine tightly. "So... back to your mystery man." Paris sighs as we weave through the throng of people going about their day.

I groan inwardly. Why did I open my mouth? "What about him?"

"Does he have a name?"

"Yes."

Paris gives me a sidelong stare, waiting for me to feed her curiosity. "Well?"

"Albert."

"What?" she sputters and stops walking, her face horrified while she stares at me... *unblinking*. The look on her face is priceless. I force away the urge to laugh. "Holy shit balls, when you say mature... did you mean eighty?"

"No! Geez, he's not *that* old," I state with a shrug. "Wait, is fifty-six old?"

Paris blanches. "Rei Rei, are you shitting me? You better be shitting me." I can't hold in my laughter any longer and I throw my head back and crack up laughing. Paris rolls her eyes and slaps my arm. "You rotten bitch. You had me concerned for your mental health there for a hot minute. I mean, don't get me wrong, some fifty-year-olds are hot, like I'm all for a hot sugar daddy, but with a name like Albert? No thank you."

"What's wrong with Albert? It's a good strong name. One of my friends from primary school was called Albert, we used to call him Albie. He was adorable."

Paris snorts. "Naming your child Albert should be considered child abuse in my opinion. How do you look at a baby and call it Albert? It's just wrong."

I chuckle, amused by her little rant. "Good thing no one asked for your opinion then, isn't it, bitch tits?"

Paris grins. "Nice try, stop trying to distract me with your nonsensical jargon. As your BFF, I demand you start dishing out some deets. How's the rompy pompy?" she questions, wagging her perfectly shaped brows at me suggestively.

I laugh at her choice of words. "Well, you remember when I told you that I've never been able to get off with any man?"

Paris nods. "I do recall." When a shit eating grin spreads across my face, Paris stops walking again and gapes at me wide-eyed. "Wait, are you telling me this mystery man of yours finally got you to *orgasm*?" When I nod, she lets out an ear shattering squeal and claps her hands.

"Not only did he make me orgasm, P, he made me squirt."

"Shut the front door." She gasps. "Oh, I am so freaking jealous right now. Betch, I'm going to need to hear every little detail, but first, let's go get your hoochie waxed." I laugh when she pulls me through the door to Belle's beauty salon.

AFTER MY WAX, PARIS AND I SPENT THE AFTERNOON SHOPPING FOR lingerie. I've never really had the confidence to ever wear lingerie for any of my boyfriends in the past, but Talon, God, he makes me feel so sexy and desired that I'm finding myself wanting to dress up for him in the sultriest outfits. I want to drive him just as crazy for me as I am for him. Like Paris said, the power of good dick can compel you into doing just about anything.

And boy was she right.

I want to experience everything with him. I want to step out of my comfort zone and try new things. Talon has opened my eyes to this whole other world and a side of me I didn't even realise had been buried under all my insecurities. I'm so tired of being the good girl, I so desperately want to explore this sultry and sensual side that I've discovered. I think he's turned me into a nymphomaniac. I honestly can't remember a time I have ever felt so sexually charged —though, I suppose four years of monotonous sex can do that to a person, especially when you come to appreciate that there is so much to explore to the act itself.

"Why do you look so nervous, boo?"

I exhale and hold the bags up that I'm holding. "Because I am nervous, P. What if I suck at the whole 'being sexy' thing? I don't want to end up making a twat of myself."

Fucking hell, it's been the longest four days waiting for my period to finish, I'm about ready to jump his bones.

Paris stops walking and turns me to face her. Her bubbly mood from moments ago flattens. "Rein, are you kidding me? You're freaking gorgeous, babe, without even trying. You've got this natural beauty about you that I know most girls would kill for. Don't over think it," she says with a warm smile, and using her fingers, she brushes my hair out of my face. "We've all got a seductress hidden away deep inside of us just waiting to come out on the prowl. I promise you, there is nothing sexier to a man than a woman who oozes confidence and isn't shy about her sensuality. The moment he sees you in that outfit he's going to want to screw you through a wall."

I visualise Talon's reaction when he sees me in this skimpy outfit and the thought alone makes me shudder visibly with desire. The feral look he gets in those fierce blue eyes... "Ooh, there you go, that's my baby girl." Paris giggles when she witnesses my cheeks flush and my body judder. "When are you seeing him next?"

"Tomorrow. He's asked me to help him shop for a gift for his mum. And then he's flying out the day after to spend Christmas with his family in Ohio. He'll be gone for two weeks," I tell her, all the while trying to mask the disappointment from my voice.

"Well then, you should surprise him tonight. You know, give him a little somethin' somethin' to think about while he's away. Like an early Christmas present."

I've got him a Christmas present already–after all he's done for me, it's the least I can do. And maybe the dress up could be a treat. I searched for what seemed like forever until I found the right gift. The moment I saw them displayed in the shop window, I just knew it was the perfect gift for him.

I wrinkle my nose. "You think?"

"Hell yeah!" Paris chirps excitedly and hooks her arm through mine. "I'm totally helping you get ready. I'm thinking wild and messy curly hair…" She starts to witter on joyously and proceeds to pull me along with her like an errant toddler.

Fuck, the nerves start to bunch up deep in my belly. What if I royally screw this up and make a fool of myself? No, no, come on, Rein. Don't let your fear talk you out of this.

You got this.

PARIS LEFT MY PLACE FORTY MINUTES AGO AFTER SHE HELPED DOLL ME up to go and get railed by my professor. I'm hoping she never finds out because I can guarantee she will murder me and find a way to bring me back just to kill me all over again for keeping it from her. It's not that I don't trust her–I do, with my deepest darkest secrets– but this isn't just about me. I have to protect Talon. I can always find another school and finish my masters, but if this ever comes out, it will go on his permanent record, and he'll never be able to teach at a college or university again.

Guilt fills me at the very thought, and I almost turn around and head back into the elevator to go back to my place. I stare at my reflection in the elevator mirror and exhale slowly.

No one's going to find out, Rein. You're being careful, and besides, you're into deep now, there's no walking away.

The brazen voice in my head whispers reassuringly. I push the button to his floor before I lose my nerve and the doors close behind me. My knees tremble uncontrollably, and I keep telling myself it's the cold and not my nerves. I did walk over the courtyard clad in the skimpiest lace lingerie, covered only by my beige trench coat in the freezing cold, in four-inch red stiletto heels.

Thankfully, Talon's apartment is like a two-minute walk from mine, so it isn't far and its mostly surrounded by grass so less chance of slipping and breaking my neck. However, my bare buttcheeks–along with my moist lady parts–are bloody freezing from the icy chill of the wind as it whips around me. How attractive showing up to his door like a block of ice dressed in red lacy lingerie.

Nevertheless, I'm certain my body will heat up the second I lay my eyes on him, it always does. The elevator slows as it arrives at his floor and my heart starts to beat up in my throat. "Here goes everything." I step out of the elevator and walk down the dimly lit corridor towards his door, and with every step, my heart pounds harder.

A shaky breath pushes past my lips, and I drag my tongue across my bottom lip, straightening myself out before I raise my hand and knock on the door.

Got no choice but to see this through now.

I hold my breath in anticipation, every sense heightened. The door unlocks and slowly opens, revealing a topless Talon with his strongly built torso, burly arms with thick coil of veins on display, wearing only a pair grey sweatpants and *glasses*.

Holy son of Ares.

That block of ice I was moments ago thaws as my body goes from sub-zero to inferno in a matter of milliseconds. Talon in a suit is hot. Talon dressed in casual jeans and tees is also hot, but Talon topless in grey sweatpants hanging loosely on his narrow hips, showing that delectable Adonis belt that gives me a lady boner accompanied by a pair of rectangle slim rimmed reading glasses and tousled hair is just… *dangerous*.

I can't not stare at him, and I make no attempt to hide it either while I blatantly gape at him. Talon's eyes slowly travel down the length of me and back up again until his cerulean eyes meet mine.

"Hello, Snowflake," he drawls gruffly, licking his lips while he lifts one arm to hold the door while his body leans against it.

Goddamn, this man. How can one human be so fucking beautiful? It's maddening. Paris was absolutely right about one thing though, when the object of your desire is standing before you, your feminal impulses kick in.

"Hi, Professor," I reply, softening my tone. I peer up at him through my lashes. "I hope I'm not disrupting your evening by just showing up unannounced."

Talon's eyes rake over me again and the corner of his lip curls into a sexy smirk. "Oh please, disrupt away."

I smile and bite down on my lower lip, my fingers untying the belt keeping my jacket closed. "Are you sure? I would hate to derail any plans you may have had." Talon watches raptly as my jacket falls open, revealing the red, cut-out harness detail lace teddy bodysuit I'm wearing underneath. His jaw drops open and once again his eyes sweep over me, his Adam's apple rising and falling when he swallows hard.

"Sweet Jesus." He groans and quickly straightens from his leaning position. My eyes catch sight of the very large and flagrant bulge at the front of his sweats, and it has me avidly licking my lips. "The only plan I'm interested in right now is the one that will end with me spending the night between those gorgeous legs of yours."

My heart swells and my pussy clenches at his response. "I'm liking the sound of that plan," I purr, sliding the jacket off my shoulders until it falls and pools around my ankles.

"Fuck me," he growls, taking a step towards me.

I smirk up at him and marvel at the unbridled lust flaming in the depths of his eyes. "Oh, I plan to."

Talon stares down into my face, his hand grips my jaw, and he leans in close, so his face is close to mine as he speaks in a low guttural tone. "I hope you've got that pussy ready for me, baby, because I'm going to split you in two."

"I'm so ready, Professor."

Talon shakes his head, his bottom lip between his teeth while his eyes scan my face and flitter up to settle on my eyes. "No, Snowflake. There's no professor, not tonight. There's only Talon. I want to hear you screaming my name while I pump that tight little cunt of yours full of my hot, thick cum," he drawls, closing the front door and backing me up against it, his well-built body covering my own. "But first..." He gathers my arms and pins them above my head. "I'm going to take a long look at you, so that I can burn the very image of you in this outfit to my mind to use while I'm away, because, baby, you look fucking sensational," he whisper-growls, his lips grazing mine with every word. "Goddamn, baby, these curves make daddy so fucking weak." I moan when he trails the backs of his fingers down the exposed skin of the dip of my small waist. I melt instantly against his featherlight touch, his words heating every drop of blood rushing through my veins.

Fuck, I came over with the intention of taking control, but this is the affect this devilishly gorgeous man has on me. I shake myself out of the trance and stare up into his eyes. "Well, daddy can appreciate my curves while I crawl on top of him and ride him until I milk every last drop of cum from his big thick dick." Talon's eyes darken and he makes a low hissing sound, his jaw clenching tight while he stares at me impiously, like a man starved. I free my hands from his hold and they explore and caress every ripple of delicious muscle on their way to his manhood protruding from his sweatpants. "And those glasses are staying *on*."

Talon smirks, pressing his forehead to mine. "And so are those heels."

I raise a brow. "Deal."

Talon's mouth comes crashing down on mine, hard and needy. Lips still fused, he lifts me into his arms and carries me over to the round spinning love seat placed beside the floor-to-ceiling window. "You do realise people can probably see us through the window, right?" I murmur against his lips.

"Good, let 'em watch and wish they were us." His eyes search mine; his gaze is daring, and my stomach stirs with the thrill of someone watching us fuck.

What has this man done to me?

Chapter 7
Talon

DEEP DIVE - ZARYAH

"Oh fuck, that's my good girl." I pant, watching Rein rocking her perfect hips back and forth while I grind my hips up into her, matching her tempo. "I fucking love watching my cock disappear into that delectably tight cunt of yours," I growl in her ear and nip at it before I suck it teasingly into my mouth. "You can't get enough of daddy's big dick, can you, baby?"

Rein tilts her head back and she whimpers, biting down on her luscious bottom lip. "No, God, I can't get enough of you, you feel so fucking good."

I can't see her face because she's facing away from me, but I can feel the heat of her flushed cheeks pressed against mine. "Who does this pussy belong to?" I hiss in her ear while I stroke her clit.

"Oh my God," she cries out, curling her fingers at the nape of my neck, her fingernails digging into my skin. "You, it belongs to you, only you."

I run my tongue up her neck. "Mine," I assert lowly in her ear. "Now, be a good girl and open up those beautiful legs wider for daddy, so I can tease your clit." Rein obeys and spreads her legs wider. My hand moves from where it's gripping her waist to caress her swollen pearl. "With each savage thrust and every rip-roaring orgasm, I'm going to erase the memory of every other worthless fucker that's ever had the pleasure of taking this pussy before me," I affirm gruffly while teasingly tracing the shell of her ear with my tongue.

Rein shudders in my arms and her nails dig into my nape a little deeper. "Oh yes, daddy, fuck me." She moans ravenously, rocking her hips impatiently. "Show me, baby, show me, I want to feel how desperate you are to claim my pussy."

Desperate doesn't even begin to cover it. The irrepressible and all-consuming desire that rapidly swarms my body with every breathy declaration that slips past those honied lips of hers is unlike anything I've ever experienced in my life. I've been fighting every urge to not allow myself to lose complete control, but when she talks to me in that manner, I can feel the feral beast inside stirring, just itching to surface and give her exactly what she's begging for.

Jesus, my self-control is waning.

I feed my cock into her slick pussy until I'm fully rooted to the hilt. Rein's gasp whirls around us for a millisecond. I close my eyes when–like a vise–her walls clamp and flutter around my cock as she stretches to accommodate me. "Oh fuck." I let out an involuntary groan, pressing my forehead to her temple when my head spins.

"Ohh, yes, right there." Rein whimpers, grinding her hips down when I push up into her. I grab hold of her thighs firmly, spreading her wider and start thrusting into her, fucking her from below, meeting her every plunge with a brutal drive of my own. Rein doesn't hold back her strident whimpers of pleasure as I drive my cock deeper into her slick cunt. "Oh shit, you're so hard. I can feel your cock throbbing."

"Mm, do you feel what you do to me? I have no control of my cock when you're in the vicinity, Snowflake. You've got me sporting a constant rock-hard stiffy in mere seconds." I almost growl in her ear, flicking her clit teasingly. "Daddy's going to fuck this pussy so good. By the time I'm done with you, you're going to have trouble remembering your own name," I assert and sink my teeth into her neck, sucking the sweet flesh hard.

We fuck each other desperately. Our moans and pants hang in the air around us, as does the melodic sound of wet flesh hitting flesh. Every violent plunge of her drenched pussy and drive of my granite dick sends us soaring towards that all-consuming rapture, that sweeter than sin release we're so urgently chasing down. "Ahh yes, yes, yes, don't stop!" she pleads, clawing at my forearms. "Right there, baby, right there, harder, fuck me harder!"

I have no intention of stopping and I show her that as I pick up my pace and shove every fucking inch of my cock deep inside her and curse audibly when her already snug cunt tautens and greedily swallows me up, gripping me so tight I forget how to fucking breathe. I can feel her wetness dripping down my balls and fuck if that doesn't spur me on to fuck her even harder. One hand grips her hip and the other comes up to fist her hair and tilt her head back while I speak lowly into her ear. "Play with that clit for me, baby, let me watch while you make yourself come. I want you to fucking shower me in your succulent girl cum."

"Yes, daddy." She whimpers, reaching her hand between her legs and playing with herself.

"That's a good girl." I growl. "Scream for me, my little cum slut."

We're both so worked up it doesn't take her long to explode around my cock, her orgasm triggers my own and she takes me over with her, milking my cock for every drop as I unleash spurt after spurt of hot cum deep inside her while she screams my name at a deafening volume while she unravels stunningly. I watch in fascination as she sprays her liquid arousal all over me, soaking my cock and thighs.

Goddamn.

With a whimper, Rein collapses against me, her gorgeous body flushed and glistening with a sheen of sweat. We're both breathless, panting to catch our breath.

"You okay, Snowflake?"

"Fucking *hell*." She pants, biting down on her bottom lip. "I think you may have fucked me into a paralytic state. I can't feel my legs. Just when I think it can't possibly get any better, you go and prove me wrong."

I smile, caressing her full tits. "I can't seem to control this flaming need I have for you. You've awakened the starved beast in me, Rein Valdez," I tell her openly while I circle my thumb over her budding nipples. "I've kept that part of me dormant for so long, but every second I spend with you, I can feel him slowly inching up to the surface, just burning to come out and fucking ruin you for all other men."

Rein smiles warmly and tilts her head back to look up at me. I lower my gaze to hers and lick my lips. "You already have," she affirms, her marvellous eyes aglow.

I stare into her eyes, and the nerves in my stomach bunch up. My eyes close, I bite my lip and tilt my head back with a throaty groan. "Fuck, what are you doing to me?"

Rein shifts and traces her lips down the length of my neck. A slow sigh pushes past my lips. The warmth of her breath against my damp flesh sends a bout of tingles cascading up and down my spine. My cock, still immersed inside her swells once again. Despite the ardent urge to thrust up into her, I slide out and she whimpers in displeasure.

I know, baby, I feel the same, but don't worry, I'm not done with you yet.

I need more of her, but in a position where I can watch the expression on her face as she falls apart on my cock. I want to stare into her eyes while I empty my seed deep inside her. "Up."

Rein peers up at me but doesn't miss a beat and obeys. I observe her while she rises up to her feet, and damn, I'm loving the look of her right now. Her usual silky hair is tousled, but in a very sexy way where I had my fingers tangled up in it while I railed her. The bruises on her neck where I've been sucking raveningly on her flesh are darkening down the length of her throat. A fine-looking reminder of our impassioned fuck session.

I fucking love seeing my marks all over her supple olive skin. As

I stand, I scoop her up into my arms–bridal style–and carry her to my bedroom. Rein's lips capture mine and we kiss hungrily, our tongues duelling all the way to the bedroom. I lay her out on my bed and pull back, breaking the kiss. We're panting, her chest rising and falling almost in perfect rhythm with mine. I sit back on my heels, spread her legs open and lower my gaze to her swollen pussy glistening mouth-wateringly.

A low growl escapes from deep within my chest when I see my cum leaking out of her pussy. "Fuck," I rasp. "Watching my cum spilling out of your tight cunt is the sexiest fucking thing, Snowflake," I admit gruffly. Using my index finger, I scoop up the thick rope of my seed. Rein watches me raptly, her eyes firing up all over again. She leans up on one elbow, curls her fingers around my wrist and brings my finger to her mouth, all the while her eyes never leaving mine. Using her tongue, she licks up the cum and moves her hand from my wrist to the nape of my neck, and she draws my face closer to hers. My lips part and I grip her face with my right hand, tilting it up before I close the miniscule space between our lips to suck on her tongue. Rein emits a moan deep in her throat, the vibrations humming right through me, to which I respond with a guttural growl of my own at the taste of myself on her tongue.

Jesus fucking Christ, my dick fills with blood almost immediately, pearls of sheen pre-cum gathering on the tip. "I'm obsessed with the taste of us," I murmur against her lips and push her back down on the bed as I crawl over her.

Rein smiles impishly in return, her wanting gaze igniting every goddamn nerve in my body. "Then allow me to quell your fixation, Professor."

I stare deep into her eyes and lick my lips. "There's no quelling this fervent addiction that I have for you, Snowflake. Believe me, I've tried. But I would love to watch you give it your best shot."

Rein rolls me over onto my back and straddles me with a wicked grin. "While I do like a challenge, there's really only one solution to your little problem," she responds roguishly, leaning down until her lips are a breath away from mine.

"What's that?" I murmur, staring up into her eyes.

"Just don't get enough of me," Rein whispers back and grinds her hips, rubbing her already drenched pussy over the length of my throbbing cock.

"Oh *fuck...*"

"Are you going to tell me where we're going?" I question curiously, following Rein out of the department store.

Rein shakes her head and takes a long sip of her caramel Frappuccino. "Nope." I stop walking and raise my brow at her. Her lips curl into a sugary smile, the straw gripped between her pearly white teeth, her eyes all wide and mischievous. "I helped you shop for a gift for your mother, now I need *your help* with something."

My brows knit. "Why do I get the feeling I'm not going to like this?" I express stiffly and groan when she grabs my wrist and tugs me toward the car park.

"You won't know until you get there, now get a move on or we'll be late."

"Late for what exactly?"

Rein pins with an exasperated look. I relent and allow her to drag me towards my car. A ten-minute drive later, we pull up outside a two story, sort of white, brick building with a badly defined gravel parking area in front, where there are various cars and pickup trucks.

"You can park in that spot right there behind the red pickup."

"What is this place?" I question, pulling into the parking bay. She only smiles brazenly and proceeds to open the door. I watch her climb out of the car, still daftly waiting for a response I know isn't coming. Rein leans forward and gestures for me to get out of the car. "All right then." I sigh with a shake of my head. I kill the engine and follow her out of the car.

Rein walks around the car towards the entrance but I grab her arm and tug her to me. An adorable little gasp emits from her as I stare down into her pretty face. "I'm still waiting for an answer."

Rein's tongue swipes across her bottom lip and her eyes narrow a little. "Patience, Professor," she drawls, cocking her head to the side while she gazes up at me.

With a smirk, I take hold of her chin and bring her face closer. "Snowflake, you're really making my palm itch, and I know you're fully aware by now that I have no qualms about dragging you into the back seat of my car, taking you over my knee and spanking you until your juicy arse is scarlet and branded with my handprint."

Rein's lips twitch ever so slightly, and just as she parts her lips to respond, the voices approaching interrupts whatever she's going to say. "Rein!" I look over her shoulder at the kid animatedly running down the steps toward us. Upon hearing her name being called her entire face lights up like a Christmas tree and she spins to face the young boy with her arms wide open. I keep back and silently observe them. The kid couldn't be older than ten or eleven years old.

"Phillip!" Rein laughs and groans a little when he practically rams his little body into hers and locks his arms tightly around her waist. "Oh my goodness, did somebody miss me?" she teases with a grin, enveloping him in a tight embrace.

"Yes," comes his muffled reply.

"Aw, well, I've missed you too, buddy. I told you I'll always come back to you guys. Have I ever let you down and not kept my promises?"

Phillip pulls his head back to look up at her but has yet to release his hold around her waist. He shakes his head, smiling adoringly up at her. "No, you're a good promise keeper." Rein smiles down at him and brushes his sandy blond hair out of his bright green eyes.

Well fuck, this is new. I've not seen this amiably affectionate side to Rein before now. Not that she's unkind in anyway, she's not got a bad bone in her body, but I suppose I'm just a little taken aback to see this tender side to her. I stand back and silently observe them.

The entire exchange melts my heart into a puddle around my feet. It seems this place means a great deal to her.

Phillip looks over at me and his fair brows crease while he eyes me curiously. "Who's that?"

Rein follows his gaze and looks back at me over her shoulder. "This is my friend, Talon. I brought him along to help me with that project I've been working on the last couple of months," Rein explains.

I smile and offer a little wave as I move a little closer to them. "Hi, Phillip, it's a real pleasure to meet you." I hold out my fist to him and he hesitates for a moment and just anxiously stares at it.

"It's okay." Rein encourages him with a nod, soothingly brushing her slender fingers through his soft blond hair. He relaxes and eventually raises his hand and fist bumps me.

"You're an artist too?"

With a nod, I glance fleetingly at Rein before I answer. "I am, yes." I kneel so I'm at eye-level with him. "What about you? Do you enjoy painting?"

Phillip shrugs. "I guess painting is cool, but I prefer to play video games."

I chuckle. "You want to know something, kid? I love to play video games too."

Phillip smiles and bounces elatedly on the balls of his feet; he takes hold of my hand. "Come, I'll show you my game collection!" he chirps animatedly, tugging me so I can follow him.

"Hell yeah!" I stand and follow him towards the entrance, throwing Rein a cocky grin over my shoulder as we pass her by.

"Wha... hello? What about me? Oh, I see how it is," she calls out after us. "Am I not good enough for you anymore, squirt? Hey! I brought him here to help me, not to play video games!" Rein complains as she jogs after us.

We wind up playing video games with Phillip for half an hour. Of course, I let him win—ah, who am I kidding, the kid is a whiz and I had my arse handed to me.

"Wow, you suck, Saxton," Rein states teasingly when Phillip KO's me yet again.

I give her side long stare and lick my lips, lowering my gaze to her lips. "That I do. A skill I'm rather proud of, Valdez. And may I remind you that you weren't complaining last night *or* this morning of that little fact." Rein's cheeks glow pink under my heated stare. Her eyes flit over to Phillip still playing his game, not paying any attention to us. I lean a touch closer and brush my nose over hers. "You're significantly adept at *sucking* too, Snowflake. Just thinking about it has me aching in my boxers," I whisper, ghosting my lips over hers. Rein parts her lips, her eyes closing, readily waiting for a kiss I'm just burning to give her.

"Yes!" We jump apart when Phillip suddenly exclaims.

Rein clears her throat and tucks a strand of her hair behind her ear. "We, uh, we should go get started on the thing."

"What thing?" I question, eyeing her amusedly, taking pleasure in watching the flush that's turning a deeper shade of red and slowly travelling down her dainty neck. My eyes linger on the love bite that's peeking up from under the collar of her pale blue polo neck sweater.

Lewd memories of the passionate night *and* morning we just spent together invades my mind. God, there is still so much I want to do to her... *with* her. What am I going to do without her for two whole weeks? I know, I know, I'm supposed to be using this time apart to distance myself from her, but fuck me, I'm not so confident I can go that long without surrendering and calling her or some shit.

Goddamn, just thinking about not seeing her pretty face, hearing her voice or smell that sweet scent of rhubarb and vanilla I've become besotted with physically pains me.

But then, so does the guilt. It stings more each time I look into her eyes and she stares back at me gorgeously and with so much affection.

I'm a piece of shit.

"If you get your butt up and follow me, you'll find out, won't you?"

I smirk and lean forward, resting my forearms on my thighs, my eyes never wavering from hers. "I'll follow you and enjoy the view every step of the way," I drawl, wagging my brows at her suggestively.

Rein rolls her eyes with a shake of her head, and despite her best effort to seem impervious, the corners of her lips twitch while she tries and fails to fight off the urge to smile.

"Are you coming or not?"

I grin. "Keep looking at me like that and you'll find out."

"Talon."

I stand and stroll over to her. Leaning closer, I take hold of her chin and tilt her head up a touch so I'm gazing deeply into her eyes. "That's right, baby, you keep my name at the ready on the tip of your tongue, because you're going to be screaming it later," I whisper to her, my lips only just grazing hers with every deliberate word.

Rein's eyes roll to the back of her head when I run my tongue teasingly along her bottom lip. "Lead the way, Snowflake." I smile and draw back. Rein's eyes snap open again, she raises a brow, and a slow lustful sigh pushes past the soft pillow of her lips.

"You're playing dirty, Professor," she utters, exasperated, and turns to walk out of Phillip's bedroom.

"Oh, how I'd love to show you how dirty I can truly play," I mutter to myself, watching her sinful arse the whole time I follow her to wherever it is she's taking me. "What is this place?" I query curiously, once we reach the top of the flight of stairs. The inside of the building isn't fairing much better than the outside, if I'm honest. It's run down and in desperate need of a face lift. The décor is ancient at best and has a very early fifties feel to it. The green carpet is worn and is starting to disintegrate, and the wallpaper is torn, mostly hanging off near enough every wall.

"It's a group home for orphan children," Rein replies, leading me down a long dimly lit corridor. My eyes take in the photos hanging on the walls of kids of different ages from toddlers to teenagers.

My heart plummets deep into my gut. "Surely, this place isn't apt enough to house children?"

Rein heaves a sigh and stops walking to turn and face me. "No, it isn't. It's far from apt, but believe me, this is an improvement compared to how it used to look. The carpets will all be ripped out and replaced with wooden floors, new beds for the kids, and they're building another two shower rooms on the third floor. Unfortunately, the building is listed so it can't be structurally altered and the funding they got to fix this place up is disgraceful. The state refuses to lend any more money and deems fifty thousand dollars to be sufficient to make this place habitable," she explains with a shrug and pulls the loose wallpaper and tears it off. "So, a couple—I say a couple, but really there's around thirty odd—volunteers that come in and offer their services where they can or do what they can to support Jack and his wife Victoria save some money and give these kids a better quality of life."

"How long have you been volunteering?" I question, following her towards the end of the corridor to a room.

"Uh, almost three months." I observe Rein turn the door handle and walk into the room. I follow her in and stop short in my tracks when my eyes take in the concoction of colour on the wall to the left of the room. The wall mural she's working on is not complete yet, she's only a quarter of the way in, but I'm spellbound by the detail she's put into her creation. I narrow my eyes and I study every flawless brush stroke. The way she's exquisitely blended the blue of the sky with the rays of sunlight or the clarity of each blade of green grass and the contrasting of tree tawny leaves of the tree's is just… impeccable. "It's going to be a surprise game room for the kids," Rein states, following me when I move over to the wall mural. "I know first-hand what it feels like to feel abandoned and lost with no idea where you belong, and as much as I would like to financially help, I can't, so I'm giving them something money can't buy."

"Your time," I finish for her, and she looks at me sideways and nods.

"Yeah. I think the greatest gift you can give someone is your time. They won't remember the ones that donate money, but they'll always remember the ones that took time out of their own lives to spend it with them or help create a little space for them to escape when life gets just a little too suffocating."

I turn my head to look at her, and our eyes interlock. I couldn't look away even if I tried. The sentiment she holds in her gaze makes my heart flutter rowdily in my chest.

Sweet Jesus, there she goes again, worming her way deeper into my heart. She's truly something out of this world. I lace my hand with hers and bring it up to my lips where I brush a kiss over knuckles. "Snowflake, I wish you would have asked me sooner, but thank you for bringing me here and inviting me to help. It would be an absolute pleasure to offer my support where and when needed."

Rein smiles, her eyes glowing enchantingly. "Really?"

I return her smile and draw her against me. "Absolutely."

Rein pushes up on her toes and wraps her arms around my neck. "Are you sure you're ready, Professor? Because I won't show you any mercy, and I will ride you hard."

"Oh, I'm counting on it."

Chapter 8
Rein

CHILLS - MICKEY VALON, JOEY MYRON

"Biggest pet peeve?"

Talon hums while he considers his answer. "People who chew with their mouths open."

I smile and glance over at him from my position on the floor. "Yeah, that's a big one for me too, or when I'm eating and someone decides they would like some and then proceeds to stick their fingers all in my food."

Talon throws his head back and laughs. "I couldn't agree more. My best friend, JT, he's the biggest culprit when it comes to that, despite him knowing how much it peeves me off. Don't get me wrong, I'm all up for sharing food, but have some manners and use a goddamn fork."

"Exactly!" I exclaim with a giggle. "My ex drove me nuts with it while we were dating, but I was just too nice to actually tell him it that I hated it in fear I would offend him," I explain with a shrug and turn my attention back to painting.

Talon pulls his brush back from the wall and looks at me, his brows fused. "Sounds like a friable relationship if you didn't even feel comfortable enough to be honest with him about things that you don't like."

I sigh and chew thoughtfully on my bottom lip while I mix the orange and yellow paint together on my palette. "Honestly? Out of all my past relationships, Hunter was probably the one I felt most uncomfortable around and too self-conscious to open up to him, and even though we were friends first, it just never felt quite right." My eyes are fixed to the palette in my hand, but I feel Talon's eyes burning a hole into my forehead as though he's trying to delve deep in my brain and rummage through my most private thoughts.

I wonder if it bothers him when I mention Hunter? Just a little? Does he have that little flare of envy that I get whenever I picture him with another woman?

"If it didn't feel right, why did you continue dating him for so long?" he questions. I force myself to look at him. It's so incredibly difficult to focus on anything let alone rub two coherent thoughts together with him standing before me topless in only a pair of dark blue denim jeans that hang temptingly low on his narrow hips.

"I thought my feelings would change, and maybe if I gave him a chance, I would feel something. I didn't, and as time went on, I felt absolutely nothing, and the longer I put it off the more challenging it became to end it, because I was nervous about hurting him... so I just didn't."

Talon rests his left shoulder against an empty white spot on the wall. "You're many things, Snowflake, but I never would have pegged you for a coward," he states coolly, watching me intently with his blue eyes narrowing at the corners.

"I'm no coward, Talon. Perhaps I can be a little naive at times, but my reservations weren't because I was fearful of confrontation, it's because I was trying to be considerate towards his feelings. Hunter was my first friend when I started at Oakhill, and I was simply trying to protect our friendship."

"It's a shame he didn't have enough respect or consideration to offer you the same courtesy," he asserts stiffly, his jaw clenching.

"Though, I'm not at all surprised, it was glaringly obviously that little twerp was intimidated by you."

I frown. "*Hunter* intimidated by *me?*" I drawl sardonically and snort on a laugh. The notion alone is absurd. "Hunter is the most sought-after guy at that school. I know you've seen the way girls pathetically fawn all over him, hoping and dreaming to be his next fuck puppet. He's good looking and has more money than he knows what to do with, so what on earth has *he* got to be intimidated by— especially of me?"

Talon straightens and he slowly advances towards me, his bottom lip between his teeth, and I openly watch him, admiring the way his muscles flex with every movement. "Exactly, every girl... but you." I stare up at him. "Why do you think he chose to date you over all the girls that he had at his disposal?"

I can't say I hadn't wondered that same thing countless times over the duration of our relationship. Whenever I brought it up, he would just say I was different to the rest and that he saw something in me that appealed to him, something he couldn't quite put into words.

"According to him, I was different than the rest."

Talon kneels in front of me, his eyes hot on mine and he nods. "And I full heartedly agree, you are different, but in ways a self-centred prick like Hunter Harris could never apprehend nor appreciate. I'll bet you my life the only difference he perceived was that you weren't tripping over yourself to get his attention and that bruised his little ego."

Well shit.

"So, his interest in me was nothing but a power play to satisfy his ego?"

Talon brushes a loose strand of my hair out of my face and tucks it gently behind my ear. "It seems so. I know guys like Hunter, they're shallow-minded egomaniacs and are incapable of staying faithful to one girl. They need and crave constant attention to feed their self-esteem, simply because they lack character and all they have to rely on are their looks," he explains, twirling my hair between his fingers.

"That's likely why you never felt attracted to him. Because to some of us, true attraction is more than skin deep. While Hunter is easy on the eyes, he didn't appeal or incite you mentally. A physical attraction is mostly desired above many things, but its fleeting. But you, you desire someone that gets under your skin, someone that seduces the deepest, darkest corner of your mind and that has the ability to provide you with a mental connection. You crave passion."

I stare at him, completely enthralled–I could listen to him talk to me in that low, appeasing tone for the rest of my life. How is he able to see right through me? Am I really that transparent? The man reads me like I'm an open book. Though, he might be right. Could this be why my past relationships have been lacklustre at best? Other than sex, we never really spent much time conversing because I never had much in common with any of them. This is why I'm so attracted to Talon.

"Hunter didn't get into Oakhill on his own merit, his father made a hefty donation."

My brows rise with intrigue. "Professor, did you go prying into his files?"

Talon's fingers skim down the length of my neck, his gaze never leaving mine. His touch sends a shiver through me. "No, of course I didn't. It's not exactly a secret among the faculty that his father is sleeping with a member of the board."

My jaw drops and I stare at him in bewilderment. "Oh damn, it's no wonder he rarely spoke about his parents." I flinch a little. "I actually feel bad for him."

Talon smiles warmly. "Enough to forgive him?"

My surprise swiftly turns into antipathy. "Honestly, I don't care enough to even waste the energy to be angry or bitter about it. It's just the fact he didn't even own up to his mistake and continued to try and mug me off with his bullshit excuses that maddened me more. But hey, I'm over it. Karma has no menu, eventually you get served what you deserve and I'm certain he'll get his, if he hasn't already," I retort tetchily.

Talon grins. "I couldn't agree more. Why deplete your energy on such trivial matters when you can focus it on other more thrilling and *pleasurable* endeavours."

My grin matches the one spread across that gorgeous face. I sultrily fix my eyes to his. "Such as..." I trail off coquettishly.

"I take you back to mine, strip you out of your clothes, and then cover your body with paint and we create our own masterpiece."

My body heats up and my pussy responds with an ache that has me moaning from someplace deep in my throat. "Paint you say?" I purr. "Sounds messy, but I do like your way of thinking, Professor." Talon leans in close and presses his forehead to mine, his eyes staring hungrily at my mouth.

"My flights not till noon tomorrow. Spend the night with me."

I'm nodding before I can stop myself. I've been trying to put the thought of not seeing him for two whole weeks out of my mind, but each time it comes up, my mood plummets and my chest fills with dejection.

Goddamn it. I've gone and grown too attached to him and now it's becoming a real problem. I wasn't supposed to catch feelings, but fuck if I can help it.

I'd blindly let this man ruin my life, then turn around and thank him for it. Like, seriously, that is so out of character for me. But just the way he looks at me is enough to make me willingly and completely surrender to him. I want him to claim me. I want him to own me, and do with me what he wants, whenever he wants, for however long he wants—because damn, no man has ever looked at me like that before, with such burning desire like he's been starved for the longest time, and the only thing that can appease his hunger is me.

I love the way he needs me.

I really like him and I'm sick of fighting my feelings or constantly trying to convince myself that it's just sex when it's evidently so much more to us both.

While I stare into his clear blue eyes, I can't help but wish I knew a way to get him to open up to me.

By the time we wrap up to leave the group home, it's gone past six. Talon and I are both complaining that we're starving, so he drives us to Gaucho's Lounge, a chic little spot tucked away in a discreet location just far enough from the city to avoid being spotted together by anyone.

Talon guides me to a booth situated at the back of the restaurant, strategically located for those who desire some seclusion while they dine. My stomach knots with nerves as I take my seat. *This is not a date, Rein. It's just a quick meal, that is all.* The waiter comes over and hands us two menus. "Thank you." I smile and take the menu from him.

"Welcome to Gaucho Lounge. Can I start you off with some drinks?" the waiter asks, pulling out his digital device to take our order.

"What would you like, baby?" Talon asks, looking at me over his menu.

What would I like? I'd like to crawl into your lap and suck on the tongue that calls me 'baby' in such a sensual manner.

I shake off my lewd thoughts and clear my throat a little. "Water, *ice cold* water, please."

Are you sure you don't want something else, some wine?" Talon offers, and I shake my head. One sip of alcohol and my already dwindling inhibitions will become non-existent, and I may just succumb to the fire burning in my belly and the throbbing between my legs and make good on my previous thought.

"I'm good with water for now." Talon doesn't push and just nods in response and looks over at the waiter.

"I'll have a beer please, mate. Bud, if you have it."

God, that Aussie accent.

"We sure do, sir. I'll be right back with your drinks." The waiter walks off and disappears in the direction of the bar.

I peruse the menu, chewing on my bottom lip thoughtfully. "Decided on what you'd like to eat?" Talon questions and slides over to sit beside me in the booth. The intoxicating smell of his aftershave surrounds me instantly and I resist the urge to bury my nose in his neck and fill my lungs with it.

"I'm deliberating over the seafood risotto or the chicken pasta. They both sound delicious," I reply, staring at the menu.

Talon chuckles. "Get both."

Get *both*? I turn my head to look at him incredulously and he smiles handsomely, his blue eyes gleaming. "I'm aware I'm no Victoria Secret model, but I assure you my appetite isn't big enough to put away two plates of food, though it may look like it," I retort, dropping the menu on the table and crossing my arms over my chest.

Talon shifts beside me and reaches out to touch me, but I scoot away from him. "Whoa, hey, Snowflake, come back here." When I make no move and ignore him, he sighs and wraps his long fingers around my upper arm and pulls me back to him. Much to my irritation, I begrudgingly slide across the shiny faux leather seat to my previous position.

"Look at me, Rein," he orders. I turn my head and look him dead in the eyes. Talon's brows are drawn together tightly–he looks just as affronted as I feel. "First of all, sweetheart, you know damn well I didn't mean it in that context. I'll take a woman that isn't shy to put away a plate of real food over a tiny bowl of salad any day. I don't care if you eat two plates of food or ten, I'll order you the entire damn menu if that's what you want, and it still won't faze me. Secondly, how many more ways am I going to have to show you that I'm obsessed with every dip and every curve of your body? You're not overweight, not even close, and even if you were, it wouldn't matter because you'll still be so goddamn beautiful, Rein," he affirms, reaching up to brush the backs of his fingers along my jaw.

"Fuck, you turn me on so much," he adds with a hoarse whisper as his lips inch closer to mine. "And the fact that you're oblivious of how gorgeous you truly are makes you that much more attractive."

My annoyance drains away just as quick as it appeared, and I'm left yet again in a state of red-hot lust for this devastatingly perfect man. My hope is that one day I'll learn to love and see myself the way he sees me. Perhaps someday I will make peace with my flaws, but right now, I crave nothing more than the feel and taste of his lips on mine.

It seems Talon has the same idea because his lips sweep over mine and he draws me into a slow, spine-tingling kiss that has my head whirling with want.

"Ahem, your drinks."

Talon and I keep kissing rather passionately, completely unaware of our surroundings and too lost in one another to acknowledge the waiter delivering our drinks. "Um, sir, can I take your food order?" the waiter tries again. This time, it seems Talon hears him and draws away, leaving me in a breathless stupor.

"A seafood risotto and chicken pasta, please, mate," he replies, never taking his eyes off mine. "And make it to go." The waiter smiles knowingly when he catches my eye, and I blush profusely and veer my gaze. "Thank you." Talon dismisses him politely and turns to look at me again and grins.

"To go? I thought we were eating here?"

Talon shakes his head and rakes his fingers through my hair. "We can if you like, but I don't want to waste what little time we have holding off the urge to not touch or kiss you. I want to spend the night and every minute leading up to the very last second till I have to leave getting my fill of you."

My heart judders in my chest. "I would like that too."

Talon smiles adoringly and leans in to kiss me, but I draw back a little and he gives me a questioning look. I pick up his bottle of Bud and suggestively run my tongue along the rim of the bottle while he watches fixedly. He groans, biting down on his lower lip. "Keep teasing me, Snowflake, and see if I don't ruin that mouth."

I smile at him impishly and take a sip of his beer, but before I even have a chance to swallow, Talon's mouth is on mine, sucking the liquid from my mouth into his with a low groan. "Finest tasting beer I've ever had," he whispers, licking up the droplets of the liquid that seeped down my chin at the exchange.

"Couldn't agree more."

"Fuck, what the hell is taking so long with this food? How long does it take to cook pasta and some rice?" Talon states impatiently while I kiss down the length of his neck, stopping to suck at the base till I leave a nice red mark behind. "Lord have mercy, I'm about to bust." He moans, taking my hand, placing it against his protruding erection, throbbing perilously like it's about to burst through the zipper of his jeans, and he grinds up against it, desperate for some friction. My pussy aches and moistens, soaking through my already damp underwear. "Christ."

"What is your biggest fantasy, Professor?" I whisper in his ear while my fingers dance teasingly over the length of him. Talon hisses and his hips roll up instinctively, demanding more contract.

Talon draws his bottom lip between his teeth and opens his eyes to look at me. "I have too many, but the one I think about the most—especially while I'm working—is you spread out wide on my desk, begging me to feast on your pussy until you shower me with your tasty girl cum."

Damn, that is hot. I'd be lying if I said that fantasy didn't cross my mind while I touched myself to the thought of him on more than one occasion. "You remember a while back when you gave me that B-minus?" Talon nods, his blue eyes searching mine. "You caught me daydreaming and called me out in front of the whole class. That's exactly what I was fantasising about."

Talon smiles lazily and wets his lips. "I knew you were thinking about something sexual, because your eyes were hot and full of lust while you were watching me."

"I'm sure all the girls in that class look at you in the same way," I reply, stroking him through the thick fabric of his jeans and relishing in the way his dick jumps with every graze of my fingertips.

"They do, but none of them have ever affected me the way you do. My body responds differently to you. There's something in the way that you look at me that sends these intense, fiery frissons pulsing through my body."

"Like an electrifying current that–despite the heat of your skin–causes every hair on your body to stand on end and fires an impious shiver through you."

Talon stares at my mouth. "God yes, exactly that." He groans hoarsely. "Do you have any idea how difficult it was for me to teach that class and keep my thoughts in coherent order while fighting off a raging hard on?"

My lips ghost over his. "You were hard for me, Professor?"

"I'm always hard for you, baby."

"I like it when you call me 'baby.'"

Talon traces his thumb along my bottom lip. "You do?"

"Mhm, it gets me so wet," I respond breathily, my eyes closing. My lips part, and I luridly suck on his thumb. The rasping sounds emitting from deep within Talon tells me it's time for us to leave or we're going to wind up fucking each other right here in this booth without a care who watches. My lips brush his apart and I glide my tongue into his hot mouth. Talon groans and sucks on my tongue, his hand wandering down my back to grab a handful of my bum and pull me closer against him.

"Ahem, so sorry, but your food, sir." The waiter pops up again and disrupts the moment. Talon pulls back, his blue eyes stormy as he stares up at the waiter.

"You're killing me, mate." He almost growls in frustration while the waiter stands there sheepishly and holds up the bag of food. Mortified, I can't contain the laughter bubbling up inside, so I bury my face in his neck to smother the giggle.

"Thank you," Talon says with a chuckle and rubs my lower back. The waiter nods awkwardly and walks off, leaving us alone.

"Take me home, Professor."

"Fuck yes." Talon drops some money on the table, grabs the bag of food and ushers me out of the booth. "Moving forward, we'll be ordering in," he asserts, lacing his fingers with mine and pulling me towards the exit.

Moving forward...

The fact he's intending to spend more time with me makes my stomach tighten with elation. I'm always on edge just waiting and anticipating him to end whatever this is between us.

We leave the restaurant in a haste and make our way towards his black mustang in the car park. While I'm expecting Talon to open the passenger side door, I'm surprised when he sets the bag of food on the roof of his car and presses me up against the car. "I'm going to need to finish that kiss," he declares, staring down at my face.

I peer up at him wantonly and brush my fingertips over his jaw, the stubble of his beard scratching my skin. "Don't. If you kiss me now, I know I won't have the strength to stop."

A slow smile spreads across his handsome face and he nods. His large hands come up from my hips and cup my face before he presses a lingering kiss to my forehead.

Whoa.

My eyes close at the sentiment and I literally feel a mystifying warmth engulf me. I melt against him and draw him closer, inhaling his scent deep into my lungs.

The drive back to Talon's apartment took twenty minutes. There's a sudden shift between us, and for the life of me, I can't place it. Perhaps it's because he's leaving for two weeks, but the entire drive back we couldn't keep our eyes off one another. Talon kept our fingers laced while his thumb soothingly caressed my knuckles, further fuelling that warmth I felt before when he kissed my forehead.

We stand, waiting for the elevator, my back pressed against Talon's strapping chest. One strong arm is wrapped around my waist, his fingers caressing the exposed flesh of my stomach where my top has ridden up while he drags his nose and peppers kisses down the side of my neck.

The elevator dings, alerting us of its arrival. I turn to face him, my cheeks flushed, and my eyes hooded. I take his hand and walk back into the elevator, pulling him in with me, my eyes interlocked with his. Talon hits the button to his floor and sets the bag of food on the floor beside us as he slowly moves towards me.

Damn, I love the way his brawny body feels pressed up against mine. An audible moan escapes me before I can suppress it when his lips feverishly capture mine. His dexterous tongue languidly glides over mine, deepening the kiss until I can't focus on anything but the addictive taste of him.

My knees turn to jelly, and if it wasn't for him holding me up, they would have given out on me. The inconceivable desire I have gushing through my body is almost too much to bear.

My lungs burn from lack of oxygen, but I can't seem to pull away long enough to suck in a drop of air. The elevator bell causes us to pull apart, panting to fill our deprived lungs. Talon stares down at my mouth and brushes the pad of his thumb over my swollen lips.

He flashes me a telling smile and my body responds readily. It's one of those slow but sexy, panty melting smiles that nonverbally conveys he's intending to turn my world inside out.

Talon takes my hand and grabs the bag as we exit the elevator and walk side by side down the corridor towards his apartment.

The butterflies take flight in my belly and flutter like crazy. Shit, why am I so nervous all of a sudden?

"We can eat now if you're hungry?" Talon asks, turning the lights on and holding up the bag of food. I shake my head.

I'm not hungry for food, I'm hungry for you.

"Are you hungry?" I question, and he smiles and shakes his head, setting the food on the kitchen island.

"I'm absolutely starving, but not for food," he affirms, walking towards me. He shrugs his leather jacket off and drapes it over the back of a chair. I watch him raptly, my eyes raking over the heavenly length of him. I swallow thickly when he towers over me. "Take off your clothes."

I don't hesitate and start removing my clothes–one item at a time–while he watches on until I'm standing before him completely exposed and as naked as the day I was born. Talon's eyes blacken as they slowly sweep over my body. Reaching back, he pulls his T-shirt off from the neck and drops it on the growing pile of clothes on the floor. *Holy shit.* Such a simple motion, but it sends red-hot shockwaves pulsing through me that pools deep in my groin.

Talon grasps my hips and lifts me into his arms as if I weigh nothing but a bag of feathers. My legs coil around him and our lips lock, kissing like our lives depend on it while he carries me though the apartment towards the third spare room he uses as an art studio. Till this day, I've never been in there. The door has always been closed and he's never invited me in. Don't get me wrong, I've been itching to get a glimpse of his work, but given his reaction whenever I ask him anything personal, I thought better to keep my mouth shut.

While patience is bitter, its fruit sure is sweet.

Chapter 9
Talon

SWEAT - ZAYN

"TALON, wow, my God. These pieces are incredible." I continue to admire her while she marvels at my paintings. The wonderment in those striking eyes while she regards each one makes my heart swell. I've not shared my paintings with anyone—well, other than Taylor, of course. Every piece holds a different meaning to me and is a projection of my private thoughts and feelings. Most of which I painted after I lost Taylor, after I isolated myself from everyone. It was the only thing that helped me manage my grief—well, that and a detrimental volume of alcohol consumption. "These paintings deserve to be exhibited in a gallery, not shoved in a corner of your studio, gathering dust. Why on earth would you hide them away?" Rein questions, her wide and curious eyes burning imploringly into my own as I move towards her.

"Because they weren't painted with the intention of ever being seen by anyone other than me," I state and take the painting from her and place it back on the floor. "I've never felt comfortable with the idea of having my work hanging up in some gallery or in some random strangers house. Particularly if they're derived by my private thoughts and feelings."

Those paintings do nothing but drag up dark memories I'd rather keep buried. Each one is a depiction of how broken and how screwed up my head was after Taylor died. My mind was a bleak and chilling place back then and just the thought of falling back into that endless pit of torment scares me shitless.

"Art is never finished, Professor, only abandoned."

I smile and rub my jaw, taking a step closer to her. "Leonardo Di Vinci." Rein nods, watching me raptly as I near her. "Oh, so you do manage to take a break from daydreaming long enough to tune into my class from time to time. That's good to know," I drawl playfully, taking hold of her forearm and tugging her flush against me.

Rein's eyes light up, glittering like two precious jewels, beguiling me through and through. Her head cocks to the side and she regards me closely, a playful smile gracing her lips. "Oh, *Professor*, I assure you, I don't miss a single word that comes out of your mouth."

My brow lifts with intrigue. I stare into her eyes. "You don't, huh?"

Rein shakes her head slowly; her eyes remain fixed on mine. "Absolutely not. The accent, the articulate manner you speak, and the smooth yet deep tone of your voice is just so…" She trails off and swallows thickly. "Erotic," she finishes with a breathy whisper, her eyes lowering to my lips when I shuffle closer. "You could read me the phonebook and I'll still be wholly immersed in every single word."

Shit. This girl is on a secret quest to drive me senseless.

"I'm familiar with the feeling. The way you feel about my voice is the way I feel about your eyes." Rein's eyes close as my lips brush against the shell of her ear when I speak to her in a low, sensual tone. "Your eyes hold such grandeur," I avow, drawing back so I can look down into her pretty face. Rein's eyes flutter open and they lock with mine, and for a moment, all I can do is gaze into them hypnotically. "When you look at me like this, I lose all train of thought and my sense of awareness wanes until I can't focus on anything but you," I confess, raking my fingers through her long, glossy waves. God, I'm besotted with the way the strands just glide through my fingers so effortlessly, like each one is formed of the finest of silk.

"How am I looking at you?"

"Like you're mine and no one else's."

Rein sucks in a slow breath and exhales with a soft 'Mm' while she stares up at me absorbedly before she pushes up on the tips of her toes, kerbing the already small gap between our lips and ghosts that sensational mouth of hers over mine. "I have no interest in being anyone else's. So, show me what it's like to be *yours*, Professor," she whispers implicitly.

Fucking Christ.

She will be my ruin.

Who the fuck am I fooling? There is no escaping this girl. I've tried continually and failed. What we have goes so much deeper than just sexual attraction. The goddamn battle I undergo on the daily trying to force her out of my mind is honestly outrageous. I can safely say I have never felt anything like this for anyone... not even Tay, and I was out of mind in love with her. But Rein—fuck, she's something else. Despite the illicit nature of our relationship, I'm starting to believe that on some cosmic level, Rein Valdez was always meant to be mine, and I am not a man that believes in fate.

Then again, how is it that every perfect inch of her body fits so seamlessly with mine? Almost like she's the key I've been inadvertently searching for my whole life, waiting to unlock the entrenched parts of me just pleading to be unravelled. Parts of me that have been closed off for so long and are damn near bursting at the seams to open up to her, to be vulnerable *with* her, even if it is for just one night.

With a sigh, I press my forehead to hers. "You have no idea what you do to me." A groan escapes me when she tortuously drags her index finger up from the base of my throbbing dick and all the way to the oozing tip.

"I may have *some* idea," she replies, gazing up at me through those lush dark lashes.

With a slow shake of my head, I swathe my fingers around her wrist and bring her hand to my lips to kiss the tips of her fingers. "Fuck, you don't. You and that succulent cunt of yours have well and truly fucked my mind, Rein Valdez."

Rein smirks and her thick dark brow arches. "And you… your enormous cock and that wicked tongue of yours have ruined me for all other men, Professor," she throws back roguishly.

I grin and slowly walk her back towards the wooden workbench at the back of the room, our eyes locked firmly on one another. "Good, because I'm going to make certain that no one will ever fuck and make you come the way I do. I want you to remember how fucking good it felt to be mine." I lift her up onto the work bench and step between her legs. "So that years later when you're laying in bed with the lucky fucker that gets to marry you, you'll think of me, and your pussy will ache, and your clit will throb just as it is right now."

Rein's eyes close and a low moan emits from deep within her. "Talon."

"That's right, baby, while he's asleep next to you, you'll touch yourself and remember this very day. And just as you reach the apex of your climax, you'll want to scream my name, but despite your best effort to stifle it, it will flow past your beautiful lips as a muffled whimper," I drawl, taking the soft pillow of her lower lip between my teeth and tugging gently. "My name will forever remain a sinful secret embedded to your sweet lips, snowflake." I whisper, my wandering hands finding her budding nipples, I brush the pads of my fingers, caressing them teasingly.

The thought alone of another man touching her makes my blood boil, because I want nothing more than to make her mine, but we need to be realistic—we have no future. Currently, we're drifting from one stolen moment to the next with the possibility of getting caught at any given moment, and while its thrilling, it's also bittersweet. In a year, she'll graduate and go back home to her life in London. *That's* our reality.

Whether it be now or later, I'm going to lose her either way.

Rein's legs enfold around me, her beautiful thick thighs tightening as she draws me closer till our bodies are pressed intimately against one another. The citrusy notes of her perfume mixed with the fruity scent of her lotion wafts around my senses, immediately amplifying my already raging arousal for her.

"You sure have an excessively high opinion of yourself there, don't you, Professor?" she states playfully while she rakes her nails lightly down the length of my chest. "Tell me, what makes you think I would settle for a man that can't satisfy me long enough to stop fantasising about my illicit tryst with my college professor?" she adds with a wayward smirk.

My lips curl into a half smile. "I have nothing of the sort, Snowflake. And I truly hope you don't settle, because you deserve a man that can fulfil all your desires. However, we all have that one person we keep secretly buried in our minds, the one that got away. The one person you share that fanatical connection with you only come across once in a lifetime," I explain, trailing the backs of my fingers along her jaw.

"If you're mine, then I suppose that makes me your once in a lifetime then?"

I stare into her eyes, and we share a smile.

My fingers grip the backs of her thighs, I tug her hips forcefully toward me, and she falls back on the workbench with a gasp. "I can promise you one thing for certain, Snowflake. I will not be forgetting you in a hurry," I declare truthfully.

Rein watches me with hooded eyes while I lift her leg and trail my lips along her calf. "Allow me to turn that 'hurry' into '*never*,'" she purrs, spreading her legs further, exposing her bare pussy glittering with her honey. "Fall to your knees and devour me, Professor," she demands sultrily. "Let me leave a taste in your mouth no other woman will ever satiate."

The raw heat that fires through me abruptly is truly dazzling. No woman has ever brought me to my knees quicker than this deity spread out before me. I've never really been religious, but if ever there's a goddess worthy of worship, it would be her. I'm happy to crawl into the church between those sensational legs and spend the night confessing my sins.

Forgive me, Snowflake, for I'm about to sin.

That first sluggish lick through her slick folds and the way her eyes roll to the back of her head, followed by that melodious moan is the only absolution I'll ever need. The sweet and salty taste of her explodes over my tastebuds. Rein arches up when my tongue glides over her engorged clit. "Oh, yes, Talon."

I love watching her expressions while I feast on her tasty cunt. The flush that spreads across her neck and face as she chases down her climax, or the way her legs twitch and the muscles in her abdomen spasm with each lick of her clit drives me insane with carnal lust. I tease the opening of her pussy with slow circles, using the pad of my index finger, making her squirm and rock her hips ravenously, demanding more contact. I slide a single digit inside her and she whimpers when I stroke her G-spot.

Another finger joins the other and I thrust them both into her rhythmically while my mouth continues the assault on her bundle of nerves, driving her closer to that sweet release she's desperately craving.

"Look at me," I order, and she lifts her head, her chest rising and falling. The heat in her eyes makes me shiver. "Play with that pussy in my face, come on, let me watch you. Show me how you play with that clit when you're thinking about me." Without a moment's hesitation, her fingers reach between her thighs, and she eagerly begins to caress her swollen nub in slow circles. "That's a good girl, there you go. Moan for me, let me hear you, fucking drive daddy crazy." I groan, absorbedly watching her pleasure herself and work my fingers deeper into her snug cavern.

"Oh yes, yes, right there, fuck me just like that."

"That feel good? Yeah?" I whisper, stroking her G-spot, and she mewls, biting down on her bottom lip. "I bet it fucking does, you insatiable little slut."

She's so close, the trickle of her creamy girl cum dripping out of her pussy and straight down to the gorgeous pearl of her arse, her muscles squeezing my fingers like a vise and her breathing becoming laboured.

"Oh yes, daddy, don't stop. Please, don't fucking stop."

This is such sweet torture. "Spread those pussy lips for me, let me see that engorged clit." Rein stops stroking and unfurls herself open for me, using her index and middle finger. My mouth salivates at the sight. "That's a good fucking pussy right there." I flick my tongue against her clit and suck it hard, making her arch up. She curls her fingers in my hair and grinds her pussy into my face.

"Fuck!" she cries out, fucking my face. "I'm coming, oh I'm fucking coming!"

I pull back and release the suction on her clit to watch her pussy contract. A stream of her creamy honey spills out of her pussy while she grunts in displeasure. "Oh my God, look at that. You've got the best fucking pussy, baby."

Rein stares up at me, eyes aflame and pleading. "Make me come."

I lean over and suck on her erect nipple, my eyes on hers. Rein hisses, watching me and raking her fingernails down my back. "No coming until I say so. Understand?"

"Where are you going?" Rein questions with a frown when I pull away and walk across the room to the drawer where I keep my brushes.

"Getting supplies. Lay back and don't you dare touch yourself." I smirk when I hear her huff and mutter incoherently to herself. I plan to tease her and make her delirious with desire until she's damn near weeping for me to fuck the soul out of her. I find the brand-new brush I bought a couple of months ago still in its case and tear it out of its plastic packaging.

Rein leans up on her elbows, legs still spread, observing me while I gather up jars of red, blue, and yellow ready mixed water paint. I pick up a pencil on my way over to her. "Here, use this to pin your hair up." Rein looks at the pencil and then at me, surprised. "Don't look so surprised, Snowflake. I told you I don't miss anything. I've seen you pin your hair up with a pencil before." Her lips curl into a beautiful smile and she takes the pencil, twists her up into a messy bun, and pins it with the pencil in less time it took for me to blink.

Fuck me, that's sexy.

"Happy?" she utters with a raised brow. "Do you think you can get over here and finish what you started now?"

I grin, walking over to her and setting the paint down on the oak workbench. "Oh my, someone is rather tetchy when they're being denied, aren't they? I'll just keep denying you, Snowflake, if you insist on being a brat."

Rein says nothing and only stares back at me when I place my hands on either side of her and hold her gaze inch for inch. I can see she's just burning to throw back a cocky remark, but she manages to bite it back. "That's what I thought," I state gruffly, my eyes sweeping down to her lips when she licks them and then moving back up to meet her eyes. "Now be a good girl and lay back for me, so I can take my time and revel in that succulently swollen snatch of yours."

Rein does as she's told and lays back, all the while keeping her wary gaze on me. A slow sigh escapes her when I feather soft kisses down her inner thigh as I push them further apart. My eyes are fixed on hers as I pick up the clean paint brush and leisurely trail it up her stomach towards the valley between her breasts. Rein moans and an array of goosebumps rise across her body, her nipples pebbling. I glide the soft bristles of the brush around the light brown areola of her breast, and she groans, lifting her arms up and over her head to hold the edge of the worktop while she instinctively arches up.

"Is that good, baby?" Rein hisses and bites down on her bottom lip when I skim the tip of the brush over her erect nipple, her moans getting loader, her breath shorter the longer I tease her nipple.

"Talon, please." She whimpers, rocking her hips up in hot pursuit of some release from the violent ache emanating between her legs.

Fuck. The mouth-watering scent of her arousal combined with the sticky cream oozing through her folds is driving me fucking insane. Nevertheless, I force away the urge to bury my face between her thighs and drink up every drop of her heavenly nectar, because watching her weep with pleasure while I leisurely take her over the edge will be worth the excruciating aching of my nads.

Crikey, I'm just burning to feed my dick and bottom out inside of her.

I bite and suck the inside of her thigh and run my tongue over the red mark I left behind. "Oh my God..." Rein wails, and her hand gripping the worktop tightens.

"Oh no, baby girl, God's not going to help you now. Plead to *me*," I tell her steadily and drag the brush around her pussy lips, intentionally missing the part she's begging me to pay attention to.

Rein sucks in a sharp breath and throws her hips up when I drag the bristles of the brush through her slick cleft and against her enflamed nub. "Oh, daddy, please…"

She's so wet that her pussy soaks the brush almost instantly, amplifying my already flaming libido tenfold. I close my eyes and take a moment to absorb the sensual sounds exuding from her, storing it away to use while I'm away and undoubtedly longing for her. I use the tip of the brush and stroke her clit in slow teasing circles again and again until I feel her body start to quake and her breathing hasten. "Talon, yes… yes." She pants as she reaches that sweet spot, rocking her hips against the brush, matching my rhythm. "Don't stop, baby, please."

"Look at you, so goddamn beautiful when you're at my mercy." I groan, licking the pearl of her arse. Rein's eyes go wide in panic, and she immediately tries to shy away, but I grip her hips tight to keep her in place. *Oh no you don't.*

Just as I suspected, she's not yet been properly introduced to anal play. Perhaps I'll give her a little taste, just tease the rim with my tongue and watch her unravel for me. "Relax for me, Snowflake, I got you." Rein stares back at me guardedly, she's hesitant, but it's hard to miss the curiosity radiating deep in her eyes. Oh, you want it all right. The soft bristles of the brush glides over her clit and she throws her head back with a breathy moan, whimpering incoherently in Spanish.

I can't take my eyes off her, she's such a mesmerising sight. "Play with your nipples for me, Snowflake. Roll them between your forefinger and thumb." Rein obeys and teases her erect nipples, sucking on her bottom lip to stifle the moan that escapes her when she tugs on them and her hips roll up, grinding herself against the brush.

My tongue hungrily laps up the cream that's dripping from the opening of her starved cunt right down to her arse. Fuck, if that isn't the most addictive taste. I circle the rim with the tip of my tongue, and Rein shudders in response, her chest rising and falling quicker as she nears her climax. "Uh, yes, right there, keep going. Fuck, daddy, you're going to make me come," she laments fervidly, longing out the 'fuck' while clutching handfuls of her bountiful tits.

"Mm, fuck yes, that's a good girl. Look at me when you come for me." Rein peels her eyes open, and she stares into my eyes. "That's my girl. Give daddy that cream, baby. I want that pussy juice down my goddamn throat." I stroke her clit a couple more times and push my tongue in her arsehole just as she's going over, burning to feel every wave and contraction that fires through her, and of course, gluttonously swallow up the warm liquid that oozes out of her pussy, and sweet Jesus does she deliver. And then, she comes undone, whimpering my name again and again while her body judders, and every surge of her sweet rapture wreaks absolute chaos upon her exquisite body.

"Holy shit..." She pants, limbs still quivering. I grip her waist and tug her towards me, grinding my erection against her. Rein mewls and sits up, curling her fingers at my nape and pressing her forehead to mine. "Kiss me."

I don't miss a beat and claim her mouth, drawing her into a zealous kiss. My hands roam over her body, squeezing her hips while my mouth continues to insatiably duel with hers. We don't come up for air, paying no attention to the signal being sent to my brain that I'm running low on oxygen. I continue to devour her mouth, moaning gutturally when she sucks on my tongue.

Fuck. I can't get enough.

Rein pulls away, breaking the kiss to suck on the base of my neck. My eyes close and my head lolls back to give her more room to continue her ministrations.

Unbelievable... I can run five kilometres and not break a sweat, but one kiss from her and I'm panting to catch my breath.

This girl literally takes my breath away.

Rein slowly pulls back to look at me, our eyes interlock, and for a moment, we just gaze longingly at one another. Shit, there she goes again, beholding me so beautifully. My stomach tautens while I'm entrapped in her gaze, unable to look away nor move.

Damn, her beauty is dumbfounding.

When she affectionately brushes her fingers along my jaw, I snap out of the thrall she's got me under. "What's on your mind, Professor?" she asks with a coy smile.

"You," I answer, staring into her eyes. "You're what's on my mind. Continually."

Rein's already flushed cheeks redden further. "Well, I'm not at all sorry to hear that," she responds with a smirk and a one shoulder shrug. "Because I really like the fact that I'm your peccadillo."

I wet my lips with a groan as I dip my index and forefinger into the jar of red paint and slowly drag them up the length of her forearm. "I'm on a highway holding a one-way ticket straight to hell because of you." Rein sucks in a soft breath and lowers her gaze to watch me smear the paint up her forearm.

"I hear heaven is overrated anyway. Why waste time being good when being bad is better..." she murmurs, drawing me in for a kiss while her hands unbutton my jeans and slowly unfasten the zipper.

Oh, fuck it all to hell. If I must burn, I'll burn.

Lips still locked, I kick my jeans off, lay her back, and crawl on top of her. Rein's knee knocks the jar of paint over and it spills all over the worktop and on the white cotton canvas under her. She pulls away with a gasp and reaches over to lift the jar before it rolls off the counter, but I lace my fingers with hers. "Leave it," I say with a groan and bruise her lips with another impassioned kiss.

The paint and the mess around us are quickly forgotten the moment I feed my dick and bottom out inside her sensationally tight pussy. Rein's legs enfold around me, keeping me as close to her as humanly possible while we rock together rhythmically.

I held it together for her as long as I could while she climaxed twice, her walls fluttering wildly around my cock, each spasm pushing me closer and closer to the release I'm so desperately yearning until I come undone and spill rope after rope of my hot seed deep inside her.

We lay, limbs twisted like a pretzel, utterly spent, chests heaving, and our hearts racing while we catch our breaths. We're an absolute mess. Stained all over in an array of colours.

Rein opens her eyes and looks up at me adoringly, her eyes glittering like gems. I can say honestly, hand on my heart, that it wound up being a night I would never forget and would cherish till my very last breath.

Chapter 10
Rein

HURTS SO GOOD - ASTRID S

"I HAVE A GIFT FOR YOU."

A gift?

I smile and turn my head to look up at Talon when he sidles up behind me in the bathroom while I towel dry my hair and he envelopes his burly arms around me. "If it's the package between your legs, I'm going to have to respectfully refuse. I love a good dicking, but my poor vagina is still throbbing from the pounding it got in the shower not even ten minutes ago," I answer impishly, and he laughs heartily. The infectious sound resonates through me, filling me up with a warmth that spreads across my chest. It's a true shame that he doesn't laugh more because his laugh is just so wholehearted, masculine, and so very sexy.

"I do love that you consider my knob a gift, Snowflake, but I don't think I could get it up even if I tried right now," he informs me and nuzzles my jaw. "You've literally milked me dry," he adds cockily and grins when I chortle.

"Well, thank heavens for that, because one more round with your mammoth cock and she'll be written off."

"Mammoth?" Talon repeats with chuckle, his eyes gleaming and looking amused and delighted at the same time. "We're honoured."

I playfully roll my eyes with a smile. Men are incorrigible, so darn easy to charm them. "Okay, *Professor*, deflate your ego and tell me more about this gift you got me."

"Actually, I have two gifts." Talon sweeps me up into his arms–bridal style–like I weigh nothing but a bag of feathers and carts me out of the bathroom towards his bedroom.

My brows rise with interest. "Two?" Talon nods and brushes a kiss on my lips before he sets me down on the bed.

Ooh, I wonder what he got me. I honestly wasn't expecting a gift from him, so to say I'm enthused is the understatement of the century. "I actually have a gift for you too," I inform him, watching him move around his super king size bed towards the bedside table.

"You do?" he questions as he opens the drawer and takes out one medium sized box wrapped in sparkly silver paper and a pale blue, letter sized envelope. The nerves in my stomach bunch up.

Oh my goodness. What's in the envelope? Is it a letter?

I chew on my lip thoughtfully. My eyes follow him eagerly as he strolls over to me clad in nothing but a pair of tight, black Hugo Boss boxer shorts that does nothing to secrete his manhood. My sore lady bits flutter with admiration. The sinewy muscles in his thighs and ripped torso flex with every step. Holy moly, the man unwittingly exudes supremacy. Talon catches me eyeing him appreciatively and he licks his lips and smirks.

"You can open the envelope, but not the gift until Christmas day," he states, fixing me with a mock glare while he hands me the box and envelope. I flash him a sugary smile and take the gifts, lifting the box by my ear and giving it a little shake. "Fine, you meanie."

My lips purse when I hear nothing. It's very light, almost like it's empty. Oh crap, this is going to bug me now. I'm the worst when it comes to waiting to open gifts. I just don't have the patience.

Even as a kid the curiosity that burned inside had me lying in bed night after night wondering what the gifts were under the

Christmas tree. Until I couldn't take it anymore, and while everyone was asleep, I'd sneak out of my bed early in the morning and tear the paper at the corner to see what was inside and then tape it back up again. I felt terrible after, but my curiosity was satiated. My poor mother was none the wiser and I acted all surprised when I saw the gifts on Christmas morning.

I know, I was a right little terror, ruining the magic of Christmas and all, but what can I say, I was a curious kid. A trait of mine that regrettably stuck.

Talon shifts almost uneasily while he waits for me to open the envelope. "You know you really didn't have to get me anythi..." The words die on my lips when I pull out the contents of the envelope.

A plane ticket.

For a very fleeting second, my heart leaps up to my throat when I presume he's asking me to go to Cincinnati with him—not sure why I got all excited, not like I could actually go, what with work and all—but my excitement plummets just as fast when I see the destination printed on the ticket.

'LHR – London Heathrow'.

I stare stock-still at the ticket between my fingers for a while and slowly lift my gaze to look up at him, blinking away the tears that are burning the backs of my eyelids.

"What is this?" My voice is barely an octave over a whisper.

Talon smiles back at me handsomely. "What does it look like? It's a ticket home to spend Christmas with your family."

When I wordlessly stare up at him, his smile slowly vanishes, and his brows knit tightly. I push the ticket back into the envelope and hold it out to him. "Thank you. I really appreciate the gesture, Talon, but I can't accept this," I declare with a shake of my head.

Talon takes a step closer and perches down till he's at eye level with me. "What do you mean you can't accept it? Of course you can. It was just the other day you were sobbing and saying you wished you could go home."

I wet my lips and veer my gaze from his to look out the window when I feel my eyes brimming with tears. "I can't."

Do I want to? Of course I do. I would love to go back home. I miss my aunt Dani and Grammy so much. I miss my bedroom, my home, but the thought of going back and having to face the memories of my mother scattered all over the house is just unbearable. It's such a sweet and considerate gesture, and his heart is in the right place, but at the same time, it feels like a handout, and Talon already knows how I feel about asking for help from others.

If I *really* wanted to go home, I would have worked day and night to save up the money and pay for it myself. I don't need nor want anyone to take pity on me. I like to pay my way, I'm not a charity case. And while I'm aware he only did this because he overheard the conversation with my grandmother and saw how upset I was over not being there with them over Christmas, it doesn't make me feel any better about myself. If anything, if I accept it, I'll feel like even more of a failure than I already do.

"Hey, Rein, will you look at me, please?" Talon reaches up and gently turns my face to his. "Why can't you go? And before you start with the 'I'm not a charity case' spiel, it's a gift, not a handout."

"An eight-hundred-dollar gift, Talon?" I ask incredulously and pull my face away from his hold. "I'm forever indebted to you. You've done enough for me as it is. Please don't get me wrong, I get it, you clearly wanted to do something nice for me, and I'm so very grateful. But this..." I hold up the envelope. "As generous and amiable as it may be, it is too much. I can't accept it but thank you." I place the envelope in his hand and drop a kiss on his cheek.

Talon sighs and his eyes remain on me when I draw back slightly. "Snowflake, you are absolutely in no way indebted to me for a goddamn thing, all right? I did what any human being with a good conscience would do."

I raise a brow and pin him with a dubious look. "Really? So, you would spend eight hundred dollars to fly home *all* your other students too, would you?"

Talon stares at me, those ocean blue eyes piercing through my own. When I raise my brows expectantly, the corner of his lip twitches and he exhales, wetting those soft kissable lips. "That's not what I mean and you know it. You can't compare yourself to my other students, Rein."

"Why not?" I fire back.

There's this look that flashes his eyes, like he wants to say something, but he hesitates and thinks better of it. "Well, for starters, I'm not fucking any of them. And..."

"And... what?" I question, urging him to finish. It bloody grates me when people don't finish their sentences.

And *what, Talon? You don't care about them? What is it about me that appeals to you above every other girl beautiful girl out there? Why me?*

My eyes search his until Talon veers his gaze from mine and shoves his hands through his damp hair. In that moment, I can't help but admire how different he looks when his hair isn't styled and slicked back as it usually is. Makes him seem more boyish and carefree when his dark blond locks are freshly washed and product free, hanging freely around his handsome face.

Oh my God, I'm such a simp. Get it together, Rein, for fuck's sake.

"It doesn't matter," he utters, brushing it off and standing. And just like that he shuts down on me again. Before I can stop myself, my hand shoots out and I grab hold of his wrist, stopping him before he can walk away. Talon looks back at me over his shoulder, his gaze slowly rising with me when I stand.

"It matters to me," I tell him and take a step toward him. "And what?"

"You really need me to spell it out for you, Rein?"

I blink, taken aback by his response. "When you refuse to open up and share things with me, yes, I'm afraid I do need you to spell it out for me," I retort irritably, dropping my hold on his wrist and crossing my arms over my chest.

Talon turns to face me properly, his facial expression hardening and his startling blue eyes now grey and stormy. "What is it you want me to share with you Rein?"

"God, you always do this. Why are you so reluctant on letting me in? You know pretty much everything about me and what I know about you I can fit on the back of a stamp, Talon."

"What are you talking about? I've shared plenty about myself. What is it that you want to know, Rein? My favourite colour? It's blue. My preferred flavour of ice cream? Mint chocolate chip. What my favourite film is? Scarface. There, know me better now? Has that assuaged your curiosity?"

I can feel the annoyance stewing inside me and my hands start to shake, so I fist them by my side. "Don't fucking patronise me. Is it a damn crime to be curious and want to know things about the man I'm spreading my legs to near enough every day? I want to know things that matter. I want to know what makes you, you!"

"For what purpose?" he snaps hotly, holding his arms out while he glares hot daggers at me. "Whether we like to admit it or not, this thing between us has an expiration date Rein, and getting to know one another will only complicate things and make walking away even harder than it already is. The less you and I know about one another the better," he states dourly.

Yikes. If that isn't a big fat 'fuck you', I don't know what is. It would have honestly hurt less if he had cut me wide open with a blunt cleaver. "I never asked nor made you feel obligated to open up to me, Rein. Everything you shared with me was of your own free will."

He's right—I did. I let my guard down and foolishly believed if I opened up, he would eventually feel comfortable enough and let me in. Like a fool, I got all caught up in the fantasy and misinterpreted his affection for something more than an inconsequential fuck.

Deep down, I know he's not saying these things to hurt me—if anything, he's trying to protect us both, but the truth is ugly, and it hurts like a bitch for the reality is just that, an illicit fling is all we'll ever really be.

My wounded heart sinks deeper into my gut with every passing second we stand there, staring heatedly at one another. I don't think I can deny it any longer. The unbearable ache spreading deep in my chest and the tears burning the backs of my eyelids all indicate the very truth I've been refuting. I've fallen for him.

I force myself to nod and drop my gaze from his to stare down at my feet. "You're absolutely right, you didn't. However, communication is a two-way thing, Talon. I don't trust people enough to open up completely, but you made it so easy to talk to you that I found myself wanting to share parts of myself voluntarily with you," I answer distantly and look back up at him again. "But I get it, you're right. You're under no obligation to do the same and we shouldn't make things harder for ourselves, especially when you've already got one foot out of the door." The storm in Talon's eyes moments ago subsides and they go back to the startling blue that I've come to love. While he stands still, his chest rises and falls as he watches me, likely trying to gage my next move.

Keep it together, Rein. Don't you dare cry.

"Rein I—"

With a shake of my head, I walk over and pick up my clothes from where they are folded on the chair by the window and proceed to get dressed. "Perhaps these two weeks apart will do us both good," I state evenly. Each word leaves a sour taste as it exits my mouth. When I turn to face him again, I can't place the look on his face. Is it guilt? A touch of relief, perhaps? Damn it, what is so bad about his past that he's so adamant on keeping it buried?

Why won't you let me in?

I walk over to him, push up on my toes and press a lingering kiss to his jaw. "Merry Christmas, Professor."

Talon's eyes close and his jaw tightens under my lips. When he says nothing and stands motionless, I pull away and walk out of his bedroom towards to the front door as quick as my legs will take me before the tears brimming in my eyes fall.

Through the slow pounding of my heart in my ears, I don't hear the footsteps behind me. I gasp audibly when I open the door to leave and his hand suddenly appears over my head, and he slams it shut, keeping me wedged between his body and the door. My body stiffens, the warmth of his body engulfing me as I stare at the wooden door, my pulse racing uncontrollably. "Snowflake…" he murmurs in my ear. My eyes close and the heat of his breath against my skin sends a shiver cascading straight through me.

My fear in that moment is walking away and never feeling with anyone else the way I do when I'm with him.

"Don't go." I take a moment to swallow the lump forming in my throat and will away the tears before I speak.

"Give me a reason to stay." I sigh.

"I want you to."

I shake my head. "Not enough."

Talon exhales slowly. "I *need* you to."

"No, you don't," I utter bitterly and open the door, but he pushes it shut again.

"What is it you want to hear? That I care about you? I thought I made that pretty clear," Talon declares and turns me so I'm facing him. His gaze locks adoringly with mine, and he skims the backs of his fingers over my cheek. "If only you knew how precious you truly are to me, Snowflake. I can't get you out of my head. You're laced in every single one of my thoughts in some way or another. And despite me trying to convince myself on the daily that these feelings I have for you are just lust and nothing more, it's becoming more and more evident with every moment I spend with you that I…" He trails off and I stare up at him, waiting with bated breath for him to continue.

Goddamn it, that you *what*?

Chapter 11
Rein

HEAVEN - FINNEAS

This man is going to be the reason I lose my sanity at the tender age of twenty-one. "That you what?" I ask.

"I really like you."

Like me? Wow. Talk about stating the obvious. That's a given, isn't it? Considering we're humping like two feral rabbits at every opportunity. When he said feelings, I daftly thought he was going to say that he's falling for me, or at least something more than just 'liking me'. That's the same as him saying he's attracted to me.

I suppose this is a rather substantial affirmation on his part. Admitting that he has *some* feelings for me is better than just being a frivolous screw to him. Talon cups my face with his large hand and his lips descend upon mine, kissing me so deeply and thoroughly that I forget my own damn name. What has he done to me? I'm not fainthearted, or a weakling. I don't like being told what to do, I don't take shit from anyone, I never have, but Talon has this baffling power over me. His kiss alone holds such tenderness and ascendency that it instantly weakens me. Those lips of his are my kryptonite. It sounds so incredibly cheesy and cliché, but that's God's truth.

Our little spat is quickly forgotten, and before I know it, I'm stripped naked and back in his super king size bed with my legs wrapped tightly around him, crying out his name while he pleads for me to come for him with every mind-shattering thrust.

It's four in the morning. I'm lying enveloped in Talon's arms, listening to his slow, even breathing and the rhythmic beating of his heart while he's fast asleep. I've been staring out of his bedroom window, watching the snow falling from the sky. Even in the dark everything glistens beautifully, almost like a fairy has sprinkled her dust all over the city.

I've not felt a sense of belonging, as I do in this moment since my mum died. Everything I've been missing most of my life, I'm finding with Talon. What's worse is, I know this is only temporary and I shouldn't feel this secure and sheltered in his arms, because as much as he says that I belong to him in a moment of passion... I don't, not really.

Talon shifts in his sleep and his arms tighten around me. My eyes close and that overwhelming warmth engulfs me again. The next time I open my eyes the sun is beaming brightly through the window. With a gladdened sigh, I hug the pillow and peel my eyes open, blinking till my eyes adjust to the brightness of the room.

Wait a minute. I lift my head and look down at the pillow I'm hugging. I sit up so fast I make myself dizzy. The other side of the bed is empty, but there's a note, the gift he got me, and the envelope with the plane ticket resting on the pillow.

I pick up the note and slowly unfold it and see Talon's neat handwriting.

'All I want for Christmas is *you*, Snowflake.'

A grin spreads across my face and I read those six words repeatedly–each time makes my heart swell that little bit more. I press the little note to my chest and sigh animatedly. I pick up the envelope and read the note on the front.

'Don't let your pride keep broken what your heart needs to fix.'

I stare down at the envelope holding the plane ticket and sigh. My pride and dignity are the only two things I really have left, and I don't plan on letting go of either for nobody.

Christmas Day

It's been two days since Talon left for Cincinnati. We're texting constantly and talking on the phone near enough every night. Eleven days to go and I'm counting down every minute till he's back.

"Yo, Rein, hello?" I'm reading a text message Talon sent me and grinning like a lovesick fool. I'm so engrossed that I don't even acknowledge the soft fluffy teddy bear hurtling towards my head till it hits me with a 'thwack'.

"Ow!" I grouse and throw Clay a glare from where I'm sitting at the end of his three-seater sofa. "What the hell, Clay?"

"What are you, tone deaf, kid? I've been calling your name the last ten minutes. Dinner is ready," he states with a shrug and tosses a dishcloth over his shoulder.

"Oh, sorry." I smirk sheepishly and stand, tucking my phone in my back pocket as I walk over to his cosy table of four. "Wow, Leila, everything looks incredible. I wish you would have let me help you."

Leila—Clay's gorgeous girlfriend–smiles warmly and waves me off while she walks over to the set the bowl of roast potatoes on the table.

"Don't be silly, girl, you're our guest. Besides, I sort of like seeing Clay in the kitchen." She giggles, throwing her boyfriend a sultry look over her shoulder, her green eyes gleaming with such love. Clay flashes her a dimple bearing grin and winks at her while he carves up the turkey. She sighs lustfully. "I'm a lucky girl."

"Are you kidding me? He's the lucky one. Boy's clearly punching." Leila smiles prettily and picks up Jackson from his crib and sits him in his highchair.

"Damn right I am." He beams proudly and kisses her cheek

before he sets down the turkey in the middle of the table. "Dinner is served. Merry Christmas everyone."

I rest my head in my hand and observe them for a couple of minutes. They're such a beautiful little family and so very happy. If they were a cartoon, you would literally see little love hearts popping around them, they're honestly that adorable. Especially little Jackson with his big green eyes, bright blond hair, and round chubby cheeks you can't help but want to bite. Ugh, he's so darn cute. Which isn't surprising really if you look at how beautiful his parents both are.

They make being in love seem so effortless, so much so that anyone looking in from the outside can't help but yearn for what they have. I know I do, and I don't even believe in love or want kids. But if I had to picture my future, I would want it to be just like this.

"Rein, red or white wine?" Clay questions, pulling me from my musings. He's holding up one bottle of merlot and one sauvignon blanc in each hand.

"Red for me, please."

My phone buzzes on the table and I see a message from Paris. I open it and smile when a selfie of her holding up a flute of champagne, standing behind a twelve-foot Christmas tree, looking stunning as always appears on my screen with the caption, 'Bored shitless, wish you were here, betch.' She's begrudgingly hauled up in the Hamptons with her family for the week. I snap a quick photo back to her of my glass of wine, and later, another one of me and Jackson to which she responded by sending me one back of her cleavage.

She's incorrigible.

After dinner, I help Clay clean up while Leila bathes Jackson and puts him down for the night. "Thank you for inviting me to join you guys. I had fun." Clay smiles and hands me a wet plate to dry.

"Of course. You think I would allow you to be all on your jack jones like some loner on Christmas Day, kid? You'll always have a place at our table," he affirms, smiling and bumping his shoulder with mine. My eyes well up and I quickly blink them away. Why am

I so emotional lately? "Rei, are you crying?" Clay questions, leaning over to look at me when he hears me sniffling.

"Pfft, no, it's the damn onions."

Clay laughs and flicks water in my face. "What onions? I don't see any onions around, you little dork. You're totally crying."

I elbow him in the ribs, and he groans. "Shut up. You breathe a word of this to anyone and I'll gut you with a butter knife. Comprender, amigo?" I warn playfully and shove my finger in his face.

Clay grins and nods, holding his soapy hands up in mock surrender. "Si, si, amiga."

"Buena. Now pass me the plate idiot." I smile when Clay hands over the plate, chuckling and shaking his head amusedly.

He's such nitwit, but I do adore him.

Adonis:
I leave you for forty-eight hours and you have a baby?'

OH, SOMEONE'S BEEN SNOOPING AROUND ON MY SOCIALS. HE'S clearly seen the picture I put on my Instagram story of Jackson and me.

Me:
Surprise! You're a daddy!

Adonis:
Oh, I'm a daddy all right. Your daddy.

Damn him. I'm all alone, soaking in the bathtub and he still manages to make me flush like some virtuous schoolgirl.

Me:
That. You. Are.

Adonis:
How is my good girl doing?

Me:
'Good. Soaking in the bath, wishing you were with me.'

My phone starts ringing, his name flashing across my screen.

'Adonis: FaceTime video'.

My stomach tightens with excitement. I take a moment to compose myself before I push the green button and his handsome face graces my screen. "Hey, you."

Talon smiles and licks his lips with a very masculine groan. "Goddamn, I miss that face."

"Just my face?" I purr impishly, and he sighs, shaking his head, pulling his bottom lip between his teeth.

"No, Snowflake, I miss every tasty inch of you," he answers, hugging his pillow and resting his chin on it. "I would give anything to be in that bathtub with you right now."

"Oh yeah?" He nods. "And what would daddy do to me if he were?" I ask, softening my tone to a breathier one. Talon's deep and throaty groan vibrates in my eardrums through the Bluetooth earphones, and it almost feels like he's right there with me.

"Oh, baby, daddy would take his sweet, sweet time making you feel so good. Teasing and pinching your nipples first. And then, I'd slowly make my way down to the gorgeous folds between your thick, juicy thighs and faintly stroke your clit in lazy circles, slowly and torturously building you up to that moment your body starts trembling and you whimper *'daddy please'* in that sexy way that you do that makes me delirious," Talon declares, watching me with hooded eyes.

An involuntary moan escapes me when my clit pulsates with need. "Mm, keep talking."

Just hearing his voice is enough to make me a hot and needy mess.

"Daddy wants to watch you come apart for him, Snowflake."

I nod, biting my bottom lip, squeezing my thighs together to aid the already unbearable ache slowly building between my legs. "Mhm."

"Show daddy what he's missing. Show him how much of a cock hungry slut you are," Talon drawls gruffly. I can't take it anymore. My free hand wanders down to the tender spot between my legs. "Stop." My eyes open and I look at him questioningly. "Set me down on the side. You're going to need both hands."

I lean up and prop up my phone on the wooden bath tray in front of me. "If my phone falls into the tub and meets its demise, you're buying me a new one," I forewarn him with a smirk, and he flashes me a sexy grin in return.

"It'll be worth every last dime," he declares, stroking his bearded jaw. "Now be a good girl, lean back and show me what is mine."

I've never been one to ever enjoy being told what to do or allowed anyone to disrespect me, but this man has unveiled a dark side to me I don't recognise. He calls me his little cum slut and I shamelessly plead for more. Never in my wildest dreams did I ever imagine I would be this girl, but here I am willingly laid bared to him at his mercy.

"You're such an exquisite sight, baby. Look at you, spread out and ready to please daddy like a good little whore." Talon groans, biting down on his lip. "Fuck, those tight, perky nipples of yours are just begging to be sucked on. Play with them and imagine it's my tongue circling and suckling on each one." The tips of my fingers circle each sensitive nipple and I roll them between my fingers.

"Oh yes…"

"That's it, baby, just like that," he hisses, watching me raptly. "Oh, that's a good girl, twist them between your thumb and forefinger so it stings just a little bit. Shit, you're making me so horny, you've got me dry humping the fucking mattress."

"Uhh, daddy, I need you *so* bad." I whimper, arching up when I tug on my nipples and the sting thrums through my body and pools deep in my groin.

Talon's breathing goes heavy, and his voice drops an octave deeper when he groans almost beseechingly. "I know. I know, baby. I need you too like you wouldn't believe," he affirms. "Sit up on the edge of the bath and spread your legs wider, show me that delectable pussy."

I grip the side of the tub and carefully lift myself up and out, perching my bum on the tiled ledge. I place one leg on either side, exposing myself to him completely. Talon curses under his breath, his Adam's apple rising and falling in his throat when he swallows thickly. Even through the phone, his hungry gaze and the way he's ravenously licking his full lips incites an inferno within me. I feel my face catch fire under his intent stare. "I know you hate to hear this, but you, Snowflake, truly are the epitome of perfection," he tells me solemnly. It's so easy to believe and accept his words as true when he's looking at me like I'm some divine creation, worthy of his admiration.

"It's not so bad hearing it from you, Professor," I admit, sultrily grazing my fingertips up and over the damp flesh of my inner thighs.

"You're seriously making me consider cutting this visit short and flying back home to you." I smile and brush my fingers around the entrance of my pussy. "You're making daddy and his big cock real hungry, baby." I slide two fingers into my pussy and gasp audibly when a surge of pleasure flows down my spine.

"Talon."

"That's a good girl, fuck those fingers into that tight cunt for daddy," he moans in response. My head falls back and my eyes close when I use my thumb and play with my clit. "Tsk tsk, no, you keep those gorgeous eyes on me. I want you to stare into my fucking soul when you come for me." I do as I'm told and force my eyes open to look at him. "That's my good girl. Now tease that sweet spot for me. I want to see those thighs shake, but don't you dare come."

I twist and curve my fingers, and using a firm yet deep pressure,

I stroke my G-spot in a rhythmic motion, which causes my body to judder and my hips to instinctively rock back and forth, slowly increasing friction while riding my fingers when I hit that soul shattering spot.

"That feel good?"

"Yes, so, so good." I whimper, biting down hard on my lip to keep from screaming when I feel that all too familiar heat building with each intense thrust of my fingers.

"Oh, I bet it does," Talon whispers. "I want you to slowly slide your fingers out and suck them clean for me."

"Talon, please, I'm so close," I lament in displeasure. I'm right there, lingering on the cusp of sweet release, just a couple more thrusts and I'll take a deep dive into that heavenly abyss.

"Rein." The manner of which my name rolls off his tongue combined with the surly warning laced in his tone sends a tremor through me. And despite the strong urge to be disobedient and finish, I begrudgingly withdraw my hand and lift my fingers to my mouth to suck them clean with a throaty moan. "Atta girl, just like that, you lap up every last drop of your honey for daddy like the starved, naughty little slut that you are." Talon growls lowly, like a feral animal that is ready to pounce and devour its prey. I keep my eyes on him as I pull my fingers out of my mouth with a loud 'pop'.

"Mm, tastes so good."

Talon nods, licking his lips. "Yes, that you do, and the instant I get back, I fully intend to crawl between your legs and have a lengthy, impassioned make-out session with that delectable cunt," he coincides with a devilish smirk.

"But for now… I want you to turn that faucet on, spread your legs wide for me and sit under it…"

Ho-ly *shit*.

Chapter 12
Talon

POISON IVY - HEMI MOORE

"Oh my... Talon, shit, shit! I can't..."

"Go ahead, Snowflake, come and lose the bet." I pant, squeezing the base of my cock with my thumb and index finger.

"Christ." Rein whimpers, breathless, throwing her head back when I turn the dial up on the phone and the vibrations start up again, causing her body to arch up. Those long slender fingers fist the bed covers and she sinks her teeth into her lower lip so hard I'm sure she's drawn blood.

"Denial is such sweet torture, and it looks so fucking good on you, Snowflake."

"Oh shit, yes, yes, yes, I'm so close," she pleads helplessly, locked between heaven and hell as I continue to edge her, each time making her believe she will be rewarded with that much desired orgasm she's been denying herself the last hour out of sheer obstinacy.

We made a bet to see who has the control to edge the longest without coming. It's coming up to almost a week since I've been away and I'm going out of my mind missing Rein both sexually and emotionally. She's on my mind constantly, in everything I do, and it's honestly jarring.

Three whole years I managed to go without sex, and it didn't faze me at all. Not one bit. One taste of Rein and I've become an out-of-control sexual deviant. Though, I can't deny, out of the sea of students, Rein has always been the one that stood out, always the one I most secretly treasured. A fantasy tucked neatly away in the depths of my mind. A gentle ebbing flame of lust gradually flourished into something more tangible. Now I can't get enough.

All it takes is a fleeting thought, at any time of the day, and my cock springs up and refuses to go down until I eventually cave and beat the beast into submission.

I'm a grown man and I often pride myself for the level of control I have—or did have before I met her. But now, I can't go a lousy day.

I've reached my limit. Seven days is just one too many without her, and as much as I love my folks, I need to go home to my girl.

My girl.

Oh, fuck me dead. When did I become such a sappy bastard?

A low melodic moan emanates from Rein, pulling my attention right back to her again. She's sprawled out on the light grey bedsheets, gripping the pillow above her head with a death grip, her chest rising and falling with every jagged breath. Those sinfully curvaceous hips rock back and forth against the vibrator attached to her pale blue, lace panties. I've never seen a more gorgeous sight; her body is glowing with a sheen layer of perspiration.

I watch on with intent and such admiration as her thighs start to shudder and her mouth hangs open with a silent scream.

God almighty, I want to be with her. I want to taste her and smell her arousal. Watching her through the screen on my phone is driving me wild. Especially that growing wet patch on the bed where she's practically oozing luscious pussy juice I'd give my left nut to be drinking right about now.

"Come on, baby, edge with me." I moan, stroking my cock. Rein opens her eyes and looks over at me, watching me with fiery eyes that spear right through me. "Don't you dare look away, or take your eyes off me. I want you to watch me while I stroke my cock for you. Good girl. I know you love to watch. You love seeing how hard my cock gets for you, don't you?" Unable to utter a word, she nods, sucking on her bottom lip. "Look what you're doing to me." I pant, fingering the beads of pre-cum gathered on the tip and slowly leaking down my throbbing shaft.

"Suck it off," she whispers in-between breaths. "Show me how good you taste."

I keep my eyes on her and bring my thumb–which is saturated with my pre-cum–to my mouth and suck it off. "Oh God, I crave the taste of you so much. Please, daddy, come home and fuck me."

Oh, I'm coming, baby. I'll be home and between those intoxicating legs real soon.

Her pleading alone sends me hurling towards the brink of release, but I squeeze my cock again and the urge to erupt ebbs away. With a groan, I stroke the sensitive crown of my cock and it jumps and pulses with need upon contact. My balls are so tight and full from edging for so long, its unbearable but fuck it's worth it. "You look so fucking delicious, so wet for daddy. I want to just hold those legs open and suck that clit until you shower me with your come."

"Oh, fucking hell, Talon. You're killing me." Rein moans as she lingers on the brink but manages to stop herself just in time before she goes over and whimpers in frustration.

"You can end this whenever you want, just give in and come for me, baby." My voice is heavy with lust while my fingers stroke up the shaft and circle the thick overly sensitive tip that throbs and causes me to moan out load as I fight to hold back the waves of pleasure that threaten to consume me.

"No, you come first."

"Fuck no. You come first…" I growl, thrusting my cock into my fist. "Always," I add with a harsh whisper when my balls tighten and that all-consuming heat starts to build through my body, driving up through the base of my cock and winding through every inch. "Oh fuck, fuck, I'm close, so fucking close. Ah, just one touch and I'll go over, Jesus fucking Christ."

Rein pants as her hips buck up and she rocks them almost fiercely against the toy. "Oh *shit, shit,* Talon, I can't...I can't hold back anymore..."

"That's right, baby, don't stop." I pant. "Edge for me. That's a good girl, ride it out, baby, ride it for daddy just like that. God, you're so goddamn beautiful, you're going to make me come."

"Come with me, daddy, please, come with me," Rein cries out, and I lose it. Between the hypnotizingly sensual way she's moving those hips and the noises she's making, my focus and control lapse fleetingly and it's too late.

"Oh fuck... Oh, I'm gonna come, I'm coming. Ah, Rein!" My limbs stiffen, and for a blissful moment, I lose all cognitive function. I forget how to breathe, how to think as I soar towards the pinnacle of my orgasm. The only things I can focus on are watching Rein come with me and the blinding pleasure firing through me, making my body convulse and shudder while I spill thick rope after thick rope of my cum all over my stomach and chest.

My body goes limp, and I collapse on the bed, panting to catch my breath. Hands down, one of the most intense and gratifying orgasms I've ever had. I felt every ripple of pleasure in my goddamn soul.

"I win." Rein pants, laying on top her bed in a heap of arms and legs, looking all wild and sexy in her post orgasmic state.

"Shit, Snowflake, you've fucking ruined me." Rein peels her eyes open and looks at me through the phone screen, her cheeks crimson, her face aglow with perspiration.

"Holy shit, that was intense. Remind me to never make a wager with you again," Rein states, licking her full lips and rolling onto her side to pick up the phone where she had it propped up on the bedside table.

I laugh and look down at the mess I've made all over myself. "Best bet I've ever lost."

Rein smiles lazily. "Mm, I told you I had more perseverance than you."

"You're not going to let me live this down now, are you?"

Rein adorably pretends to mull over it for a second before she shakes her head. "Nope, I think I'll hold onto this victory for as long as possible, Professor." My eyes lower to the shimmering necklace around her neck. The necklace I bought her for Christmas. "I like seeing that necklace on you."

Rein looks down at it and brushes her finger over the crystal snowflake attached to the white gold chain. "I really like it too, especially with you being so far away, it's comforting having something from you so close to me."

"Rein Valdez, are you getting sentimental on me?" I tease.

Up goes that sexy brow. "Are you really going to sit there and tell me you've not got the cufflinks I gifted you nearby?" she questions eloquently and grins when my eyes flit over to the black box sitting on the bedside table. "You're so busted, Professor."

"Okay, fine, I'll admit that your exuberant cheesiness may be rubbing off on me a little bit. And I may also like the fact that we unknowingly bought each other similar gifts. Fucking sue me." I completely forgot she bought me a gift. Not until she told me to check the front zipper of my bag on Christmas day. I've never been so elated to open a gift in my life. We agreed to open our gifts together later that evening on a video call. When we saw what the other had bought, we sat in silence for a second, just staring at the boxes in our hands in pure astonishment before looking up at one another and grinning. Rein bought me a pair of silver *snowflake* cufflinks.

After all, great minds tend to think alike, but lovers think as one, and that whole encounter is a perfect example of that conception and how well-suited Rein and I really are for one another.

Rein emits a cute little snort with her laugh. She covers her face with her hand in sheer embarrassment while I crack up laughing. "What the hell? Did you just snort?"

"No!" she denies profusely between peals of laughter.

"Yes, you did, you adorable little dork. Don't you try and deny it, I heard it, I heard it all," I tease her with a chuckle. Rein shakes her head, her reply muffled by her hand covering her face.

"Oh my God, shut up, I did not snort."

"And just like that, Sexy Saxton is back in the game ladies and gentlemen. Now we both have things to hold over each other," I state with a wicked grin and wag my brows at her while she stares at me, looking less than pleased.

"I really hate you."

"Sorry, what did you say?" I tuck my fingers behind my ear and narrow my eyes. "I couldn't hear you through the snorting," I reply cheekily. Rein's desperately trying her best to keep a straight face, but the corner of her lip is twitching.

"Might I remind you that you're an academic, Talon Saxton."

"This may come as a shock to you, Snowflake, but we academics are permitted to have a persona off school grounds, you know?"

Rein rolls her eyes good naturedly. "Had someone told me that I would hear the illustrious Professor Talon Saxton crack a joke, I would have booked them an appointment to have their head examined."

I smirk. "Had someone told me that I would be fucking my student, I would have told them to join in at that examination, yet here we are at one in the morning, a hot naked mess after a rather passionate phone sex session."

A pretty flush spreads from Rein's cheeks, slowly making its way down to her slender neck and across her chest at my response. "Touché, Professor."

I flash her my signature panty melting grin and she bites her lip and grins back sultrily before she sits upright. "Any regrets?"

My smile matches Rein's. I don't hesitate. I tuck my right hand behind my head and keep my eyes on her. "My only regret is not being there with you right now."

"Well, only eleven thousand, five hundred and twenty minutes till you're back." Rein sighs.

My brows rise swiftly, and I'm sure they disappear into my hairline as I stare back at her, stunned. "That's... incredibly precise."

Rein shrugs and smiles tenderly before climbing off the bed. "Tell me about it. That's how desperately I want to see you, Professor. You've got me counting down minutes."

"I'll be damn sure to make up for the twenty thousand, one hundred and sixty minutes that I've been gone when I get back, Snowflake."

Rein laughs, and I find myself soaking up the sound. "I'll be holding you to that promise."

"You better," I reply with a groan when I stretch my body out on top of my bed. "What are your plans for tomorrow night?"

"Uhm..." Rein sets me down on the counter by the sink in the ensuite bathroom while she pulls on an over-sized plain black T-shirt, covering her naked body from my appreciative eyes. Damn, I was thoroughly enjoying the view of her full and bare tits bouncing enticingly with every movement. I cringe inwardly at how aberrant that sounded, but God, can you blame me? Just look at her. "There's this New Year's Eve masquerade bash at Aura that Paris is dragging me too. I really don't want to go," she explains with a roll of her eyes. "And I was happy to be working, but she begged Clay relentlessly to cover me so I could have the night off. Paris can be annoyingly persistent when she wants to be, so now, I've got no choice but to go."

Ah, that's right, JT had been going on and on about this party when I spoke to him the other night. Sounds like it might be a good night. "What about you?"

"Nothing exciting, just dinner and drinks with family and some old friends."

Rein smiles prettily and nods in understanding. "Don't overexert yourself now, old man," she utters with a smirk and pushes the toothbrush between her luscious lips.

"I don't even have the privilege to be offended, because compared to you, I am old." Rein's brows draw together and she shakes her head while she brushes her teeth. "Don't be absurd. You're twenty-eight. In what universe is that considered old?"

"Mine," I tell her pointedly as I crawl off the bed towards my own bathroom. As lazy as I'm feeling, I made a real mess over myself–the spunk is starting to dry on my skin and I can't sit in it any longer. "You want to tell that to the grey hair I found in my beard the other day?" I grumble, rubbing a hand over the overgrown stubble on my cheek.

Hm, perhaps I should go have a shave when I head back tomorrow, I muse while I watch Rein rinse out her mouth and pat it dry with a towel as I make my way over to my own bathroom.

"My Abuela says every grey hair tells a story. Having grey hair doesn't make you old, it makes you wise in the ways of the world," she explains amiably and lowers her eyes to look down at the phone briefly. "And sexier," she adds with a wink.

With an amused chuckle, I prop my phone up against the mirror on the counter by the sink and place my hands flat down on the surface before I lower my head to look down at her. "Sexier, huh? I suppose that means you're into the whole silver fox thing… Another fantasy of yours, perhaps?"

Rein says nothing and only smiles widely, evincing her pearly white teeth.

Interesting. I'm going to take her silence as a yes then.

Chapter 13
Rein

UMBERELLA - RHIANNA

NEW YEAR'S EVE.

"Betch, we're going to get white girl trashed tonight." I look at Paris through the mirror in the bathroom while I curl my hair with the wand and shake my head.

"Uh, P, I assure you, I am absolutely not getting trashed tonight."

Paris applies swipes of her blush across her cheek and looks at me as though I've sprouted a second head. "Don't be a snore, it's new year's, Rei Rei."

"Nah uh, no way, there was no mention of getting trashed when you begged me to come out tonight. P, you promised me a fun night out that doesn't wind up with me having my head buried in the toilet, chucking my guts up."

Paris sniggers. "Oh, come on, Rei, step out of dullsville and live a little will you, please? It's New Year's Eve, it's been a lousy year, so let's start the new one on a positive note. Get fucking shitfaced, kiss some strangers and possibly get railed till you can't walk straight in a dark corner of the club. The night is ours, the possibilities are endless, bitch tits." I almost burn my neck with the damn curling wand when I break out into peals of laughter.

"Honestly, how you and I became best friends, I'll never know, P. We're literally chalk and cheese," I say, wrapping the final piece of my hair onto the wand. Paris grins and brushes her fingers through her freshly straightened hair.

"Honey, God himself took one look at your lacklustre life and thought to himself, nah, I missed some pizzazz when I created this betch, so he put me in your life to add some spice, senorita," she explains with a giggle.

Laughing, I pick up one of my beauty blenders and throw it at her, which to my dismay, she skilfully dodges. "I promise you, P, my life is anything but dull. Some of us are actually capable of having fun without drinking ourselves into a drunken stupor, you promiscuous tart," I fire back playfully, and she beams back at me proudly while pouring us a glass of champagne. We've been friends long enough to not get offended by things we say to each other, because it's never meant in a malicious manner. This is just our way of affectionately bantering with one another. I love the girl dearly and couldn't care less to whom or how many guys or girls she's slept with.

"What can I say... my coochie and I take great pleasure in spreading joy," Paris declares cheekily with a wink and holds out the flute of champagne to me. "Besides, why stick to plain vanilla when there are so many different and exotic flavours out there to taste and appreciate?"

The woman has a point.

"I tried the whole one-night stand thing, and it did not bode well for me, so all the more power to you, bitch tits."

"Nah uh. This is going to be our year. We are going to make twenty-twenty-two our bitch, sugar tits."

"Now that, I'll drink to."

"Salud!" we sing in unison and clink our glasses before we down our glasses of champagne like the refined young women we are.

We didn't get to Aura till a quarter after nine o'clock. Paris arranged a town car to pick us up and drive us to the club. "Stop squirming, you look smokin' hot, Rei Rei," Paris assures me when I uneasily tug the hem down to the sheer black mini dress Paris convinced me to wear. Probably the most risqué outfit I've ever worn out in public. My entire body—save for my tits and half my bum cheeks—are exposed, covered only by a thin sheer mesh. It's a hot outfit, but I'm just not sure I have the body to pull it off. I feel practically naked and like everyone is looking at me.

"I feel like everyone is looking at me," I tell her warily as we link arms and walk towards the entrance of the club.

"You're damn right they're looking at you. You look to die for, and that dress is made to fit your curves, bestie, so flaunt what your mama gave you, and by the end of the night, you're going to have a long line of guys begging to kiss you."

"I don't want to kiss other guys. I want to kiss *my guy* who is currently in another state right now."

Paris stops and looks at me questioningly. "Wait a minute, I thought you said this thing between you and your mystery guy was nothing but sex?"

I don't mean to, but I hesitate, and like a blood hound, she picks up on it instantly. "I mean, it is, but that doesn't mean I have to go around snogging random guys."

I couldn't see much of her face because her white mask is covering most of it, but Paris narrows her hazel eyes at me in scrutiny. "That sounds an awful lot like monogamy, Rei," she asserts, pulling me to the side when a couple try passing by us. "You really like this guy, don't you?"

I wince and readjust the black lace mask veiling my eyes. "I really don't know, P, it's all very... *complicated.*"

"Nothing is ever complicated, *people* complicate things," Paris replies as we continue to walk through the crowd towards the entrance. "You've always been a go-getter, Rei, that's one of the many traits I admire the most about you. If you like this guy, be upfront and tell him, what's the worst that could happen? You're still screwing the guy, so clearly he likes you or he would have been gotten bored by now."

"I know he likes me; he's told me that."

"Well, there you go. What are you worrying about then?"

I sigh and shake my head, looking over at the long line of people queuing to get into the club. I can already feel the bass of the music playing inside, vibrating through the floor as we near the VIP entrance. "I don't really know much about him. Every time the conversation about his past or anything personal comes up, he closes off on me."

"I mean, that does sound like a red flag, but I wouldn't worry about it too much. Men generally take longer than women to feel comfortable enough to share things. Especially if he thinks it's just a fling."

'Rein, this thing between us has an expiration date.'

Talon's words from our argument a week ago creeps back in my mind, and I nod distantly. "Yeah, I suppose that could be it." God, why can't I shake this feeling that he's keeping something from me?

Paris stops just before we reach the two burly security guards at the door and takes hold of my shoulders. "Hey, tonight is ours, we're going to tear shit up, and you, Chica, are not going to waste a second of it stewing over a man. Are you with me?"

I smile and nod. "Yes, I'm with you."

"That's my betch." She grins. "You look glorious, darling," she drawls, embellishing her already horrifying British accent while she fixes my hair.

"As do you, mon cheri." We lace our hands and make our way over to the security guards.

"Hey, big D," Paris purrs as she nears the burlier one of the two. The immediate smile that spreads across his handsome face indicates he's well acquainted with her.

"Hey, beautiful," he responds, giving Paris the once over and licking his lips appreciatively. No one can blame him, my bestie is looking like every man's wet dream in that nude Christian Dior, glitter mini dress. "How is it you manage to get hotter every time I see you, Paris Dalton?"

Paris titters when his large hand takes hers and he brushes a kiss over her knuckles. "Dennis, you very well know that flattery will get you everywhere. But a gentleman never asks, and a lady never tells," she teases with a flirty wink. I stand idly while they practically fuck each other with their eyes. "Oh, this is my best friend, Rein Valdez. Rei, this is Dennis, he's the head of security at Aura." Oh, I was starting to wonder if she forgot that I'm standing right beside her. I smile and give him a little wave when he finally manages to tear his eyes away from Paris.

Dennis' eyes roam down the length of me, and he smiles. Dennis is big enough to crush every bone in my body with a one arm hug, and I find myself wondering how on earth Paris kept up with this titan of a man with her small frame. Though, there seems to be something kind behind those meltingly soft, chocolate brown eyes. "Nice to meet you, sweetheart."

"Likewise."

"Have a good night, ladies." Paris gives Dennis' beefy arm a squeeze when he opens the red rope for us to enter. Their eyes remain interlocked until she passes by. Damn, the sexual tension between them is so palpable it makes me miss Talon terribly. I check my phone screen again for the millionth time in the space of an hour.

No calls or messages.

While Paris and I check in our jackets and handbags, I keep my phone with me. A part of me is wondering and secretly hoping he'll call or even text me at midnight. I suppose this will once and for all establish how into me he really is.

"So, Big D?" I probe with a knowing smirk.

Paris smiles sheepishly, her eyes flitting over to the entrance at the mention of his name. "Betch, don't look at me like that, it was just a random hook up a few weeks ago," Paris shouts over the music before she pulls me towards the staircase up to the VIP floor.

"What? I'm not judging. I'm just surprised, he's not exactly your usual type. You're into pretty boys, not muscular, bodybuilder types." Paris shrugs.

"I know, but I was drunk and horny, he was just there and up for a wild night. I have no regrets, that man almost fucked me into a coma. I couldn't walk straight the next day." She giggles, tossing her hair over her shoulder. I know that feeling. "I need a drink, or ten. Let's do shots! Come on!"

I groan and follow her through the swarm of people towards the crowded bar. While we wait at the bar, my eyes roam the overflowing club. The room is filled with a beautiful array of dresses and smartly dressed men in suits and tuxedos. Everywhere I look, I see party goers in different types of masks from lace to venetian– concealing their faces. While we wait to get some drinks, I sway along to the music. "Let's take a photo for the gram!" Paris shouts over the music and pulls me towards her and holds the camera up, snapping a couple of photos of us.

After about ten minutes, Paris finally manages to get the attention of one of the bar staff to order a drink. "Ariel, hey," she greets the redhead behind the bar with a sugary smile. I smirk when I hear her name. It's very fitting, what with the bright fire truck red hair and bright blue eyes. She almost looks like a tattooed, rebel version of Ariel from the little mermaid.

Ariel walks over to us, smiling. I admire the full sleeve tattoo down her arm of roses, the face of an attractive older woman, and various tribal designs. "Hey, babe, it's been a minute since you showed your pretty face up in here," Ariel shouts over the music with a grin, shaking the cocktail shaker and displaying a deep dimple on her left cheek.

"I know, I've been hauled up in the Hampton's playing the dutiful daughter with the folks over Christmas," Paris replies with a roll of her eyes.

Ariel winces and pours the luminous blue liquid into a martini glass. "Yowch, sounds harrowingly tedious. Let me ease your pain, what's your poison tonight, gorgeous? The usual?"

Paris nods and pulls me to stand beside her. "Hit us with two red-headed sluts followed by screaming orgasms and keep 'em coming, baby." I look between Paris and Ariel who are exchanging meaningful glances.

"You got it, hun."

Paris' eyes follow Ariel as she walks off to prepare our drinks. I observe them exchange flirty glances across the bar. When she turns to look at me, her smile grows–noticing my quizzical look. "What?"

"Is there anyone in this club you haven't shagged?"

Paris throws her head back and laughs heartily. "Yeah, that hottie over there. He's married. A big bummer because I bet he can fuck like a rockstar. Also, doesn't he remind you of Clay?" I look over at the cute bartender shaking up cocktails like Tom Cruise from the movie *'Cocktail'* and nod. I do see a resemblance, but Clay is far better looking.

"Yeah, he sort of does, actually."

"Ladies, your drinks." Ariel comes back with our cocktails and sets them on the bar. I stare down at them and groan. Cocktails are lethal for me, they taste like juice going down, and before you know it, you're shit-faced and unable to stand straight. "On the house," she adds with a wink and leans over the bar towards Paris. "Come find me at midnight."

Paris smiles, her cheeks flushing under her mask. "I can't. I'm with my girl tonight, but I'll definitely call you," she replies, brushing a slender finger along Ariel's arm.

"Look forward to it." Ariel walks off to serve another customer. We take our drinks and make our way through to the VIP section–based on the second floor.

"You are so going to find her at midnight," I assert with a snort, taking a long sip of my cocktail. Oh, very fruity with a hint of tequila.

Yum.

"Absolutely not. I told you tonight is about us, no hook ups," Paris states with a shake of her head and takes a sip of her drink also.

"Bitch, please, you think I don't know you? You're itching to go and see her. Don't worry about me, go do your thing and get your midnight kiss. At least one of us will see the new year in, in the right way."

Paris smiles into her glass and shakes her head. "Or I could just kiss you?" she suggests impishly, and I almost choke on the mouthful of cocktail mid-sip.

Coughing and sputtering, I shake my head while she cackles. Evil betch. "That's a hell of an offer, but I think I'll pass, sugar tits. You're practically a sister to me, and incest isn't my thing."

"Boo, you whore."

"Shut up and swallow your orgasm, bitch."

FIFTEEN MINUTES TO MIDNIGHT, I'VE HAD ABOUT SIX DIFFERENT cocktails, each one with an obscener name than the last. I've hit my limit, one more sip of any alcohol and I'll go from happy and tipsy to full-on trashed. Those last two pussy lickers made me my stomach lurch threateningly, but I managed to keep it down. I'm not a lover of creamy cocktails.

My feet are aching in these goddamn five-inch heels from dancing the past two and a half hours, but I'm having such a great time with Paris. It's been good while since we've both had this much fun together on a night out.

"Five minutes to countdown!" The DJ announces and plays 'Umbrella' by Rhianna. Paris throws her hands in the air and almost topples over.

"Aw, hell yes! This is our jam, bitch tits!" she shouts over the music and throws her arms around my neck. We sing along to the lyrics at the top of our lungs. "Love you forever, bitch tits!"

"One minute!"

"Love you always, sugar tits!" I hug her tight. "Go find your girl."

"Rei, no!"

I nod and cup her beautiful sweaty face with my hands. "Yes! Go, right now and get the soul kissed out of your skanky self."

"Rei, are you sure? What about you?" Paris pouts, and I nod, smiling reassuringly.

"Thirty seconds."

"Absolutely, I'm good here. Go, betch, go." I usher her and she kisses my cheek and hurries off into the crowd towards the bar to find Ariel. With a sigh, I look down at my phone, and when I see no messages or missed calls from Talon, my heart sinks deep into my gut with dejection. The music changes to a chiming bell, similar to Big Ben back home, while people around me excitedly countdown.

"Are you ready? Here we go!"

"Three!"

In a sea of couples, there I stand, all alone, staring down at my phone and hoping for a call or a text I know won't come.

"Two!"

Electric fireworks light up the club around the dance floor at the final stroke to midnight.

"One!"

I gasp out loud when I feel a warm yet firm grip on my arm upper arm. I'm swiftly spun around and drawn into a strong frame. My head's still in the midst of processing when a pair of soft lips claim mine. I immediately stiffen and place my hands on the person's chest, ready to shove them away, when something stops me.

Actually, I say something, but it's a number of things. First, the aftershave. Second, the familiar sense of comfort that consumes me the moment his strong arms wrap around me. And thirdly, the kiss. I'd recognise that kiss if I were blind and braindead. I'm very well acquainted with these lips. This kiss is familiar, too familiar.

Talon.

My body relaxes and the butterflies in my belly go wild as elation fills me from the tips of my toes all the way to the top of my head while our lips move together in a habitual yet feverish kiss.

"Happy New Year!"

The crowd erupts around us, and my boozed-up brain picks up the sound of *'Auld Lang Syne'* playing in the background, but neither Talon nor I are fazed or have any desire to stop kissing—least until our lungs protest with lack of oxygen. "Talon." I pant.

Talon presses his forehead to mine and smiles handsomely. "Happy New Year, Snowflake. Daddy's home."

Chapter 14
Talon

...FUCK- JHONNY RAIN

I CAN'T TELL you how good it felt to kiss her again. It's only been seven days, but it felt like a lifetime had passed since I last tasted her lips.

"What on earth are you doing here?" she questions with a soft laugh. "I thought you said you were spending New Year's with your family and friends?"

"And I fully intended to, but honestly, I've just been itching to get back since I left. I couldn't enjoy my time away when my mind was constantly here… with you," I reply earnestly.

Rein's smile is wide. Even through the mask veiling her pretty face and the dim lighting of the club, I can see her eyes glittering beautifully. She suddenly gasps, her eyes scanning the club. "Shit, Paris is here with me. What if she recognises you?"

"That's the beauty of a masquerade bash, Snowflake. Anonymity." Rein laughs and snakes her arms around my neck and takes a step closer till our bodies are flush against one another.

"I wouldn't underestimate Paris if I were you. She's more

perceptive than she lets on. She can pick out a needle from a haystack."

"Shall we get out of here then?" I groan, dragging my nose down the length of her elegant neck. Rein's eyes close and her head falls back to give me more room to feather kisses down to her collarbone.

"While I would love to, I can't. Not tonight." Frowning, I draw back a little and look down at her questioningly. "I'm here with Paris and we made a promise that tonight will be ours. I've barely spent time with her lately as it is. I can't just up and ditch her. Girl code, hoes before bros and all that," she states, her tone remorseful.

I respond with an understanding smile and cup her face with my hands. "That's fair enough. May I at least steal you away for a little bit then?" I suggest with a side smirk.

Rein bites her bottom lip and considers my request. "I might be persuaded."

"Well then, Miss Valdez, come with me and I'll be happy to illustrate my power of persuasion." I lift her hand to my lips and kiss her knuckles, my eyes never leaving hers.

"Lead the way, Professor."

I lace my hand with hers and guide her through the large crowd of people dancing and towards the staircase leading up to the office on the third floor. I'm sure Craig won't mind me using his office for a couple of minutes. In fact, if I know my mate, he'll absolutely encourage it.

"Where are you taking me?" Rein questions as we step into the elevator, and she watches me push the code in for the third floor.

"Someplace private where we'll be away from prying eyes." Rein takes a step towards me, her eyes sweeping over the length of me.

"Tell me, Professor..." Rein purrs, running her index finger down and over my chest while she gazes up at me through her lashes. "I'm curious how you managed to find me within the sea of people in this club, especially with a mask on."

My right arm curls around her small waist and I tug her up, locking her body against mine. "You are not a woman that's easy to overlook, Snowflake. I'm well conversant with every dip and curve of your body. You also have an assertive presence that is compelling. Especially dressed in an outfit that leaves very little to the imagination," I drawl, ghosting my lips over hers as I speak to her in a low gruff tone. "I've been watching you from afar. Biding my time, envisioning all the things I'm going to do to you, all the while fighting off the feral urge to walk over and knock the teeth out of every man whose gaze lingered on you for longer than necessary," I affirm, lifting her mask, revealing her beautiful face.

"What happened to you not being a neanderthal, Professor? I thought you didn't believe in imposing upon a woman?" she questions, tongue-in cheek, raising a brow in an inquisitive manner.

"Need I remind you, Miss Valdez, that you *pleaded* to know what it feels like to be mine. Well, I'm a man that looks after what's his, and you, baby, solely belong to me and me alone," I answer solemnly while walking her backwards out of the elevator that opens directly into the spacious office.

"I have absolutely no objections to that, Professor."

"That's good to hear, because we'd have a real big problem if you did."

Rein blinks up at me and skims her tongue along her bottom lip, forcing my eyes down to watch her do so. I'm going to devour that mouth of hers. "Right now, all I can think about is pressing you up against that glass over-looking the entire club and showing each and every person down there how good you look when you come for daddy."

Rein breaks away from me, her eyes scanning the office nervously. "Talon, whose office is this? Won't we get into trouble if we get caught?" she questions hesitantly.

My feet follow her, and I smirk challengingly. "Are you fearful of a little danger, Snowflake?"

"It's a hell of a risk to take considering our situation, don't you think?" Rein's back meets the glass pane of the window, and she sucks in a short breath. I tug her lace mask back down over her eyes and brush my fingers along her jawline.

"Who in this club will know who we are if we keep our masks on the entire time?"

Rein say's nothing and only stares up at me contemplatively, her lower lip clasped between her teeth. Despite her hesitancy, the wayward girl inside her is intrigued. "What do you say?" I ask, brushing my fingers up the silky, caramel flesh of her inner thigh. The soft moan and impish smile on her face is all the consent that I need. "Turn." She obeys and spins to face the window. I lift both her arms over her head and place them against the glass. "Keep your hands there, understand?"

"Yes."

"Good girl." I nip at the flesh just behind her ear and she moans for me softly. "Spread your legs for me."

The heat emitting from between her legs makes my head whirl. I just know the moment I glide my fingers through her folds they're going to be soaked with her arousal. "You're going to show every person watching on from down below how good it feels to ride and come all over my fingers," I growl in her ear as I slip my hand through the elastic of her skimpy brief bottoms. I couldn't tell if they were underwear or bikini bottoms. If I'm honest, and in this moment, I couldn't give a fuck. "I want every man down there sporting a rock hard stiffy, wishing they were the one up here with you."

"Yes, daddy." Rein sighs when my fingers glide through her slick folds. Fuck, I was right—she's so damn wet.

First, I start by teasing her clit, stroking her swollen pearl with slow torturous circles. "I love that squelching sound your cunt makes when you're hungry for me."

Rein's head lulls back. "I love the way you play with my cunt. Ah, yes, right there."

"You like it right here?" I groan in her ear, and she nods, her thighs juddering with each stroke of my fingers. "Does that feel good, baby?"

"Oh, daddy, yes, it feels *so good*." She whimpers, rocking and rolling her hips, rubbing herself against my fingers for more friction. A swell of pleasure surges through me, and my cock pulses impatiently, reminding me once again of my continual desire for her when her juicy bum gyrates against me. Rein's adorable grunt of displeasure when my fingers abandon her clit pleases me. I smile, licking the shell of her ear, my fingers circling the entrance of her pussy.

I give her pussy a slap and Rein draws in a quick breath, her hips thrusting up. "That's a good girl, Snowflake."

Rein looks back at me over her shoulder, no words are spoken–nor is it needed. Those exquisite eyes are telling me exactly what she needs, and I eagerly abide. Feeding one long digit into her snug cunt, which insatiably swallows it up, her walls clench around my middle finger like a vise. "Want another?"

Rein nods, wetting her lips. "Yes."

My index finger joins, and there's no way I could suppress the groan that escapes me when she flutters around my fingers when I push them knuckle deep and she starts sensually rocking her hips back and forth, riding them.

"Oh, daddy, fuck me."

Christ, baby, I plan to. I'm going to fuck the ever-living soul right out of you. My eyes scan the club to see if anyone has noticed us yet. I can't see anyone watching, but it won't be long before we catch someone's attention. My hand is covering Rein's modesty so she's not exposed to the entire club, but anyone looking can clearly see I'm fingering her. Particularly, with the way her lips are parted, her head thrown back against my chest, and the very carnal movement of her hips.

She's a goddamn glorious sight indeed.

When my thumb finds her clit and we fall into a rhythm, it doesn't take her very long to come. "Ay dios mio, papi. Don't stop, please, please, you're going to make me come."

"I know. I can feel you getting tighter. Your pussy is squeezing my fingers like it wants to break them off entirely." I moan and my free hand grips her jaw. I turn her face to mine so I can devour that mouth of hers. Rein responds to the kiss with equal fervour. "That's a good girl. Let's give them something to be envious about... come undone for daddy, Snowflake." My fingers stroke her G-spot with more pressure, pushing her closer and closer to the precipice of release. Her body starts to quiver, and her breathing hastens when she skyrockets towards the pinnacle of her orgasm. I feel her girl cum dripping down from my fingers towards my wrist with every deep thrust.

"Shit, oh, I'm coming... fuck, Talon, I'm coming!"

The pleasure laced in her tone when she screams my name resonates right through me. "Yes, you are. Give it to me, don't hold back. I've got you, baby."

With every squeeze and contraction of her walls around my fingers, my arousal intensifies tenfold. My dick pulses and strains zealously against the zipper of my black slacks with every upsurge of her orgasm. My fingers remain buried deep inside her pussy while she slowly rocks against them, riding out those last few seconds of her climax.

Rein collapses against me with a breathy moan, her face flushed, panting to catch her breath. My lips brush a kiss on her warm and clammy temple. "You did so good, Snowflake. Look at our audience," I murmur in her ear. Rein's eyes open and she looks down to see the large group of drunken patrons watching us. Two of them being her best friend, Paris, and my best friend, JT, both looking equally as stunned as each other.

"Shit." Rein quickly straightens and goes to pull my hand away from between her legs. "Talon, that's a lot of people. Oh, my goodness... are they recording us?"

I keep her against me and slowly slide my fingers out of her pussy. "Mhm, it seems they are."

Rein twists her head to look up at me, eyes wide and fretful. "Aren't you worried?"

"Do I look worried?" Her panic-stricken eyes scan my face before she slowly shakes her head. "Ninety-eight percent of these people we'll never see again, and besides that, our faces are covered, the club is dark, and the glass is lightly tinted, so they can't identify us from all the way up here," I clarify and almost instantly feel her body relax.

Holding her gaze, I lift the two fingers that were inside her and bring them to my mouth, sucking them clean with a throaty groan. Rein watches raptly, and when I pull them out, she curls a finger around the collar of my shirt and draws my mouth to hers, tasing herself with a hot and hungry kiss.

That's my girl.

I LOVE MY JOB AND I WOULDN'T CHANGE WHAT I DO FOR A LIVING because it's something I'm truly passionate about, but that first day back after a long break is honestly so gruelling to me. The inbox full of emails from faculty members and students, the preparation for the week of classes is just taxing until you turn off the vacation mode and get back into the routine of work life.

The last couple of days I spent with Rein, just before the start-up of school, was truly remarkable. We more than made up for lost time and I realised that I can't fight the truth anymore. I'm in love with her and I want us to make a real go of things. I'm considering taking the next step and asking her to be my girlfriend.

My girlfriend.

Damn, just thinking about it, my stomach does somersaults.

While my computer fires up, I take a sip of my coffee and send her a good morning text. My class with her isn't till the afternoon, though I hope I'll see her beautiful face in the corridor in-between classes.

I skim through the fuckload of emails sitting in my inbox and stop scrolling when I see one from the Eclipse Art gallery, announcing the results of the winners for the competition. I don't think I've ever clocked an email so fast in my life.

My eyes skim through the email and stop when I see the result of the winner.

HOOK, LINE, PROFESSOR

'First place – Rein Valdez'.

"Fuck yes!" I almost leap out of my chair with pure elation. I knew she would win; her artistic ability is truly something to be admired, and of course they would pick her. I had absolutely no doubt. I can't wait to tell her; she's going to be so fucking happy and I can't think of a more deserving person.

A knock sounds on my door and a part of me is hoping it's her. "Come in."

The door opens and my stomach plummets into my gut when I see Polly standing at the door, a file in her hand and a rather smug smirk on her face.

Jesus Christ, I've not even had my damn coffee yet and she's already on my case. It's too early for this shit. "Morning, Professor Saxton. Happy new year."

I slap a phony smile on my face and nod in a civil greeting. "Good morning, Miss Montgomery. Happy new year to you also. I trust your Christmas break went well?"

"Yes, it was. In fact, Professor, it was rather... enlightening."

"Enlightening?" Who the hell has an enlightening Christmas?

"Yes, you know, when you have a gut feeling and you find out that your intuitions were correct all along. You ever get that feeling, Professor?"

Oh, give me strength. Where is she going with this? "Maybe once or twice," I reply tightly. "I actually have to prepare for my classes... was there something I can do for you, Miss Montgomery?"

Polly's smirk grows into a full-on calculating grin, and she nods, closing the door behind her before she haughtily saunters over to my desk. There is something about her demeanour that I don't like —so much so that the hairs on the back of my neck stand on end.

"Matter of fact, you absolutely can. I'd like to discuss your relationship with Miss Valdez."

Fuck.

"I'm sorry... my relationship?" I question, leaning forward in my seat, keeping my voice as cool and composed as I can. "Miss Valdez is my student." My answer is stony. I keep my gaze on hers, holding it inch for inch. I don't even think I'm blinking while I stare her the fuck down.

Polly rubs her lips together and takes a seat in one of the chairs opposite my desk and crosses her legs. "Come on, Talon, you can drop the righteous act. I know all about your relationship with Rein Valdez."

How the hell could she know? We've been careful. Keep your shit together, Talon, she could very well be bluffing.

"Oh well, please enlighten me, Polly. Exactly what type of 'relationship' is it that you seem to believe I have with Miss Valdez?"

Polly smirks. "One where you're fucking her."

My fingers go numb where I have them laced together so tightly on top of my desk. Of all the people to get found out by, why did it have to be this conniving bitch? And more importantly, how did she find out?

Don't go on the defence, Talon. It's her word against yours and Rein's, and she could very well be blowing smoke. I smile and lower my gaze to my hands for a moment to gather my thoughts. "Wow, well, that's one hell of an accusation, Polly. Now, I'm not exactly sure what gave you this ludicrous impression that I'm consorting with a fellow student, but—"

"I saw you, Talon," she claims. "It's amazing what you can see when you learn to read between the lines."

"And what pray tell did you see?"

Polly crosses her weedy arms over her flat chest, and she sighs, swinging her leg back and forth gently while she maintains eye contact with me. I can see the fucking exultation in her eyes, and it makes my stomach turn, because deep down, I know this bitch has got me by the short and curlies.

"I've always admired how good you were at hiding your emotions, Talon. The past two years or so that we've been working together, I've observed you from afar. I've seen the way you interact with your students and it's always the same, curt yet courteous. However, over time I noticed that you always seem to look at Rein a little differently. Your eyes linger on her a little longer. There's this look of admiration lurking behind those stony eyes of yours whenever you look at her. And I've not seen you look at anyone else like that."

My eyes narrow while I rub my index finger along the freshly trimmed beard I got the day before. "Well, it seems you've spent a significant amount of time observing me, Polly. You don't find that to be a tad bit obsessive and intrusive?"

Polly stands and wanders around my office. She stops and admires the paintings hung on my wall. "I've never been shy about voicing my interest in you, Talon. So, it shouldn't really come as a surprise to you that I may have admired you from afar. It's only natural, isn't it? To pay attention to those you like."

I pinch the bridge of my nose and exhale slowly to kerb the annoyance I can feel teeming. "Polly, look, I agreed to go on a date with you, and I thought I made myself pretty clear right after that I don't date, nor do I have any desire to. I can understand that my lack of interest in you and the outcome of the date didn't exactly go as you'd hoped and that would have been upsetting to you—and I'm sorry for that—but I will not stand here and have you accuse me of having an improper relationship with a student, simply because you're pissed that I turned you down."

Polly spins on her heel and gives me a sharp look before her features soften again. "Maybe I was a little sour that you turned me down, but that has nothing to do with this. This isn't an allegation, Professor, I know for a fact that you are having illicit relations with a student."

"Oh, you know for a fact... so where are these facts of yours?"

Polly walks back over to my desk, her hands placed on her narrow hips.

"I'll get to that. Would you like to know the moment I realised? When Rein walked into that restaurant with her date, your entire demeanour changed. Your eyes were on her when you thought I wasn't paying attention, and then you went off towards the bathroom and she followed shortly after. I'm not stupid and I don't appreciate being treated as such. I sussed out the sexual chemistry between the two of you the second she walked into that restaurant, but I wanted to give you the benefit of the doubt."

Fucking hell, this conniving bitch is craftier than she lets on. Well, she's met her match, because I can be just as cunning when I want to be.

"Right. So, let me get this straight, you're basing all of this on what exactly? A hunch? Because my eyes lingering a little too long on Rein and some phony chemistry you 'picked up on' all equates to me having an affair with her, does it?" I respond astutely. "Surely, an intellectual such as yourself can grasp how ludicrous that sounds, right?" I add, rocking back and forth on my chair, the hint of a supercilious smirk on my face while I stare up at her looming over my desk, looking mildly exasperated.

What did she think I was going to do? Fall apart under pressure and confess all to her while down on my knees begging for her mercy? Fuck that. I'd rather go straight to the Dean myself.

"You're right, Talon, I am an intellectual, which is why I made sure I have these." She leans over and picks up a brown envelope she has sitting on her chair and drops it on my desk.

What the fuck are these now?

"And these are…?"

"It would do you good to take a look."

The knot in my stomach tightens as I pick up the envelope and open it. Photos fall out first and I pick them up to see it's from the night of our date, the night I pulled Rein out of the car after she almost had the accident. Photo after photo of me running towards the car, then another six of me dragging Dean out of the car and punching him. With each photo, the blood in my veins turns icy and my annoyance intensifies.

"You followed me?" I question, flipping through the photos and turning my stony gaze to stare up at her. "This is all you have?" I question, holding up the stack of photos. "These photos prove nothing, Polly. I was simply driving home and saw my student in a dangerous situation and went to her aid, that's all. I didn't like the look of the guy she was with, and I was simply looking out for her. Good thing too because he could have killed her." I toss them back at her. "I would have done the same for any of my other students."

Polly uses her index finger and pushes aside the gold desk sign so she can place her hands down on my desk and lean over.

"And what does the university's rulebook say about spending the night with a student, Professor?" she probes further. "If my memory serves correct, any fraternising with a student outside of school grounds is prohibited, am I right?"

I've never wanted to hurt a woman in my life the way I want to ram this crazy bitch's head through the goddamn wall. "And I wouldn't waste my breath trying to come up with a clever ruse to justify going up to her apartment—I'm not even going to bring up how a student on a full scholarship, living on a waitress' income can afford to rent a luxury apartment on the same complex as yours, because we both know that's no coincidence."

My anger gets the better of me and I slam my hands down on the table before I rise to my feet. "I've heard about enough of this absurdity. I think we both know what's going on here, Polly, you're pissed you didn't get what you wanted from me, and you've decided to start a vendetta and make up these fabricated stories to ruin my reputation. If you believe these will hold, please, by all means, go to the Dean, go to fucking board for all I care, but don't forget that the entire school—including the faculty members—all know of your infatuation with me. So, in the end, you'll end up looking like some obsessive stalker that can't take no for an answer."

Polly blanches and I notice the smugness from before drain away from her face before she gains composure and straightens again and wets her lips. "Oh, Talon, you misunderstand. It's not my intention to ruin your reputation. In fact, it's quite the opposite. I'm trying to look out for you, sweetie," she expresses and reaches up to touch my jaw, but I catch her wrist and glare at her menacingly. "You might be able to blag your way out of those photos, but I see the way you look at her. I wonder how your precious Rein will react when she finds out that your beloved late fiancée is the donor to the heart that's currently beating inside her chest."

No, it's not possible. That information isn't available nor open to the public, so how the fuck did she find out?

My impervious façade slips, and the haughty smirk plastered on her face silently affirms that she's now got the ball securely in her court and I've got no choice but to play the game by her rules.

"The look on your face, Professor, confirms my suspicions that she has not a clue and probably thinks she's special for catching the attention of the infamous Professor Saxton. Little does she know, it's not her you're holding onto, it's the last thing you have left of your fiancée, isn't it?"

My mind is screaming what my mouth should be, but I can't seem to get the words out. It's like my trap is being forced shut, and however hard I try, I can't seem to utter a single word. All I can do is stare at her as my world comes falling around me one bit at a time.

"It's real handy having friends in high places. Can you imagine how devastated she will be when she finds out the truth? Poor girl." Polly places a hand on her chest and feigns a sorrowful look. "Considering all the demeaning things you said to me before, I should go straight to Rein and the Dean, but because I'm nice and still have a little soft spot for you, I'll do you a solid and keep your secret, but on one condition."

Fuck me, here we go.

"What do you want?"

"You put an end to your little illicit tryst with her."

Chapter 15
Rein

I LOVE YOU - BILLIE EILISH

Adonis:
'Good morning, baby.'

"You're awfully chipper this morning."

I leap out of my skin when Paris suddenly appears beside me, holding two large cups of Starbucks. "What's got you grinning like the Cheshire cat, hm?"

"What?" I feign innocence and she pins me with a pointed look in return that clearly expresses she's not buying it. "I wasn't grinning."

Paris giggles. "Oh, you were, and you still are, look at you. I can see your damn wisdom teeth from here you're grinning so wide!"

I cackle and take the Styrofoam coffee cup from her. "Since when is being in a good mood a crime?" I defend while we walk through the corridor, side by side, waving at a couple of our classmates on our way to business class. Just thinking about sitting there and listening to Mr Charlton droning on is making me sleepy. I love the class, I'm not a fan of him.

"No, you grinning like the cat that caught the canary isn't a crime but keeping the deets from your little show at Aura last week fucking is. I still can't get over it, my straight and narrow best friend willingly got finger fucked in front of the entire club. It was such a proud moment for me," Paris gushes, placing her hand on her chest and sniffling roguishly.

Blood fills my cheeks every time my mind evokes that night. As nerve-wracking as it felt, the thrill of it all was so worth it. That self-conscious part of me that has been holding me back all these years is slowly fading away one bit at a time, thanks to Talon.

Think of the devil and he shall appear. Talon is walking towards his first class looking mighty edible in his charcoal grey suit. "Here comes the brooding God of Oakhill, blessing my eyes first thing in the morning. Good God, is it me or does this man just get hotter? Also, something is different about him."

"It's the beard." The words fall out of my mouth before I can catch them, and Paris turns to look at me, brows raised with interest. "What?"

"How very perceptive of you to notice so fast," Paris states with an amused grin. "Are we maybe a little too fascinated with Professor Hottie?"

Yes. I scoff and shake my head, unable to look away from him as he nears us. "Don't be ridiculous, I'm an artist, we notice these things."

"Uh huh, whatever you say, sugar tits." Talon walks right by us, and usually, he would make eye contact or nod in acknowledgement, but something feels off. Perhaps I'm overthinking it–he could be playing it safe because I'm with Paris.

At least that's what I tell myself to help ease the knot of nerves bunching tighter in my gut.

"Good afternoon class, I trust you've all had a good Christmas and New Year?" A round of mumbled responses echo in the lecture hall and Talon nods. "Excellent. Now you're all back, well rested and fresh, we'll kick start the lesson with a quiz to get your juices flowing."

Talon's eyes meet mine for less than a millisecond when he cites the part about flowing juices. "Professor, we're loving the new look. The beard really suits you," Francesca Sutton pipes up, nibbling at the end of her pen and batting her lashes at him flirtatiously.

Talon scratches his bearded jaw and nods. "Thank you, Miss Sutton. I'm overjoyed you approve of the beard," he responds scathingly and drops a stack of papers on her desk. The sarcastic tone of his voice indicates that her opinion means jack squat to him, and he made a point to make that copiously clear. "Now, it would make me happier if you put as much effort into nailing this quiz as you have observing my beard. Please pass these quiz papers around to your peers."

I forgot what a frosty prick he can be when he wants to be. Not so long ago, I was also on the brunt end of his venomous tongue. While I feel bad for the girl for getting called out in front of the entire class, the mildly covetous girl inside does a little victory dance.

Talon walks over to his desk while the papers are being passed around and very fleetingly looks up and catches my eye. I smirk and lean back against my chair.

Something feels off. When he looks at me, his eyes usually radiate such need and desire that heats me up from the inside out. Today, his eyes are distant and hold a deep look of sorrow. It's almost as though he's avoiding looking at me.

As the day went on, the feeling of dread intensified, and my good mood got shot to hell. I sent him a text, asking if he's okay, and he's read it but not bothered to respond. I contemplated going over to his place but thought better of it. What if he's just having an off day and needs some time alone? The last thing I want to do is come off as needy and desperate—even if I am both those things and burning inside to see him.

I continued to patiently wait for him to call or come over, but he didn't. Instead, on Tuesday evening I got a text message from him. When I see his name come up on my screen while working at Zen's, the elation that floods me is inexplicable. The bar is absolutely heaving, so I can't check the message until it quietens down a couple of hours later.

"Clay, I'm going to take five," I tell him, and he nods while pulling a pint of beer. I step into the back of the bar reserved for staff and open the message from Talon.

Adonis:
Hi, Rein.
I apologise for not coming back to your messages until now.
I've been reflecting the past few days and I think it's time we put an end to this thing between us. We've taken enough of a risk, and we agreed we would let it run its course. It's best for us to walk away before we get caught and lose everything. Please know that I'll cherish every moment I spent with you, and you'll continue to be very special to me.

I re-read the message repeatedly and sink down onto the sofa when my knees shake like they are about to give away. Did he just break it off with me over a fucking text message? I'm so 'special' to him, yet I'm not worthy of a goddamn conversation? I knew something was off, he's been distant the last couple of days. I should have seen this coming. Has he grown bored of me now that he's gotten what he wants from me? Am I no longer desirable to him? Or has he met someone else? Someone he can have a future with and not risk losing everything.

I've still got two hours for my shift to end, but I know I won't be able to focus on anything if I stay. I need to go and speak to him. Find out what's changed all of a sudden, when a couple of days ago he couldn't bear to be apart from me.

There's an emotional storm brewing inside of me. Feelings that are foreign to me threaten to consume me, the deep ache that spreads across my chest like wildfire restricts my airways while I fight back the tears of anger.

I pick up my jacket and shove my phone into my pocket and walk out of the back room towards the bar. "Rein?" Clay catches my arm and looks me over. What's the matter? Where are you going?"

"Something important has come up, I'm really sorry but I have to go."

Clay nods and loosens his hold on my arm. "Are you sure you're okay? I don't like the look of you," he states, his expression showing his concern for me.

I force a smile on my face and give his hand a squeeze. "I will be. I'll make up the hours tomorrow night, I promise."

"I've got you, go on. It's chucking it down, take a cab!" he calls out after me, but I rush out of the bar and stop when I see the rain pouring with force. There are no signs of a taxi anywhere and I'm too agitated to wait around. I'll hail one on the way. It's a twenty-minute walk from Zen's to our complex anyway. Not like I've not done the walk daily for the last couple of months.

The rain is battering down on me, soaking through me in mere minutes. I pay no mind to the January chill that seeps into my bones while I walk through the city. My mind is occupied, going through what I'm going to say to him when I see him. I'll resemble a drowned rat by the time I get there, but who gives a flying fuck what I look like? He needs to fucking explain himself. Who the hell does he think he is breaking up with me over a text message?

The more I think about that text, the angrier I feel. My entire body is shaking, not from the cold or getting soaked through but from pure infuriation.

After a long walk, I finally make it to his apartment building. I rap my knuckles on the door rather hard. My hands are shaking uncontrollably. In fact, I think my entire body is, but I can't focus on that. The door opens and Talon stands before me, looking worse than I've ever seen him. Still clad in his work attire, the white shirt unbuttoned revealing his strapping chest and washboard abs, and blue suit trousers he wore earlier today with the belt undone and hanging loosely. A woeful look mars his handsome features. He's holding a glass of amber liquid in his right hand, which I'm assuming is scotch—he does love a single malt.

Talon looks surprised to see me. His blue eyes go wide, and they flit over me. "Rein?"

"Don't you Rein me," I hiss hotly as I walk into his apartment. I kick the door shut forcefully with my boot clad foot. The loud sound of the door slamming shut lingers and echoes around us for a second or two. "It's over, is it, Professor?" I ask, lifting my arms and shoving him back while advancing towards him. Talon watches me raptly, he says nothing, but his eyes remain locked on mine the entire time. "You think you can just drop me at the click of your fingers and come crawling back when you're horny again?" I question stormily and shove him again. The glass in his hand slips and smashes on the floor. Talon's jaw clenches tight but he still says nothing to defend himself, he only looks at me apologetically.

"Do you think I'm the type of girl that falls to her knees, crawls and begs and allows just any fucking man to degrade and use her?" I add furiously and continue advancing toward him. "Do I?!" I shout and shove him harder. "You know what you can do with your precious morals, Talon? You can shove them right up your arse because no one breaks up with me over a fucking text message!"

"Rein—" Talon tries to interject but I shake my head vehemently.

"A text message, Talon? I thought you were different, but you're no better than the rest of the heartless bastards out there. You didn't even have enough respect nor the fucking decency to break things off with me like a respectable human being!" I push him again, and this time, he grabs hold of my wrists and squeezes.

"Stop!" We glare at one another angrily, both our chests rising and falling quickly with every brutal breath. "It's over. Of course I would have had a conversation with you but every argument we have ends with us fucking, we keep following the same pattern, Rein, and it had to stop. It has nothing to do with me not having any respect for you. Believe me, I have a lot of respect for you and care a great deal about you," he affirms, staring into my eyes like he wants to see into my soul. "Does it matter how it ends? Whether a text message or a conversation, the outcome will still be the same."

"What's changed? It was only a couple of days ago that you were telling me you couldn't bear to be away from me. Did you just wake up Monday and decide you've grown tired of me?"

Talon swallows thickly, and his hands holding onto my wrists tighten. "Is that what you need to hear to accept that it's done? Then yes, that's exactly it. This was never permanent, Rein. We've gotten all we can out of each other, there's no point in dragging this out. I did what's best for us both and that's for this to end," he croaks, looking over my head.

I shake my head slowly. "No, don't look away. You look me in the eyes when you break up with me." My voice, despite my best effort to keep it taciturn, comes out as a broken whisper. "Look me in the eyes and tell me it's over, Talon."

Please don't.

Talon's ocean blue eyes lower to mine, and for a long moment, we just stare at one another. The Adam's apple in his throat rises and falls, and I hold my breath, waiting, praying those two words get lodged in his throat the way my emotions are choking me. "It's over."

The backs of my eyelids sting, but I refuse to show him that he has the power to break me. I yank my hands out of his hold and shove him away from me before I turn and walk towards the door. My heart is in ruins, beating deafeningly in my ear as I open the door and walk out without so much as a look back.

Like a fool, I stand, staring down the corridor towards his door, a small part of me hoping he will come after me, but he doesn't.

It's really over. I'll never get to kiss him or have him touch me and hear him call me 'Snowflake' again. I'll go back to just being 'Miss Valdez' to him.

It isn't until the doors to the elevators close that I choke on the sob that's been suffocating me. Like a dam, I open the flood gates and let the tears flow free.

The last time I felt agonising pain this severe was when I was told my mum had died. My limbs grow weak, and I can barely keep myself upright while I silently sob into my hand.

My mother always used to say that one day there's going to be a boy that will come along and rip apart your world and you're going to feel like dying. Not only your eyes but your heart will weep for him, but don't you ever let anyone hear you cry, especially him. If you must cry, cry your heart out in silence so he'll never know he broke you.

I made her promise that day that I would never allow a boy to break my heart. I broke that promise because my heart is not only broken, its devastated.

How am I going to sit in his class and endure this suffocating ache in my chest daily and act like it's not slowly killing me?

Chapter 16
Talon

EYES OFF YOU - PRETTYMUCH

I watch Rein staring up into my eyes, and the devastation written all over her face is unmistakable. And if I'm honest, I'm fighting tooth and nail to hold back every emotion that is screaming at me to tell her that I'm in love with her and the last thing I want is to let her go. But I have no choice. I'm staring down the barrel of a loaded gun. If I tell her everything about Taylor being her heart donor, she'll never trust nor forgive me. She'll think that's the only reason I'm attached to her when it's the furthest from the truth.

Also, that snake Polly will go straight to the Dean and Rein will lose her scholarship and her future will go down the drain. I can't risk hurting her more. If I keep my mouth shut and stay the fuck away, she'll just think me a heartless bastard and eventually get over it.

"Talon, you can run and tell your little love bird the truth, but she'll never forgive you. She'll end up hating you. You'll be the reason her future goes up in flames. The way I see it, there's really one logical option. You end it, I keep my mouth shut, and Rein gets to keep her scholarship and *you get to keep your job. Everyone's happy. I'd even be happy to play along like we're dating just to get the message across, and she'll leave you alone."*

"Get the fuck out of my office."

My hands shake so I fist them by my sides. The words refuse to come out, especially with the beseeching way she's looking at me.

Forgive me, Snowflake.

"It's over," I force out. Rein's shoulders drop, and her fingers are trembling. I can feel the iciness of her body where it's pressed against mine from getting soaked. The chill makes me shiver inwardly. There's not a drop of warmth to her, her teeth are chattering, and I'm worried she'll get hypothermia. I'm just about to tell her to come in and dry off, but she rips her hands free from mine and pushes me away before turning and walking out of the door.

The door slams shut behind her. My eyes close and I release the excruciating breath I've been holding. Before I know it, my feet are following her. I get to the door but stop myself before I turn the doorknob.

You need to let her go.

Let her go.

I punch the door and press my forehead against it. My breathing hastens when my emotions start to overwhelm me. "I'm sorry, Snowflake," I whisper, sinking to the floor and staring into the empty apartment. I've made a fucking mess of everything. I should have trusted my gut and stayed the fuck away and spared us both the heartache, but my heart nor my knob didn't listen to reason.

How ill is my fate to first lose the woman I love, the one who was meant to be the mother of my child and my future wife, and then–by some miracle–I find a piece of her in another and fall out of my arse in love with her only to lose her too?

What have I done? What am I being reprimanded for? Why is it that I cannot just be happy?

The rage I'm feeling, I could honestly rip that shrew Polly limb from fucking limb. I've never harboured such disdain for one person in my life. I'd kill her and happily go down for it. For the life of me, I cannot comprehend what it is that she's getting out of any of this. It's truly irksome, the shit that goes through some people's heads. She's seriously unhinged and in desperate need of psychological help.

I could resign, but that won't stop her from going straight to Rein and telling her everything. That psychotic tramp will do everything in her power to make sure we don't end up together, and moreover, I'm genuinely concerned what she will do to Rein if I don't abide by her irrational demands.

I need to protect Rein; I won't allow what happened to Taylor to happen to her.

Three glasses of scotch later and nursing the fourth, I stare out of the window towards her building. I wonder if she's home, and if she is what she's doing.

Fuck, I'm missing her like crazy already and it's only been an hour. Actually, it's coming up to thirty odd hours if we count Monday too–where we've been apart.

Ugh, the temptation to just pick up the phone and call her gets stronger with every drop of scotch I consume. There's a knock on my door and I straighten. My heart kick starts and beats wildly in my chest. "Snowflake." I rush over to the door and pull it open. My stomach drops when I see JT at the door, the wide smile on his face dropping when he takes in my dishevelled appearance.

"Whoa, dude, what the fuck happened to you?"

Without a word, I turn and walk towards the living room to pour myself another drink. "T, hey, you all right, bro?"

"I'm fan-fucking-tastic," I grouse, unscrewing the cap to the bottle of fifteen-year-old single malt. "Drink?" I offer him a glass and he takes it from me, followed by the bottle after I down one glass and pour another.

"Yo, easy, slow down, mate." I stare down at his hand when he takes hold of my arm and pulls me towards the sofa. "Come and sit." JT sits on the sofa beside me and watches while I lean over and cradle my head in my hands. "T, what's going on with you? Why are you in this state, bro?"

"I fucked up, mate." I sigh heavily and shake my head. "I fucked up big time and I don't know how the hell I'm going to get out of this web I'm tangled up in."

JT leans over and taps my shoulder supportively. "What did you do?"

"I've been sleeping with my student." JT's hand falls away, and when I look over at him, I see the stunned look on his face.

"You did what?"

"That's not even the worse part," I admit sullenly and lay back on the sofa.

"Don't tell me you've been busted and lost your job?" I snort bitterly and shake my head.

"No, that would have been much easier," I tell him. "Remember when I told you I had a P.I. look into where Taylor's organs were donated?" JT nods silently, and I continue. "Well, he found them. Her lungs went to some guy with terminal lung cancer. Her kidneys to a middle-aged woman in Florida, and her heart... to a teenage girl in London who almost died in a car accident, just like her."

JT frowns. "Okay..."

"That girl is Rein Valdez. She landed a full scholarship to Oakhill University. She's an art major and my student," I declare. JT stares at me with his eyes almost bulging out of his skull and his mouth ajar.

"You're having me on, right? This is a wind up, because that's the sort of shit you see in chick flick movies, bro." When I only look up at him, he continues to gape at me in scepticism. "Is she... is the donor girl the one you're sleeping with? Was she the one at Aura on New Year's Eve?"

I nod.

"Oh my God, you've gone and lost your goddamn mind?! T, sleeping with a student is one thing but sleeping with the girl who has your dead fiancée's heart is just downright strange, bro. What the fuck are you thinking?" JT rants while pacing back and forth. "Fucking Christ, Talon, I thought you were starting to get over your grief of losing Taylor, but this... this is some next level obsessive bullshit."

"Hey, dickhead, you don't just 'get over' losing someone you love! Have I dealt with my grief? Yes, I have, and I've made my peace with losing her," I retort hotly.

"Have you?" JT snaps. "Because to me it sounds like you've only superseded your grief with another fixation as a mean to cope, and that's not healthy, bro, not for you and certainly not for that girl."

I scowl up at him and sit upright. "What the fuck are you talking about? You're acting like I'm some mental headcase who went out of his way to find this girl and fuck her just because she's got Tay's heart."

"Didn't you?"

"No!" I bellow irately. "Rein was already my student when I found out who she was. She was already under my fucking nose for a year and a half. I've been fighting my attraction for her since the day she came crashing into me on my first day at the fucking school, you dickhead!"

JT sighs and stares back at me wordlessly while he rubs a hand over his jaw. "Why her?"

I glare at him, my brows drawn tightly. "What do you mean?"

"Why her? Of all your students at that school, why is it you're attracted to her when she's the opposite of everything you're into? We've been friends for years; I know your type, and that girl is the furthest from it. You've always been into blondes who are petite and slim, just like Taylor, and Alexia from before her, and even Haley. So, why her, bro?" I stare at the ground and shake my head. "You may not know it but subconsciously you're attracted to this girl because she has a part of Taylor, and you find that comforting."

"That's not true," I dispute with a shake of my head. "It's just an organ, it's not Taylor. A part of me will always love Tay, but I'm in love with Rein. I'm in love with her mind, her smile, every curve of her body, and fuck, I'm crazy about her eyes. None of those things have a damn thing to do with Taylor. I'm in love with Rein, completely, heart or no heart."

THE FOLLOWING MORNING, I'M WALKING THROUGH THE CORRIDORS, feeling and likely resembling a zombie. I've barely slept, which has left me feeling exhausted with zero energy and hanging out of my arse after consuming one too many glasses of scotch. It's been a while since I've felt this low and out of touch with myself and it's only been a day.

My eyes roam around the corridors on the way to my office, hopeful to get a glimpse of Rein, but she's not around. I wonder if she's okay... I didn't like the state of her last night. What if she's sick? I've got a class with her after lunch, I'll have to wait till then to see her. Fuck me, when did I start sounding like a pathetic lovesick teenager?

Get it together, Talon, for fuck's sake.

"Good morning, Professor." I halt just as I reach my office and close my eyes to count to five in a desperate attempt to stifle the overwhelming urge to turn around and punch this aggravating woman's head off her chin. The pesky sound of her voice makes my skin crawl with agitation. "Oh my, you don't look so good. Are you okay?" she questions, reaching up to touch my face. I bat her hand away and fix her with a death glare.

"Don't fucking touch me," I growl and turn to unlock the door to my office.

"Ooh, someone's grouchy this morning. Who peed in your cheerios, buttercup?"

Never hit a woman, never hit a woman.

"Are you taking the fucking piss? Get lost, Polly. You're the last person I want to see right now, or ever for that matter."

Polly's smile falters ever so slightly, but then she shrugs off my outburst and smiles again. "And here's me thinking we could be friends." She bats her lashes at me. This woman has lost her marbles. Or was she always crazy and I didn't notice? How on God's green earth did she even get a job here?

"Over my dead body," I grouse, pushing the door open, walking in and then kicking it shut in her face. "Crazy bitch."

HOOK, LINE, PROFESSOR

My bag and jacket get tossed onto the chair in front of my desk while I pace back and forth, rubbing my throbbing temples.

The classes in the morning drag on and it seems time has slowed to a snail's pace. I don't see Rein at lunch either. Where the fuck is she? I've seen Paris but she's nowhere to be seen and they're always together at lunch. I could make up an excuse and go ask Paris, but that would raise eyebrows. Why would a professor be asking for the whereabouts of a student?

I'm on the verge of losing my mind. "Rei Rei, over here!" My ears perk up and I almost drop the bottle of water in my hand when I hear Paris call her name. I look over my shoulder and see her walking towards Paris and her friends gathered around a table in the middle of the cafeteria.

Rein usually has this light surrounding her that draws you in, but today, that light has dimmed. She looks worn out and pale. Wearing an oversized black hoodie dress with the slogan 'be kind always' on the front and leather ankle boots, her hair is pulled up into two messy buns on either side of her head, like Minnie mouse.

"Professor?" I start out of my thoughts and turn my head back to look at the cashier lady holding out my coffee. "Your coffee."

"Oh, thank you."

Stop staring at her and get out of here, you moron.

The hour I have for lunch I spent staring at the antique clock on my wall, my quinoa salad sitting untouched in front of me, my finger tapping impatiently against my desk while watching the seconds tick on by—with every minute that passes, my gut gets tighter in anticipation of facing Rein.

Turns out, Professor Sommers won't be back for another six months due to her injury, so I'll be covering her classes till then.

Well, I suppose there's no point in delaying the inevitable. It's time to face reality.

Gathering my papers and laptop, I stuff them into my bag and leave my office to head to class. I get to the studio with ten minutes to spare and halt in the doorway. The studio's still empty, only one person in there, sitting in the bay window ledge, gazing out the window.

Rein.

It seems she's immersed deep in her thoughts, completely oblivious to her surroundings. I take a moment to admire her while she's not paying attention. Hard pill to swallow when a couple of days ago we were both happy and looking forward to every second we got to spend together, and now look at the state of us. Christ, if only I knew the last time I kissed her would be the last, I would have savoured every second. Fuck, I hate this. I hate how abruptly things have changed. Had things gone how I planned; Rein could have been my girlfriend right now and those captivating eyes would be shining brightly with such devotion every time she looks at me.

While I'm transfixed and studying her, she finally notices me standing there. I say notices but she full on catches me watching her and I don't look away when her eyes interlock with mine. The dejection emanating in her gaze feels like a stiff punch right to the gut. It literally knocks the wind right out of me.

Rein is the first to break eye contact. She jumps off the ledge to take her seat, concealing herself behind her canvas.

The studio fills up with all the usual faces a couple of minutes later. "Good afternoon, everyone. Welcome back. I hope you've all had a relaxing Christmas and New year," I say, moving around the desk to stand at the front of the class.

"How was your break, Professor?" one of the students to the left of the class questions.

"My break was very... memorable. Probably one of the best I've had in a very long time. Thank you for asking," I reply, my eyes of their own accord quickly veering to Rein. She bites her lip and stares back at me wide eyed, her soft full lips parted. "Now, before we start, I'm sure you all recall I announced a competition that was running just before we broke up for Christmas break. I want to thank you all for your submissions. It was a tough choice for me because all your pieces were truly exceptional. However, as you know, only the top three candidates were chosen by me personally.

The winner of the competition was chosen directly by the organisers themselves. And I got the results back Monday," I explain, walking back and forth as I speak. "I'm pleased to announce the winner of the competition is…" I trail off, looking at every student waiting impatiently for the results. "Rein Valdez."

Rein's head pops up and she looks around the class then at me with eyes wide with disbelief. The other students clap and congratulate her. "I won?"

I nod and offer her a smile. "You sure did. A well-deserved win too. Your piece was truly spectacular. Congratulations, Miss Valdez. Your painting will be exhibited in the gallery in two weeks. You will be presented with the check for the five-thousand-dollar prize, and if your painting is sold, you'll receive the money for that too." Rein continues to gape at me, and for the first time since we called things off, I can see the light of exhilaration glittering in her eyes again, and I'm truly ecstatic for her.

"Okay, for today's class we'll be taking a look at strip art…"

WHENEVER I WALK PAST REIN IN CLASS, THE SMELL OF HER SHAMPOO blended with the citrusy notes of her perfume wafts around me. It takes every ounce of my self-control to not concede and bury my nose in her neck and inhale as deep as my lungs will allow till I fill my lungs with the intoxicating scent of her.

I stand behind her, observing her work. She's got her head cocked to the left, her lower lip between her teeth while she creates her abstract design using the masking tape, but where the tape isn't sticking where she needs it to, she's getting frustrated with it. After the third attempt, Rein senses my presence and turns to look back at me over her shoulder.

"Would you like a hand, Miss Valdez?" Rein's face drops and she turns her gaze back to her work.

"No."

I take a step towards her when she's about to tear off the entire strip of tape, but I stop her by covering her hand with mine. Rein stares at our hands for a couple of seconds then slowly looks up at me. "Patience, Snowflake," I murmur in her ear. "Remember, you can't rush art. Take a breath and don't give up, you can do it." Rein's eyes close, her breathing slows, and she licks her lips. My thumb brushes across her knuckles before I let go and step away again. "Carry on." Her eyes are burning a hole into the back of my skull as I walk back to my desk and take my seat.

That's it, Talon, you just keep on digging that hole you're already confined in deeper. Because that will certainly make things better for the both of you, you absolute dipshit.

By some miracle, I make it to Friday without any more mishaps, and I successfully manage to avoid Rein. That is, of course, until I hear commotion coming from the art studio Friday afternoon. I push through the crowd and walk into the studio and see a crowd of students surrounding Rein and her friend, Paris. What the hell is going on here?

Rein is standing at the back of studio stock-still, staring at something while Paris rubs her back. When I veer my gaze to what she's looking at, my arms go slack, and I almost drop everything I'm holding. Rein's painting—the one that won the competition has the word 'slut' painted across it in big thick red paint.

Fuck.

The red-hot rage that swiftly consumes me is unfathomable. When I get my hands on the fucker who did this, they're going to have hell to pay.

Christ, the poor girl just can't catch a goddamn break. It's just one devastation after another. I set my bag and documents in my hands on the table rather forcefully and everyone in the room—including Rein—turns to look at me. The devastation in her eyes only adds to my anger. "Everyone but Rein back to your classes." I dismiss them but they all look at Rein and make no move to leave us. "Now!" I bark and they all start to file out. "If anyone knows any information about who did this, come and see me in my office at the end of the day."

I push the door shut after the last student exits and I walk over to Rein. Her bottom lip trembles and her eyes brim with tears when I near her. "Come here." I wrap my arms around her and draw her to me. "I'm going to find who did this, I swear to you," I declare, my arms protectively tightening around her when she chokes on a sob. "Shh, hey, come on, Snowflake, please don't cry," I murmur, my lips pressed against her temple. Rein says something but it comes out muffled where her face is nestled against my chest. "Look at me, Rein." She lifts her head and looks up at me. Tears spill over and stream down her cheeks.

"The person that did this won't get away with it, I'll make sure of it," I tell her earnestly and lift my hand to brush away the tears that continue to fall. "Please don't cry. Something this minor isn't worth your tears."

"What have I ever done to anyone to warrant something like this?" She weeps, bowing her head. "I worked so hard on that painting, and for the first time in my life, I actually achieved something that I was so proud of... and just like that it's taken away from me. Why does everything in my life have to be such a tribulation? Why can't I just be happy for once, Talon? Why?"

The pain and sorrow in her voice makes me ache deep within. "Snowflake, they can only take from you what you allow. You've not done anything to anyone. This is the action of someone who is tactless and very clearly envious of you." I cup her face with my hands and lift her head so she can meet my gaze. "Hey, where's that beautiful tenacious girl that takes no shit from any one? You're Rein Valdez, you're no quitter. You're going to deal with this the same way you do everything else and come out better than ever."

Rein shakes her head and pulls her face away from my hold. "What's the point? I can't fix this, Talon. It's too late. That painting is supposed to be picked up next Friday. It took me almost a month to perfect and finish. How am I supposed to recreate it in *seven days*? Between school and work, even if I paint day and night, I'll still struggle to finish it on time," Rein justifies. "You know as well as I do it's a lost cause. Just like everything else in my life," she adds bitterly with a shake of her head.

I catch her arm when she tries to walk off and tug her back to me. "No, it's not a lost cause. You are not giving up, you hear me? You don't have to do it on your own. We'll do it together," I offer, brushing a strand of her hair out of her face. Rein stares up into my eyes, searching for surety.

"I thought you said you've gotten all you can from me, so why are you still trying to save me, Professor?"

Because I'm in love with you.

Those six words almost fall out of my mouth, but I manage to catch myself just in time. "Because you're worthy of saving, and as long as you need me to, I'll be there to keep saving you, Snowflake." Fresh tears gather and seep from the corners of her eyes while she continues to gaze up me. Maybe we can't be what we were, but I'll always be hers.

Goddamn it, I need to pull away. I should pull away, but my fingers are gliding along the side of her face and slowly moving down to trace the outline of the soft pillow of her bottom lip. Rein's eyes close and her lips part ever so slightly, drawing my gaze down to her perfect mouth. The familiar scent of her makes me light-headed, and before I know it, the already minuscule gap between our lips is diminishing as my lips inch closer and closer to hers.

Chapter 17 — Rein

EYES ON YOU - TWENTY7

WHY IS my life such a mess? Like, seriously, have I been put on this earth specifically to suffer? Because it sure as shit feels like it.

For the second time this week, my world comes tumbling around me when I see my painting is marred with the word 'slut' painted over it in large bright red letters. It may be insignificant or minor, but to me, it means everything. It's the dream I spent so long working towards, and by some miracle, I achieved it. My painting was going to be exhibited in an art gallery. That's a huge deal to me.

When I think about the very small percentage of people that dislike me enough to do something so immoral, only one name comes to mind.

Sydney Dalton.

No one else at this school would get more pleasure out of seeing me suffer than Sydney, so it makes sense that she would sabotage me. If she thinks she's going to get away with this, she's got another thing coming. I've truly had it up to my fucking eyeballs with her and its high time she gets a taste of my Spanish disposition.

Right now, though, the only thing I can focus on is the familiar warmth of Talon's robust body pressed against mine. The sexy masculine smell of his aftershave that scrambles my senses without fail. My body immediately recognises and reacts to his touch, making me shiver inwardly against the fire that ignites within me.

I know we broke up and I should hate him, but I desperately need his lips on mine as though they're my lifeline, my means to go on.

Kiss me, Professor. Kiss me like you're afraid you're about to lose me.

Our lips only just touch when a loud crash outside the door causes us to jump apart. My eyes flutter open and disappointment swamps me when he pulls away and quickly averts his gaze, looking everywhere but at me. "You should head back to class."

I nod and walk past him to the door. "Rein." When I hear him call my name, I turn and look at him.

"We'll figure this out, I promise."

'The painting, or us?' is what I wanted to ask but swallow the words as they come up.

Instead, I shrug. "I won't be holding my breath."

On either count. With one last shared look, I open the door and walk out of the studio. Paris is waiting for me in the corridor, leant against the lockers. She straightens when she sees me and rushes over to pull me in for a hug. "Are you okay, Rei Rei?"

"I'll be fine, P." I sigh against her shoulder. Talon walks out of the studio a couple of seconds after me. My eyes meet his while I'm locked in Paris' embrace. "What did Professor Hottie say? Gosh, he looked livid when he saw your painting," Paris questions, pulling away and watching him walk off down the corridor. "He didn't say a whole lot. Just the usual teacher pep talk of how they'll find who did it and I shouldn't let this discourage me, etcetera."

"I don't understand who would do something like this to you?" When I give her a pointed look, her hazel eyes go wide with realisation, and she shakes her head. "No, surely she wouldn't go this far?"

"Would you put it past her? Aside from Sydney–and possibly Hunter–who else at this school dislikes me enough to sabotage me?"

Paris winces. "Fair point. I swear to God if she's the one responsible, I'm going to rip those cheap extensions right out of her skull," she fumes.

"Don't worry, P, I'll deal with Sydney."

Paris gives me a side look full of concern while we walk through the corridors. "Well, be sure to let me know if you need an alibi, sugar tits."

EARLY SATURDAY MORNING, I LAY IN BED, STARING UP AT THE CEILING after spending the night tossing and turning restlessly. My shift at Zen's isn't till four and it's currently six-fifty in the morning. Talon's words from yesterday keep going around and around in my mind. *"They can only take from you what you allow, Snowflake."*

Can I really recreate the painting in time? Even if I wanted to try, I don't have the supplies at hand and I can't use the ones at school, and I sure as hell don't have the money to buy new ones. Shit. With a frustrated groan, I pull the covers over my head. No, it's impossible. It's going to take a divine intervention, and knowing my luck, I'll only be setting myself up for more disappointment.

My phone vibrates on the bedside table, alerting me of a message or notification. I roll onto my back with a sigh and reach for my phone, wincing when the brightness of the screen blinds me temporarily.

Adonis:
3484 W Armitage Ave.
Meet me at eight a.m.
Don't be late.

I blink a couple of times and sit up so fast my head spins. I read the message again, and then two more times. Why is he asking me to meet him? I quickly search up the address–it's just a building about thirty minutes from our complex.

I send him a quick text back, telling him I'll be there before I jump out of bed to get ready.

I get to the address by seven fifty-nine. No sign of Talon anywhere. I look up at the brown residential building with a frown.

Me:
I'm here.

Adonis
Come on up, third floor.

The main entrance door to the building buzzes and suddenly opens. I push it open and walk inside and jump when the heavy wooden door slams shut behind me. My eyes roam around the well-lit foyer leading towards the elevators. Looking in from the outside, this place doesn't look like much but once you step in its rather quaint.

As soon as the doors open to the third floor, I see Talon standing there, hands in the pockets of his dark blue jeans, looking like he just stepped out of an Abercrombie and Fitch magazine cover.

"Morning," he greets with a handsome smile. A smile that makes me want to melt into a puddle at his feet. The beautiful bastard.

I narrow my eyes as I step out of the elevator and observe him warily. "Morning. Care to explain why you lured me all the way across town at the arse crack of dawn?"

Talon chuckles and my stomach goes tight at the sound. He gestures with his head for me to follow him. "Come with me and I'll show you."

I'm not proud of this, nor am I one to objectify anyone, but my eyes longingly marvel at the shape of his taut bum in those jeans. I recall what it felt like grasping those firm cheeks, my nails digging into them while he violently thrusts into me, driving me closer to sweet release.

"Rein?"

My eyes flit up, and I see him watching me with an amused smirk. "Huh?"

"I said, I hope I didn't wake you."

I shake my head. "No, you didn't. I was already awake. Why are we here so early?"

Talon unlocks the door at the far end of the corridor and gestures for me to walk in. It's an apartment that moonlights as an art studio. My senses pick up on the distinct smell of paint the moment I step into the apartment. "My friend, Marco, he gives private lessons here in his apartment and has kindly allowed us to use his studio space to work on your piece while he's away in Vegas for the week."

I turn and look up at Talon. "Why come all the way across town? You have a studio in your apartment," I question curiously, and he nods, veering his eyes from me again to look around the studio space.

"I do, but I'd rather we don't take the risk of being seen together. It's always best to proceed with caution than make senseless mistakes and regret it later."

"If you're so concerned about us getting caught, Professor, why are you taking the risk to help me?"

Talon turns to face me and sighs. "Because you've got what it takes to make it and I can't bear to see you throw it all away when I know how much you want it. I want to see you succeed and help you accomplish your dream," he admits, taking a step closer to me. The sincerity in his eyes makes me momentarily forget the days and nights I spent crying over him.

"At the expense of you losing yours."

Talon smiles and tucks his fingers under my chin, tilting my head up. "Neither of us are going to lose anything, all right? Now, you have two choices; you can walk right out of here and kick back the opportunity that has been presented to you to get one step closer to achieving your dreams, or you can pick up that brush and show those worthless arseholes how resilient and relentless Rein Valdez truly is."

"You really believe I can do this?"

"Absolutely," he declares without hesitation. "Lucky for you, I have a photographic memory, so recreating the painting won't be too much of a problem."

My brows rise. "Wait, you do?" I utter, watching him dumbfounded as he turns and shrugs his leather jacket off and tosses some overalls at me.

"I sure do." The tell-tale grin on his gorgeous face when he looks back at me causes the butterflies to take flight in my belly.

Fifteen minutes later, clad in our beige overalls, we're both standing side by side in front of the blank canvas, brushes and palettes in hand. I exhale deeply and look up at him. Talon turns to look at me, our eyes meet, and he nods encouragingly. "For the outlawed love of the Moon and Sun."

He's got me locked me in his gaze. I can't tear my eyes away from his, and the way he's looking at me honestly robs every ounce of oxygen from my lungs.

"For forbidden love," I add mellifluously. Talon licks and bites down on his lower lip, his eyes narrowing at the corners while his eyes sweep over my face, as if he wants to say something but he thinks better of it and smiles, shaking his head.

"Shall we?" I nod, and we swirl our brushes through the paint and get to work.

EVERY SPARE MOMENT WE HAVE WITHIN THAT WEEK WE SPEND HAULED up together in that studio. I must admit, of all the moments I've shared with Talon over the last couple of months, these are by far my favourite. Stolen glances when we think the other isn't watching, or the little ways we're finding to innocently touch one another, whether it be our fingers brushing against each other or playfully elbowing each other.

"What?" I ask when I catch him staring at me with a goofy grin plastered on his face while we eat our pizzas.

"You've got some tomato sauce on your face." He chuckles when I gape at him wide eyed. I pick up a napkin and wipe my mouth.

"Did I get it?" I ask, and he shakes his head, still grinning at me like an idiot. "It would be helpful if you were a tad more specific, you know?"

Talon scoots closer and reaches over to wipe the tomato sauce off my chin with his finger. His roguish blue eyes linger on mine when he brings his finger to his mouth and sucks the sauce off. Talk about your cliché chick flick moment. This would be that point the main characters finally cave in and kiss. Does that happen with us? Absolutely not. We keep staring at each other like we're moments away from tearing one another's clothes off and fuck the insufferable sexual tension out of our system. Only, neither of us are willing to make the first move so the tension between is just continuing to build. I've honestly taken all I can at this point.

"Are you just going to keep staring at my lips or do you plan on doing something about it?" I ask him brazenly. Talon lifts his gaze from my mouth to look me in the eyes and wets his lips.

"You have no idea how badly I wish I could," he rasps. "But I can't, Snowflake."

I sigh. "Why not, Talon? In the space of four days, we've almost kissed five bloody times but each time you stop yourself. It's obvious you want to, so why fight it?"

"Because if I kiss you just once, I won't stop at just kissing, and we can't go back to how things were," Talon justifies, raking a finger through his already messy hair in frustration. "It's so damn easy for me to forget my accountabilities when I'm around you, but we can't keep overlooking the reality that you're my student, Rein. All it takes is one person to suss out that there's something going on between us and we're both royally fucked."

"So, what then? We just continue to ignore whatever this is between us and pretend like we don't want each other?"

Talon nods. "Yes, because I'm tired of sneaking around and constantly looking over my shoulder, Rein. It's not a matter of if we'll get caught, it's a matter of when. The right thing to do is stay away from each other."

"Like we are right now?" I ask.

"We're working on a project."

"Is that all we're doing?" I drop the napkin in my hand and shift so I can straddle him. Talon inhales sharply and places his large hands on my hips and squeezes, looking at me with fire in his eyes.

"Rein."

I place my hands on either side of his face and press my forehead to his. "Tell me you don't want me."

Talon's eyes close and he swallows hard when my lips ghost over his. "Fuck, I don't want you." He groans, rocking himself up into me.

"Liar." I moan, brushing my lips over his.

"Tell me you haven't missed me." Talon's hands come up from my hips and push the straps to my overalls over my shoulders.

"I haven't missed you," he whispers while he drags his fingers over the exposed flesh of my waist, making me shiver visibly in his arms.

"Liar," I whisper back, and he curls his fingers at the nape of my neck and draws my mouth to his, claiming my lips with a fiery kiss we've both been aching deeply for. "Make love to me." I pant, staring into his eyes. "Consume me, tell me I'm your only one. I want to know what it feels like to be loved by you, Talon."

"Baby, you're my moon."

My heart swells with such joy it feels like it's about to explode in my chest. Talon verifies his words when he lays me down on the floor in the studio and makes slow and passionate love to me. I knew that night while I lay a breathless and sweaty mess wrapped up in his arms that he's worth risking everything for.

I tilt my head up to look up at him when he presses a kiss to my forehead. He opens his eyes and looks at me. "I love you, Talon."

His pupils expand when he hears those three words from me. I can't believe how good it feels to say those words to someone and really mean it. Talon smiles and caresses my jaw with his thumb.

"I love you, Snowflake," he proclaims and brushes a kiss over my lips.

For the first time in my life, I genuinely feel like I belong somewhere. I just hope for the sake of us both that we figure out a way to make this work, because I don't even want to imagine being anywhere else but in his arms.

Chapter 18
Rein

WHEN I LOOK AT YOU - MILEY CYRUS

"I can't believe it," I utter, standing before the finished painting and staring at it in wonder.

"I can," Talon states, coming up and wrapping his arms around me from behind. "I told you that you could do it. You need to start believing in yourself a little more, Snowflake," he murmurs, kissing down the side of my neck.

I sigh and let my head drop back against his shoulder. "It's easy to find inspiration when you're around. Motivation, however, is a whole other matter." I moan breathily when he sinks his teeth into the base of my neck and sucks the flesh into his mouth.

"I have methods for that too." He groans, slipping his fingers in the lace of my already soaked panties.

"Ahh, I bet you do." I gasp, rocking my myself against his fingers when they caress my clit.

"You're so fucking beautiful, you know that?" Talon speaks lowly in my ear as his fingers continue to stroke me, making my knees weak with each brush of his fingers.

"Thanks to you, I do know."

It's a miracle we managed to finish this painting with all the 'distractions' in-between. I'm really starting to believe that when we put our minds to it, there isn't a thing we can't overcome together.

Talon whispers sweet nothings in my ear while he continues to stroke me until my knees go weak and I'm unravelling for him, his name an unremitting whisper on my lips with every wave of orgasm that crashes through me. "Shit, I'm late for my shift," I murmur into his mouth when he kisses me. Talon pulls back and looks into my flushed face.

"What?"

"I'm late for work... again." I pull away from him and he tugs me back.

"Oh no you don't, get back here. My fingers are still soaked with your come and you're thinking about work while I'm kissing you," he states dryly. "You better finish that kiss if you want to get out of here, Snowflake."

I smile up at him sultrily and draw him in for a passionate kiss that leaves him groaning in displeasure when I pull away. "Better?" I ask, licking my lips to savour the taste of him.

"For now, yes. But I'm sure you'll make up for it for it later when you slip into my bed after your shift."

"I'm on till closing tonight."

Talon shrugs and brushes a strand of my hair away from my face and delicately tucks it behind my ear. "So? Whatever the time, I want my girlfriend to end the night where she belongs, in my arms, in my bed."

Hold the fucking phone. Did he just call me his *girlfriend*? Don't squeal, Rein, even though you're dying to, don't you dare fucking squeal.

"Your girlfriend?"

Talon nods, eyes full of mirth. "Yes, my girlfriend. You got a problem with that?"

There's no suppressing the shit-eating grin that spreads across my face. "Not one."

Talon's grin matches mine. He grips my chin and kisses me

chastely. "Good, now get dressed. I'll drive you, so you don't waste time waiting for a cab."

MY GRAMMY ALWAYS SAYS WHATEVER MAKES YOUR SOUL HAPPY, GO with that. And Talon doesn't just make me happy, he makes my soul happy. Is this the high that everyone talks about when you're in love? If so, I don't want it to ever end. Turns out, love has a way of sneaking through a door you didn't even know you left open. I'm glad I unwittingly left mine wide open or I would have gone through life missing this feeling.

While Talon drives me to work, I stare out of the window and lift my gaze up to the sky and smile.

I bet you're sitting there laughing at me right now, aren't you, Mum? Yes, your cynic daughter has gone and fallen in love. You were right all along, falling in love is inevitable. But it's not being in love that makes me happy, it's the person I'm in love with.

I look over at Talon, admiring him as he drives. He pulls his eyes from the road for a second and catches me watching him. He smiles at me charmingly and brushes a kiss over my knuckles, making my heart quiver.

Oh yes, it's him all right.

"Ray is going to fire your ass if you keep showing up late for your shifts, kid," Clay chastises me when I walk over to the bar. "There's only a limited number of lies I can pull out of my ass to cover for you. The man's a buffoon but he'll catch on eventually."

I wince and chew on my bottom lip sheepishly, "I know, I'm sorry. I'll explain later but thank you for covering for me."

"Yes, you will, but as a punishment, you can start your shift by cleaning the gents." He smirks and hands me the cleaning caddy. I gape at him, and he dismisses me with his hand. "Off you go, love, those skid marks won't clean themselves."

My stomach lurches at the mere thought of cleaning up the toilets. "Oh, I really hate you."

"You'll think twice before you're late next time. I'd wear a mask if were you."

"Shut up," I grumble, turning to walk off towards the men's bathroom. The moment I push the door open the putrid stink wafts towards me and I dry heave. Clay throws his head back, laughing uncontrollably.

"Oh my God, what the fuck died in here?!"

Clay laughs. "Wednesday's chilli night, kiddo."

"Fuck me, my eyes are burning," I complain, pulling my shirt to cover my mouth and nose.

I'm no princess but my stomach couldn't handle the catastrophic state of that bathroom. I threw up twice the moment I walked in and saw the shit marks all over the seat and on the rim of the first toilet.

Thankfully, Clay couldn't be too cruel and showed some mercy on me and let me off the bathroom duties. Though it's a lesson learnt for sure. I will not be late for my shift ever again.

The rest of the night went by in blur. When I finally make it to Talon's, it's gone three in the morning. Between work, school, and the hours in-between finishing the painting, I'm left feeling rather burnt out and my body is aching. The moment my head hit the pillow, I was out, and five hours later, I'm being shaken awake by Talon holding a fresh cup of coffee under my nose. "Mm."

"I know you're tired, baby, but you need to wake up or you'll be late for school." I groan and pout.

"Five more minutes."

Talon smiles and kisses my pouting lips. "I already gave you five minutes when I woke you the first time."

"I was awake before? I don't remember that." I yawn and stretch out in his super comfortable, super king size bed.

Talon chuckles and hands me the coffee when I sit up. "No kidding. You practically crawled to bed last night and conked right out."

"It's been a hell of a week," I mumble into the steaming cup of coffee. Talon cocks his head to the side and presses the backs of his fingers to my forehead.

"Snowflake, are you sure you're feeling okay?"

"Mhm, just tired."

"Okay. I left you some breakfast on the dining table in the kitchen. Please eat something before you head out. I'll see you at school." I nod and smile tiredly when he presses a kiss to my lips. "I love you."

"I love you."

"Don't go back to sleep," Talon warns, pinning me with a knowing look.

I smile. "I won't." He kisses me one last time before he heads out, leaving me lusting after him.

That is one fine man.

After two cups of coffee and the omelette made for me by my devilishly handsome boyfriend, I finally manage to scrape together enough energy to head home and shower to get ready for school.

It isn't until halfway to school that I realise I left my phone at home where I left in a rush. I can't go back to get it and risk being late.

Off to great start, Rein. But nothing can ruin my day today because the painting has been collected safe and sound and is currently en route to the gallery.

I shouldn't have spoken too soon, because the scene that awaits me the moment I step into the corridor is something I will never fully recover from.

I feel that icy chill in my bones when I enter the school and students keep looking at me oddly and whispering amongst themselves. There's something unmistakably tangible in the air and it's certainly not the good kind. The nerves in my stomach bunch tighter with every small step I take.

And then I walk into the art department and cease when all eyes turn to look at me. The entire corridor goes silent–save for a few whispers amongst the students. There's a flyer in near enough everyone's hands and littered all over the walls and floors. What the hell is going on? It takes my tired brain a moment to catch up when I notice the posters all over the walls. I rip one off and stare at it in absolute horror. It's a photo of me and Talon in his friend's studio. In the photo, Talon and I are both topless and my head is thrown back while he kisses down my throat.

That's not what not shakes me, it's the words under written in big bold letters.

"Professor Hottie caught screwing the student carrying his late-fiancée's heart."

My—or should I say Taylor's—heart slows significantly and I'm sure it's about to stop entirely. My vision blurs with unshed tears while I stare completely frozen at the words. "Rein!" I barely hear Paris' voice calling my name. "Oh my God, Rein, I've calling you since this morning to warn you, but you didn't answer."

This can't be true. It's a vicious lie, it must be. Talon wouldn't do this to me, he wouldn't keep something this significant from me, he wouldn't.

Oh my God, what if this is the reason he wouldn't talk about his past? Because he knew all along and that's why he got defensive every time I brought it up.

The poster slips from my trembling fingers and my knees almost buckle where they turn to jelly at the realisation that he's been using me all along. The devastation that I feel in that moment is unlike anything I've ever felt in my life.

"Rein Valdez, your immediate presence is requested at the Dean's office..." The hallway echoes with the secretary's voice over the tannoy system.

When I finally look up, I see Talon standing at the end of the corridor with campus security and Principal Anderson.

All eyes in that corridor are on us, each one with a different expression, but all I see is the apologetic eyes of the man I fell in love with. The same man that taught me to love not only him but myself. The very man that eventually became my ruin.

Talon tries to take a step towards me but security grab hold of his arm like he's a felon about to escape.

My stomach turns and I feel the breakfast I had earlier coming up. I turn and run through the crowd of people towards the bathroom, with Paris hot on my heels pushing people out of her way to get to me.

I hit my knees in the cubicle and empty everything in my stomach until there is nothing left. "Everyone out, now!" Paris shouts and comes into the cubicle to hold my hair back as she rubs my back soothingly.

I choke on the sob that's been suffocating me and weep uncontrollably into my hand. At that moment, I don't care who hears me– I'm hurting. Everything in my being is hurting, and I don't know how to make it stop.

"Oh, babe, I'm so sorry." Paris wraps her arms around me, and I sob helplessly into her chest. "I can't believe this all happening."

"How could he do this to me? He looked me in the eyes and told me he loved me, P. He told me he loved *me,* and I believed him! Like an idiot, I believed every word," I cry.

"Shh, it's going to be okay, babe. You're going to get through this," Paris says soothingly, and I shake my head.

"No, I'm not!" I shout angrily. "How am I going to be okay knowing I have his dead fiancée's heart beating inside of me? How am I ever going to be okay with that?!" Paris winces and wipes away the endless tears. "I'm such an idiot. It all makes sense why he chose me out of all the students and why he was so fiercely protective. It was never about me, not really, he was protecting her all along."

"Rein, come on, I'm sure that's not true. I saw the way he just looked at you, that's not the face of a man that doesn't care about you. Maybe if you talk to him, I'm sure there's an explanation."

I shake my head furiously. "No, I don't want to talk to him. I don't even want to see his face. I just want to get as far away from him as possible. I want to go back home," I whimper forlornly.

Paris brushes my hair away from my face and sighs, her own eyes watering. "Come on, you need to pull yourself together and go talk to the Dean. We'll figure everything else out after that. Okay?" I nod and she helps me up to my feet.

Fifteen minutes later, I'm sat in a leather chair outside the Dean's office, my hands and legs shaking, an endless stream of tears spilling down my cheeks. I keep going over every moment in my mind again and again, trying to rationalise his actions, but I keep coming up blank.

How could something like this happen? Never in my wildest dreams did I ever imagine he would do this to me. It's crazy how wrong you can be about a person. Everything about him seemed so genuine to me, when all the while he was using me as means to pacify his grief for the woman he truly loves, the one he's loved all along.

The door to the Dean's office opens and Talon walks out. My breath hitches in my throat when our eyes meet. "Rein." His voice is so broken when he says my name that it breaks something deep within me. I shake my head and look away, not having the stomach to look at him. "Rein, I know it sounds awful, but it's not what you think, I swear."

"How could you do this to me?" I sob wretchedly when I turn to look at him. Talon breaks out the of security's hold and walks over to me. He falls to his knees in front of me, his blue eyes watering when our eyes meet.

"I didn't tell you because I was trying to protect you. I didn't want you to think that was the reason because it's not, baby, I swear to you. Rein, I'm in love with you, please, you have to believe that," he pleads, taking hold of my hands.

I rip my hands of out his and shake my head. "I don't believe you; you had every opportunity to tell me, I even asked you and you said nothing!"

Talon sighs and looks at me woefully. "I should have told you, I wanted to so many times, but I couldn't bear to see this betrayed look in your eyes. When I found out you were the one that got her heart, I was shocked, but it didn't matter because I was already attracted to you. What I feel for you has nothing to with Taylor. Yes,

I loved her once and I was devastated when I lost her and our baby but then I met you and you fixed every broken part of me, Snowflake."

"Miss Valdez?" I tear my eyes away from Talon to look at Principal Anderson. "You can escort Professor Saxton off the premises." The security guards walk over and grab hold of Talon's arms, lifting him to his feet.

"Rein…" I look up at him and sob helplessly as they drag him away. The ache in my chest is unbearable, like someone is squeezing the life out of me one breath at a time. I almost get up and run into his arms, but my wounded pride stops me. Talon whispers, "I'm sorry," while they drag him out of the room, his eyes never leaving mine until he's out of sight.

I bury my head in my hands and weep. I weep for the dignity that's he's single handedly ripped to shreds and my stupidity for believing a man like him would ever truly love me for me.

Hours ago, I was the happiest I've ever been in my life, and now I'm sitting in the Dean's office being told that my scholarship has been revoked and I'm no longer permitted to enter the premises.

While I sit there, all I can think about is the promise I made to my Grammy about not throwing my life away for a man like my mother did.

At least I got to experience what it felt like to be in love, even if it was short lived, so that I never make the same stupid mistake again.

After all, they do say that it is better to have loved and lost than to have never loved at all, right?

Epilogue
Rein

TAKE ON THE WORLD- YOU ME AT SIX

SIX MONTHS LATER.

"Seriously, again, Abuela?" I sigh in exasperation when my Grammy walks around the house, chanting in Spanish and burning a sage stick which sets off the fire alarm for the third time that morning. "Every day this week you're stinking up the house with all these superstitions."

"I'm telling you, the women in this family are cursed!" My Grammy grumbles while waving around the burning sage stick.

"Ma, you're going to burn the house down, put that thing out," my aunt Dani complains, waving her arm around to the clear up the smoke gathering in the living room. "Ay Dios Mio! I was going to use that sage for the chicken tonight, Ma!"

Grammy ignores her youngest daughter and proceeds to wave the sage over my head. "Give me that." I cough and take the burning herbs off her and hand it to my aunt Dani.

"You think this is stupid, but look what happened to you, you follow your mother's fate and let some boy trick you." I pinch the bridge of my nose and sigh.

"Abuela, please, I don't want to talk about this anymore. What's done is done. I'm doing fine now, I'm starting my job, my life is still on track."

"You call this on track?" she bemoans, pointing at my protruding belly. "Mi hija, you were destined for greatness. I sent you to America to become something, not to get kicked out and show up back home pregnant just like your mother did at your age!"

My eyes water and I place my hand on my stomach when the baby stirs. "I'm sorry I disappointed you, Abuela, but I'm not sorry that I fell in love and got pregnant, just like mother wasn't sorry when she had me. I'm perfectly capable of being a mother and having a career as long as I have you both to help me."

"Rein, of course we're going to be there for you both. Don't pay no mind to Abuela, she's just high on all the sage," she says with a smile and nudges me with her shoulder. "We're both happy you're home where you belong. The both of you," she adds, placing her hand over mine on my stomach. "Isn't that right, Ma?"

"Si, of course we are, mi hija. I just wanted better for you, that's all."

"Well, I'm happy with the way things are, so don't worry yourself. I'm going to be okay."

"That's what your mother said too and look what happened to her," my Grammy utters, looking over at the photo of my mother on the wall. "May she rest in peace."

I sigh, "You don't need to worry, Abuela, I got a taste of what love is really like and I got burned bad. From here on out, the only boy that will ever have my unconditional love is my son."

"I sure hope so because I would hate for your son to see you suffer the way you did your mother." I walk over and wrap my arms around my Grammy's neck and kiss her cheek.

"That's not going to happen, Abuela, I promise you."

She smiles and pats my back. "Okay, mi hija, go before you are late for your first day."

"Good luck, we love you." My Aunt Dani waves me off. I get into my little red mini cooper and exhale.

"We're going to be okay, right, kiddo?" I smile when my son stirs again inside me.

When I found out I was pregnant just a week after the whole ordeal with Talon, I was truly shocked. I sat there for days staring at the line of pregnancy tests before me, wondering what the hell I was going to do. I couldn't stay in Chicago and raise Talon's baby. That was out of the question. The last time I saw him was at the Dean's office that day. I sent Paris back to my apartment to pack up my stuff and swore her to secrecy. I stayed in a hotel for two weeks while I got things sorted to fly back home to London.

Is it selfish of me to keep Talon in the dark about his child? Yes, of course it is—not just him but to the baby too–but how was I supposed to go and tell him that I'm pregnant after the way he wrecked me with his deceit? I'm still hurt by his betrayal, and despite me telling my family that I'm doing fine, I'm really not. I miss him so much and that giant gaping hole he's left behind aches every single day.

The only comfort I have is that I have a piece of him with me. The seed of our transitory love is growing inside of me, and I'll use that love to raise our son, so he never feels the way I felt growing up without my dad.

Maybe when he's old enough to understand I'll tell him, but right now the wounds are still very deep and having him in my life will only hurt. I've forever locked Talon away in a box buried deep in my heart and thrown away the key, and that's where he'll remain.

Today is the first day of my new life. I got a job as an art teacher at the University of Art in London. I'm still studying to get my degree at the same time, but it's a part time online course which is helpful and means I can work while I finish up school. While I'm excited, I'm also scared shitless to stand in front of a bunch of judgey students and act like I've got my shit together, when the truth is, I'm just barely keeping it together.

"Hi, Rein, are you excited for you first day?" Penny, the receptionist greets me when I walk into the building. I met her on the day of the interview and warmed to her instantly. She's someone I can see myself becoming friends with. I like her energy; she reminds me of Paris. God, I miss her. I can't wait for her to fly out here in a few weeks.

"Hi, Penny, I'm so nervous I might actually hurl, if I'm honest," I admit, and she cackles.

"Just don't show the vultures that you're nervous. Good heavens, they'll eat you alive, honey."

"That's comforting," I utter under my breath as she leads me towards the staff room. "Oh, we also have a new Professor, he joined us last week. He's an artist like you."

"Oh? Well, I'm sure we'll have plenty to talk about then."

"Between you and me, he's really fit. Makes a nice change from all the old farts we have around here," Penny explains with a girlish giggle.

I smirk and shake my head. "Honestly, not in the least bit bothered."

"More for me then, girl."

Because all I need in my life is another hot professor. Just uttering the word 'professor' leaves a sour taste in my mouth. "Where do I find my schedule?"

Penny touches her key card to the reader for the staff room door and pulls it open. The smell of coffee and freshly baked shortbread biscuits fills my senses, taking me back to my secondary school years. "Your schedule will be given to you by the head of year just before the start of the day."

"Oh, I see." I nod and wander over to the coffee machine. "Is there any decaf coffee around here?"

Penny nods and pushes the blue button. "The blue means decaf. See, there's one beside each option."

"Decaf latte, come to mama." I moan elatedly. Penny gives me a questioning look. "My Grammy is superstitious and doesn't allow me to consume any caffeine because of the pregnancy, so this a highlight for me. Pretty sad, right?"

Penny smiles in understanding and sips her coffee. "I get it, my sister has kids and she's the same. Everything must be organic; God forbid the kids have sugar. It's like World War three."

I snicker into my coffee cup and take a long sip. The staff room door opens, and I almost choke on my mouthful of coffee when I see the tall, devastatingly beautiful man walk in.

Oh my God.

My world as I know it stops spinning on its axis when he turns, and in a room full of people, like two magnets, our eyes interlock.

It can't be.

The coffee cup slips out of my fingers and hits the floor with a dull thud while I stand, motionless, staring at the man who wrecked my world not that long ago.

The father of my unborn child.

Talon looks just as shell-shocked to see me standing before him. That box I said I kept locked deep in my heart bursts open and I'm hit with every single emotion I've been avoiding since I left Chicago.

Instinctively, my hand moves to my stomach and his eyes follow. A deep frown forms on his handsome face when he sees the baby bump.

"Rein."

Oh shit, no, don't you dare cry, Rein.

I swallow the lump that forms in my throat and blink away the tears that gather in my eyes before anyone notices. Talon slowly moves over to me in front of everyone, he takes my hand, and pulls me out of the staff room.

Once we're out of the staff room, I rip my hand out of his and glare up at him. "What the hell are you doing here?"

Talon ignores my question and stares at my stomach, his brows knitted together tightly. "You're pregnant?"

"What are you doing here, Talon? How did you even find me? I don't even know why I'm asking. Paris told you where to find me, didn't she? I'm going to kill her." I fume and turn to leave, but he curls his fingers around my upper arm and stops me.

We glare at one another, his blue eyes boring into mine with a concoction of surprise and irritation. "She didn't. Despite me pleading with her. In fact, she told me to go and politely fuck myself."

That's my girl.

"Is that baby mine, Rein?"

"Is that really all you have to say to me right now?!" I snap hotly.

"Answer me," he demands, taking a step toward me.

"Yes!" I shout, shoving him back again. "Of course the baby is yours." Talon's shoulders drop and he stares down at my stomach again, shocked.

"You said you were on the pill." He utters.

"I was on the pill, but its only ninety-one percent effective and if you remember we spent a lot of time having sex." Talon shoves a hand through his hair and exhales heavily.

"You're pregnant with my baby and you weren't going to tell me?" The clipped tone of his voice cuts straight through me like a razor blade.

My eyes narrow. "Oh, that's rich coming from you. You really want to be throwing stones while you're in a greenhouse, Talon? Last I recall, you just love to keep secrets. Hurts, doesn't it?" I snarl.

"That was different!"

"How?"

"I never set out to intentionally hurt you, Rein. I tried to explain but you wouldn't even listen to me. You up and fucking disappeared on me. It didn't matter to me that I lost my job and everything I worked so hard for, what killed me was losing you."

I scoff angrily, averting my gaze from his penetrating one. "You seem perfectly fine to me."

"The fuck I am," Talon declares. He takes hold of my shoulders and turns my face, so I'm forced to look up at him again. "I've not been okay since you walked out of my life, Snowflake. I spent months going out of my mind trying to find you. All this time and I've never for a moment stopped loving you."

I can't contain the tears that fill my eyes at his profession. *Stupid hormones.* Talon cups my face with his large hands and brushes away the tears that stream down my cheeks. "Tell me you don't love me, baby," he whispers, pressing his forehead to mine.

"I don't love you," I lie, my voice wavering.

"Liar," he whispers against my lips. "Taylor was my past, but you were always meant to be my future, Rein, and the fact I'm standing here today is proof of that. I gave up hope of ever finding you and here you are. The entire universe has conspired to help me to find you and I'm not making the mistake of letting you go this time. I don't care if I have to grovel on my hands and knees for the rest of my life to prove to you that my love for you is true," he expresses earnestly. "I want you and I want our baby." The moment his lips descend upon mine all my defences slip away one bit at a time and damn, it feels so good to be kissed by him again.

I place my hands at his chest and push him away, shaking my head. "Stop." I sigh. "You can't just fix everything with a kiss, Talon. You really hurt me."

"I know, and I'm truly sorry for not being honest with you from the start. I was going to tell you. I was, but then other shit kept getting in the way and…I bottled it. I couldn't bear the thought of losing you. Forgive me."

I stare up into his eyes. "Why couldn't you just trust me and been honest from the start? I would have understood." I cry, placing my hand over my chest. "I know better than anyone what it's like to lose someone you love."

Talon pulls me into his arms, "No, don't." I fight in his hold, but he tightens his arms keeping me against me.

"I'm sorry. I'm not letting you go this time. You hear me?" he murmurs in my ear, "You can keep fighting me all you want, but I'm going to do everything in my power to win your trust back." He proclaims.

I draw my head back and look up at him, Talon brushes his fingers along my jaw affectionately. "You'll be waiting a long time."

"Have you forgotten how persistent I can be? Or would you like me to drag you into that bathroom and remind you?" He states cockily and smirks when blood fills my face instantly. Talon places his hand on my stomach and the way his eyes lit up made me my heart soar. "Everything I want is right here. A life with you and our baby." Almost like he sensed his father the baby kicks firmly against Talon's hand, and he stares down it in awe. "Whoa."

"It's a boy."

Talon smiles brightly, his eyes watering. "I'm having a son."

I roll my eyes, "No, *we're* having a son." I correct him and gasp when sweeps down and kiss me again.

Oh, to hell with it, I'll continue being angry with him later. My arms snake around his neck and I kiss him back with equal zeal in the middle of the school hallway without a care who sees or what anyone thinks.

While my heart and pride are both still wounded, I owe it to our unborn baby to at least hear him out. I won't make it easy for him, but I know what I want, and it's him.

We have a lot of building to do, but the one thing I never really doubted was the way he felt about me, because his actions always spoke volumes.

Falling in love with my professor wasn't something I ever expected but being in love with Talon is something I couldn't ever stop even if I tried.

In the end, Professor Talon Saxton truly was worth risking it all for and if I had to relive it all over again, despite the devastation, I would in a heartbeat.

As my beloved mother always said, love doesn't need to be perfect, it only needs to be true.

While our love story is far from traditional, it's as true and crazy as it gets.

And I would have it no other way.

THE END

Thank you For Reading

Dear reader,

Thank you for taking the time to read my book. I truly hope you enjoyed reading Talon and Rein's whirlwind love story.

The love you have shown these characters and their story has honestly blown me away! I'm truly so very thankful to each and every one of you.

You're feeling pretty bummed their story is over, right? Well, don't be, because you'll be seeing more from Professor Hottie and his snowflake in their upcoming novella! No date has been set yet, but I promise you their story is not over yet.

If you enjoyed the book please do a review as this helps others find my work and I appreciate and take on any feedback, good or bad.

I'll see you real soon with the next book!

Love always,

Shayla Hart.

Printed in Great Britain
by Amazon